Chronicles of Leight

Book Two

Fang Wars

By Evan Kelling

This is a work of fiction. Unless otherwise indicated, all the names, characters, businesses, places, events, and incidents in this book are either the product of the author's imagination or used in a fictitious manner. Any resemblance to actual persons, living or dead, or actual events is purely coincidental.
No generative artificial intelligence (AI) was used in the writing of this work. The author expressly prohibits any entity from using this publication for purposes of training AI technologies to generate text, including with limitation technologies that are capable of generating works in the same style or genre as this publication. The author reserves all rights to license uses of this work for generative AI training and development of machine learning language models.
Copyright © 2024 by Evan Kelling
All rights reserved.
No portion of this book may be reproduced in any form without written permission from the publisher or author, except as permitted by U.S. copyright law.

Chapter 1

My name is Tobias Caesar Leight. By now, I'm sure you've heard of me, right? Okay, maybe not. For just over a year now, I've been apprenticing under my uncle as a wizard.

Yeah, that's right, wizard. I'm talking spells, potions, and everything in between. Last year, I had to face off with a monster who called himself the devil. Somehow, I'd barely managed to win. Since then, I've learned a lot about magic and monsters. My uncle and I are tasked with protecting the greater Seattle area from anything that goes bump in the night. Sure, they're no devil, but I've dealt with many nasty mooks, who'd love nothing more than to tear my face off.

But there's one thing I'd take on a thousand face-melting squirrel demons to avoid: high school. I'm not exactly what you would call a social butterfly. I wasn't before the wizarding stuff either, but it sure as hell didn't help. I mostly kept to myself and a handful of friends. I didn't play any sports, and I didn't join any clubs. Hell, I wasn't even in any AP classes. Not that I had the grades that would get me in those classes anyhow.

It was a Tuesday, the last week of April of my senior year. My eighteenth birthday had passed a few weeks ago, and I didn't want to make a big deal about it. My uncle, my best friend Claire, and I went for burgers and a movie—nothing crazy. But today, I was in my last class of the day, math.

God, math is indescribably dull. I'd rather have my fingernails pulled out one by one with red hot tweezers. The teacher, whose name I couldn't be bothered to recall, was droning on and on about how to prove a triangle was a triangle or something. Then, after damn near an eternity, I heard the final bell ring throughout the school. Students scurried to gather their things and escape the deepest pit of hell that was high school. That was when the teacher raised a hand and let out a swift, concise whistle.

Mrs. Barton, that was her name, held up a hand and spoke loudly to gather everyone's attention. "Now, hold on, students. I want to remind you all that prom is coming up in just four days. You have until the day before to purchase your tickets to attend. I wouldn't want any of you missing out."

Prom, yeah, right. Talk about an introvert's nightmare. Mrs. Barton had nothing more to say, so she allowed us to leave after that. I threw on my black denim jacket, and as I walked down the halls, I had a brief flashback of the moment an insectoid demon ripped through my last denim jacket in these very halls. The memory sent a shiver down my spine. I was abruptly brought back to reality when a girl just scarce of a hundred pounds practically threw herself at me in a hug.

Claire Williams was a tiny little person, only an inch taller than the five-foot mark. She'd been wearing her shoulder-length blond hair down lately and had her bangs done, which made her look even younger. Her thin-frame glasses were perched low on her tiny, freckle-spotted nose. Claire was notorious for wearing apparel, usually sweaters, from various colleges. She had a tradition of visiting colleges across the country and taking home a shirt, sweater, or jogging pants to add to her ever-growing collection. I didn't doubt that she'd eventually collect something from every college in the States.

"Toby!" Claire's voice came out as a cheer of excitement.

"Hey Claire, what's up?" I chuckled. I could never match her energy. She was so full of life and happiness, and while I was no Debbie Downer, I sure as hell wasn't Gleeful McHappypants.

"Oh, nothing." Claire sighed in a very woe-is-me tone. "It's just that prom is in like four days. All my friends have dates, except for me. I've got my dress and everything, but I don't know if I'm even gonna bother at this point.

"Man, that sucks," I remarked.

Okay, I know what you're thinking. And in retrospect, I still cringe at what an idiot I was at that particular moment. But I'm what you would call an idiot, especially when it comes to courting the opposite sex, or the same sex for that matter.

Claire crossed her arms and gave me a look that might've been intimidating on someone a few inches taller. After a few seconds, a dingy, dusty lightbulb blinked somewhere in the deep recesses of my mind. Oh. Ohhhhhh.

"Well, uh, if you'd been willing to suffer through it, I guess I could take you." I offered a little more than half-heartedly.

"You guess?" Claire chided. Her eyebrow rose as she began to rise on her tippy toes.

Oops.

"Uh, I mean, if you'd do me the honor...?" I corrected myself, albeit hesitantly. I'm not good at this, okay?

Claire's expression changed instantly; her deadly glare was replaced with a wide grin too large for her face. "Yay! Okay, pick me up at six on Saturday. Don't forget! I sure hope you got a tux, wizard boy."

With that, she gave me another hug with alarming strength. I felt some bones pop as she squeezed. She released me, flashing another huge grin up at me. She turned and then practically skipped down the hall.

What have you gotten yourself into this time, Leight? Like I said, I was no good at this type of thing and the idea of fighting off rabid squirrel demons sounded way more appealing right about now. My mind was fuzzy with mixed emotions. As previously established, I had no interest in prom. But the idea of sharing a nice, romantic night with Claire was rather appealing. I shook my head, momentarily dispelling the confusion while I devised a game plan.

Okay, so I was going to prom now. Great. I had several obstacles to overcome within a few days. First of all, I did not own anything resembling a suit. If my uncle did, it sure as hell wouldn't fit me. My uncle was a few inches taller than me and built with a lot more muscle. I'd look like a small child playing dress-up. Secondly, how the hell was I going to actually take

Claire to prom? I didn't have a car or my license, nor did my uncle. I could ask Bishop to rent us a limo, but that was just more cost that I'd have to spring on him on such short notice.

I had a couple hundred dollars saved up from doing chores and the occasional odd job for my neighbors, so I decided to hit the local thrift shop in hopes that they might have some old suits that I could peruse. With a course of action decided, I exited King's View High, turned my collar up against the breeze, and made my way down the street in the direction of a small shopping center I knew of.

I stepped in a deceptively deep puddle as I arrived at the shopping center. I shook my leg a bit in an attempt to get some of the excess water off. My Chuck Taylors had been run into the ground, so there was nothing to stop the water from seeping into my sock and turning my foot into a popsicle. Fantastic.

The Wave Crest Shopping Center was a small conglomerate of small businesses, not a name brand in sight. They were organized in a U-shape with several smaller stands in the courtyard that also was home to a rundown playground where kids could run and play. There was a killer pizza shop to my right that I frequented. It had a small arcade off to the side that had a handful of old games like Pac-Man and Street Fighter II. Next to it, coincidentally, was a game shop that specialized in both tabletop games and video games. There, you could find dice, figurines, retro consoles, new games, and everything in between. I had admittedly spent way too much time and money there.

But today, I ventured to the left side of the U-formation of shops, which I frequented a lot less. A couple of doors down was where the thrift shop sat. The storefront was simple, framed by wooden pillars and a big red-on-white sign that read "The Humble Boutique." Half of the back lights were out, and the paneling looked like it was ready to fall off, but I thought the place was charming, nevertheless.

I pulled open the glass door and walked in. To my dismay, Macklemore was not in today. The thrift shop was an overstuffed mess of junk. When I walked in, I immediately tripped over a crate of old comic books. I hit the ground face first and felt a trickle from my nose. I groaned as I picked myself up, coming to a knee. I rubbed my shin to relieve myself of a stabbing pain right in the middle of the bone. My nose was filled with heat as something trickled down my lip. I rubbed my face, and my hand was promptly streaked with crimson.

"You've got to be kidding me," I said, my voice came out a bit nasally.

"Need a hand?" said a woman's voice.

I looked up to see a beautiful woman who was probably closer to Bishop's age than mine, maybe forty-something. She was of Hispanic descent but had lost her accent probably years ago. She had long, curly brown hair that fell around her round face. She wore round-rimmed glasses that made her brown eyes look bigger than they were. Her lips were small and supple; they reminded me of a doll. Her name was Gloria Ramirez. Her family owned and operated The Humble Boutique for years before I was born.

When Bishop first became my legal guardian, he bought many of my clothes and toys here. The shop was one of the few stores I frequented in the shopping center. I'd practically grown up there. There had been a few occasions when Bishop was going to be home late that I spent at the shop under the watchful gaze of Gloria and her family.

Gloria held out a hand to help. I took it with my clean hand and stood up. She pulled out a packet of tissues from her pocket and handed me a few.

"Thank you," I muttered sheepishly as I cleaned myself up. I stuck one of the remaining tissues up the bleeding nostril.

"Of course, *mijo*," Gloria said, touching my nose lightly with two fingers. "It doesn't appear to be broken. I'm so sorry about that. I was in the middle of moving some things around."

I waved a hand dismissively. "Don't worry about it. I should've been paying attention to where I was going."

"Well, what brings you in today?" She asked me. "You don't come in very often anymore."

I scratched awkwardly at the back of my head and did my best to look charming despite the tissue stuffed up my nose. My voice came out nasally. "Well, plans have changed at the last minute, and I'm gonna be going to prom."

Gloria smiled at me with a knowing look. "Ah, a young lady catches your eye, *mijo*? Or a young man?"

I blushed. I couldn't help it. "Err, well, I'm taking my best friend, Claire."

"Oh, yes." Gloria nodded. "She's come around before, right?"

"Yeah, a few times," I confirmed. That being said, I kind of need a monkey suit on short notice."

Gloria twisted her face into something thoughtful, touching a finger to her chin in thought. "Mmm, yes, I think we have a few towards the back. You're more than welcome to take a look."

She pointed me towards a secluded section towards the back of the small shop. I waved a gesture of polite thanks and made my way to the back of the thrift shop. As Gloria had said, there were several old suits hanging on a rack. None of them were particularly stellar or anything, but for my purposes, they'd pass. I started looking through the several suits that were hanging there. I hated trying on clothes, so I was doing my best to eyeball which suit would fit me best.

After maybe ten minutes of going back and forth between a few of the suits, I settled on one worth giving a try. There was an improvised dressing room in the back of the store. It was made out of three pieces of plywood, with the third attached to a hinge so it could function as a door. I slid inside and struggled with the door for a second. It wasn't professionally made, so the door occasionally got wedged against the floor.

A mirror was secured to the wall and a hook on the plywood to hang clothing from. I shuffled out of my clothes and fumbled my way into the suit, save for the tie. I hated ties. That was one thing Claire would have to let me go without. Please don't ask me why I hated them because I couldn't give you a good reason. It was a pretty standard two-piece navy blue suit and even came with a collared white shirt to complete the look. To my surprise, it fit surprisingly well. The pants and jacket sleeves were a little long, but I could roll them up in a way that was still fashionably appropriate.

I had to admit, I looked pretty good. It wouldn't put me on the cover of any magazines or anything like that, but it was sure as hell good enough to take a lady to a dance. It would do just fine. I changed back into my normal clothes, and I hissed at the damp, cold spot on the cuff of my jeans as it slid over my foot and my ankle. After hanging the suit properly back on the hanger, I took it back to the front, where Gloria was manning the register.

"Oooh, a good pick, *mijo*." Gloria smiled. She seemed pleased. Proud, even. She hit a few keys on the register, and I noticed the price that came up on the pin pad was significantly lower than the price on the tag hanging from the suit's jacket.

"Uh, Gloria. I think you hit the wrong keys." I pointed out politely.

She waved her hand dismissively. "No, Tobias. Consider it a late birthday discount. Plus, you're not too old for me to still take care of you just a tiny bit."

I tried to argue with her, but she wouldn't budge. So, I accepted the extreme discount and handed her the money. It was just as well, anyhow. The suit's original price would've drained my allowance completely.

"Thank you, Gloria." I bowed my head in a polite nod. I collected the change from the counter and stuffed it in my pocket.

Gloria had draped a sheet of protective plastic around the suit, like at the dry cleaners, and she handed it back to me. "Of course, *mijo*. Enjoy your prom, and make sure it's a night that young lady won't forget."

I promised I would and waved goodbye to her. Then, I exited the store and started making my way to the sidewalk that ran parallel to the main road. That had been easy enough. I held the suit draped over my shoulder and began walking in the general direction toward the apartment that my uncle rented.

My mind was drifting off into an idealized fantasy of how the upcoming night would be. A sweet ride to the venue, hell, maybe a limo if I could swing it. Then, a formal dinner followed by dancing under the moonlight. Claire would be wearing a beautiful dress, maybe something red and sparkly. I wasn't exactly sure what Claire would be wearing or if red and sparkly was appropriate for prom. As the last slow song of the night would fade away, our faces would inch closer together, and then...

The hairs on the back of my neck stood on end as my instincts screamed a warning. I turned around just in time to see a black car of unknown make roar around the corner. It surged down the street towards me, and I had only a moment to notice the rolled down window. It was moving too fast to get any details of who was driving or even a license plate. But what I did see was a long, thin black barrel peek out of the window.

Holy crap. I reacted purely on instinct, crouching to the ground, ducking my head so that it was shielded by my back. I scrambled to gather any amount of magical energy and frantically yelped, "*Duro!*"

No sooner had my skin hardened up like steel did I heard several distant sounding pangs of noise as a gun was fired. I was hit by what felt like sharp precise punches to my lower back. The force of the blows knocked me to the ground and a couple more blows hit me. Then the car rushed off and turned around the next corner.

"Holy..." I choked out. The blows, no, the gunshots, had knocked the wind out of me. It took a few moments of manual, steady breaths to get the air back in my lungs. I felt my skin hardening spell fade away, returning my skin to its normal consistency.

I looked around slowly, wary of another potential attack. But the car had driven off. I took a general account of myself. Luckily, I didn't have any new holes in my body, and my insides were all still inside. That was a relief, to say the least. I could already feel some major soreness seeping in all across my back and radiating to the rest of my body. I stood up slowly, my body protesting with pain. That was going to hurt for a few days, that's for sure.

I took one more look over myself, just to be sure I was fully intact. I was. The hardening spell had done its job. That's when reality set in. Holy shit. Someone had just shot at me. Little, old high schooler turned wizard, me. But why? The only people who could've possibly been gunning for me were the acolytes of the fallen angel, Azazel. And surely, they had methods more on the arcane side if they wanted to take a whack at me.

I knelt down again and picked up one of the bullets, or what was left of it. They had flattened against my hardened skin as if they had hit Kevlar. I pocketed the flattened round and stood up once more. As I did, I briefly remembered my recently purchased tuxedo, which I'd draped over my back. Frantically, I lifted it up to inspect it. To my dismay, the suit had taken a lot of the damage meant for me. It had been shredded. Not to unrecognizable bits or anything, but it sure as hell wasn't passable for prom use or anything.

"You've got to be kidding me." I sighed.

I looked around and realized that quite a crowd had gathered around. No doubt, attracted by the muffled gunfire. Someone must've already called the police because, in the distance, I heard sirens. I had no desire to get caught up with local law enforcement and decided to make myself scarce.

A long day in the books, and all I had to show for it was a sore back and a shredded suit. And if I didn't get out of here, I'd have a line of questioning with the police as well. So, someone was trying to kill me. That was neat. I was worried my life was starting to get a little too boring.

I had another realization and let out a defeated sigh.

"I forgot to get the receipt," I muttered.

I slung my ruined suit back over my shoulder and hurried down the sidewalk as quickly as I could back to my uncle's apartment.

Chapter 2

The walk back to the apartment felt longer than ever. My pant leg was still soaked, my nose had bled through the tissue I'd stuffed up my nostril, my entire torso was stiff with soreness, and my prom suit had been shredded by bullets. Oh, and someone had tried to kill me.

Today was going spectacularly. I shambled into the apartment to find Bishop sitting in his recliner. He was wearing reading glasses and held open a thick book with one hand. He held a steaming cup of joe in the other hand. My uncle was a well-built man, a few inches taller than six feet. He had salt and pepper hair that was neatly cut and slicked back to keep it out of his brown eyes. Don't ask me how, but somehow, some way, my uncle had a permanent five o'clock shadow.

As I opened the door, he rested the book on his leg and raised his mug in a greeting. It took him a moment to realize that I looked like absolute garbage. In a flash, he'd risen from where he was sitting and helped me over to the couch, relieving me of the tattered suit and my school bag as he did.

"What happened to you, Tobias?" Bishop asked me.

"Uh, well, I'm pretty sure someone just tried to shoot me," I said. My voice came out a bit slow and stilted. Maybe it was the pain or the shock.

I gave him a brief rundown of my day, careful not to leave a single detail out. Everything from agreeing to go to prom with Claire to the bullets my suit had taken for me.

Bishop scratched his chin in thought. "This is concerning, to be sure. I have to wonder if it has anything to do with an assignment, I just got from the big wigs at the Mystic Order."

The Mystic Order was an organization run by the wizards of the world. I didn't exactly have a grasp on just how large it was, but from what I'd learned from Bishop, they had amassed enough power and resources to be comparable to a small country. From what I'd seen, it was made up of human wizards, as well as dwarves, elves, and pixies. Bishop was a fairly high-ranking member and was in charge of maintaining peace amongst the magical factions who had put down roots here in Seattle. If they'd given Bishop an assignment of some sort, that meant something was up.

"What assignment?" I asked, speaking through a pang of pain that reverberated throughout my body.

Bishop nodded. "I received a message from the Order about conflict stirring up amongst the vampire clans in town. They've been stirring up quite the ruckus, engaging in open warfare in back alleys and abandoned buildings, but whatever's going on, it's starting to seep into the mortal side of things. Local news stations have been reporting on increased gang activity."

"Vampires, huh?" I raised my eyebrows.

Over the last year or so, I'd learned a lot about the magical world that made its home alongside our own. Mostly small-time stuff, though. Nature spirits, restless ghosts, and one seriously cracked-out goblin. Don't ask. But vampires were one we hadn't gotten to yet.

"Yeah," Bishop confirmed. "The local chapters of the clans seem to be pissed off at each other about something. Otherwise, they wouldn't risk acting so openly. And of course, that means it falls to me, and by me, I mean us, to figure out what's going on and what needs to be done to resolve the situation."

"Oh, how exciting." I let out a shallow breath. It hurt to breathe. "So, what do I need to know about vampires?"

Bishop let out a small, knowing chuckle. "What a loaded question that is. First of all, there are three distinct types of vampires that we know about, separated into the three clans: Blood, Emotion, and Soul."

I realized that now was note-taking time, but I couldn't remember where I'd left my little notebook that I'd been writing down anything and everything magic-related. Bishop noticed my momentary panic and held up a hand.

"I'll write this down for you later, and you can add it to your notebook," Bishop assured me, and I relaxed again.

"Sanguine Vampires are the most common vampire type in our city. I've already arranged a meeting with the local Don," Bishop began. "The Sanguine Vampires are your typical bloodsuckers. They feed on human blood to live, as well as to fuel their supernatural physiology. The blood acts as a conduit for their brand of magic to provide them with superhuman strength, speed, flight, and healing. Most of the time, they can appear human, but when using their abilities, they become something less so. But hopefully, you won't have to see that."

I took the information in, mentally filing it away for later use.

"The Sanguine Vampire are not born into their abilities, however, though they do tend to stick to bloodlines. When the offspring of a Sanguine Vampire reaches the age of sixteen, they are injected with their father's venom and transformed. But it isn't limited to their own children. If it suits them, the Blood Clan will inject any victim with their venom in order to expand their ranks. Obviously, their victims aren't always willing, but the confusion and isolation of the sudden change usually leads to them joining the clan."

"Wait a second, so these guys, the Blood Clan, they feed on and convert innocent people, right?" I asked rhetorically. "Why would the Mystic Order allow that? Shouldn't we blow them up or something? Wipe them out?"

"If it was that simple, I'm sure the Mystic Order would have by now." Bishop confirmed. "However, for one, the Mystic Order just doesn't have the firepower necessary to destroy them. And there are just far too many of them across the planet to wipe out effectively, and the last thing we need is open war with them; they far outnumber us. And secondly, it's simply not our place. We can't just go around exterminating what amounts to entire separate nations just because of their nature. We've come to certain terms with the Blood Clan that limits how much damage they can do, but there's not much more we can do with that."

Rationally, I supposed I agreed with him. Wiping out an entire clan just for doing what they have to to survive was not okay one bit. But at the same time, I couldn't help but think of all the people who were hurt, killed, or worse, because of these monsters. I had a feeling I was not going to get along very well with them going forward. I highly doubted this would be my only interaction with them, after all.

"Anything else I should know?" I asked. I wanted to make sure I wasn't going into this meeting he mentioned blind.

"Well, I hope it doesn't come to this, but you should probably know the best ways to hurt them." Bishop said carefully. "Should you have to fend off a Sanguine Vampire, try and get to open sunlight. It won't kill them instantly, but it will burn them and cause them great pain. Fire has a similar effect, and running water can wash away most magic, but the Sanguine Vampires seem to be especially vulnerable to it. But the only, sure-fire way to kill them is by decapitation."

Well, that was good to know, although I wasn't exactly sure how I was going to decapitate a vampire if I needed to. It's not like I had a sword or anything. Fire was almost off the table as well. I'd only produced fire a couple of times on my own, and one of those times had been in the depths of my own mind. Which only left sunlight and running water. I'd learned a thing or two about water magic in the past year. It came to me surprisingly easily, quite the opposite of fire magic. But I agreed with Bishop's sentiment, hopefully it wouldn't come to that.

"Okay, got it. Bloodsuckers, super strong, don't like sunlight and stuff." I did my best to commit everything Bishop had shared to memory. It would definitely take some studying. "What about the other two?"

"The Motus Vampires and the Jiangshi," Bishop said. "But we'll address them later. Don't want to load your head with too much information at once. Not when I need your head in the game. I've seen your test scores, after all.

My ears burned with slight embarrassment from his jab at my academic shortcomings, but I quickly forced it to the back of my mind.

"Alright then, take a few minutes, get yourself cleaned up, and gather your gear. We leave within the hour." Bishop said.

I nodded and slowly sat up. My body protested but I told it to shove it and get me moving. My body surrendered and I managed to get up and shambled towards the stairs. Bishop returned to his book and coffee. Climbing the stairs felt like an eternity. Every movement was met with another wave of dull pain throughout my body. My legs protested each step, and my stiff shoulders burned as I leaned on the handrail. And to top off my annoyingly tortuous day, now there were vampires to deal with.

Before even reaching my room, I stopped in my bathroom and opened the medicine cabinet. I found the Advil bottle stored in there and poured out four small pills that vaguely reminded me of M&M's. I tossed them back and swallowed them without water. I should stress that you probably shouldn't take more than two of these, but I hurt like hell and figured my body wouldn't argue with the extra help. I cleaned up my nose as well, which had finally stopped bleeding. Besides the bleeding, my nose looked relatively fine. Maybe it was a little crooked, but it didn't feel broken. I fixed up my brown hair, which had been messed up a bit from my exciting day. I took a moment to look myself over a bit, making sure I was at the very least, presentable.

I left the bathroom and walked a few steps down the hall to my room. Before I could even turn on the light, I saw a brief flash of movement in the darkness. A second later, a dark shaped tackled me and damn nearly knocked me over. The shape was in fact, my dog, Scout. He appeared as a German Shepherd that had recently grown out of puppyhood. But in reality, Scout was actually a hellhound that Bishop had taken from the underworld a few years ago. He was a shrimp, compared to most hellhounds, or so I was told. And since Bishop had raised him since he was a hellpuppy, he was loyal to us and our allies. He was very strong and good at fighting bad guys, so it was always a relief to know we had him around. A memory flashed in my mind, to the first time Scout had revealed his true nature to save me from a nagini.

Scout was snuffling excitedly as I pet him. I knelt down to his level, and he immediately drenched me with doggy slobber as he licked my face. I sputtered and gagged. I tried to push him off, but even in his disguised form, he was still much stronger than the average dog.

I finally got Scout to settle down. "It's good to see you too, boy." I patted his head affectionately and eventually Scout settled down.

Scout walked a few steps away and then sat down, giving me some space. I shed my clothes. My denim jacket was still intact, but the material seemed worn where the bullets had struck, same with the shirt I'd been wearing under it. I sighed. The bad guys had no respect for my wardrobe. I shivered again as I took off my pants, the leg was still a bit wet.

I put on a fresh pair of jeans and a green Power Ranger t-shirt with a golden emblem on the front. Then I grabbed the fun stuff. First was a silver bracelet that had two charms hanging from it. I called it my charms bracelet. In short, the charms themselves were stored with the magical blueprints for certain spells that I wasn't very good at casting on my own. I could pour my magic into a charm and then the bracelet would help me fire the spell off without too much more thought than that.

Next were my eskrima sticks, which I kept in a holster of sorts that I could strap to my leg, which made me feel like a cowboy in an Old West flick. They were designed to help me channel my magic into more precise effects that I had in mind. Without them, my spells were a little more out of control and would behave somewhat on their own. One time, I'd accidentally set fire to a small section of forest in the nearby national park. That was awkward to explain to the park ranger. Also, they were really good for whacking people on the head. I strapped the satchel to my right thigh where they'd be easy to reach in a moment's notice.

Finally, was my sheepskin bomber jacket. Not only was it very warm and cozy, but the tan leather was etched with runes that maintained spells that made it very durable, even more so than my skin-hardening spell. It could take a lot of punishment. I wish I'd worn it to school today. It definitely would have come in handy. In addition, it could be used to enhance my own physical strength, not to any crazy supernatural degree or nothing. I wouldn't be lifting cars or anything like that, but most magical baddies and beasties were a lot stronger than me, and the jacket could give me an edge in a fight.

Bishop gave me both the jacket and the charms bracelet as presents for my eighteenth birthday, so I hadn't gotten to use them much yet, but I supposed today was as good a day as any.

Now in fresh clothes and geared up, I headed downstairs. Scout recognized that I was getting ready to deal with some brand of magical mumbo jumbo or another. When I got downstairs, Bishop had changed out of his loungewear and into something more presentable. He was wearing a purple on gray flannel shirt, dark jeans, and rugged-looking steel-toed boots. Bishop was a wizard, but he was also practical. Sure, flinging fire and lightning around was the go-to strategy for a wizard in a fight, but kicking a ravenous Lovecraftian monster in the face with a steel-toe would do just as well. It was the same principle as my eskrima. Nothing beats a good whack to the face with a blunt instrument.

"You ready?" Bishop asked, looking me up and down.

Was I ready to go into a meeting with a gang of super dangerous, bloodsucking monsters? No. Absolutely not. I'd rather be doing pretty much anything else.

"Yep, sure am."
Nope! I definitely was not ready.

Scout had already gone over to where his leash hung on a coat rack. To my surprise, Bishop shook his head at the dog. Scout cocked his head and somehow had a disappointed look on his face.

"Sorry, boy." Bishop said gruffly. "We're going to be dealing with vampires, and they might get a little jumpy if we walk through the door with a hellhound on our heels. Hellhounds and vampires don't play nice. Maybe next time, if things go south."

Scout sneezed disapprovingly, jumped up onto Bishop's recliner, and curled up comfortably. He glared at the both of us the entire time. I was a little worried about that. We'd pretty much always brought Scout around on our supernatural ventures. To be going without him this time around made me feel somewhat naked. But I trusted Bishop's judgment. If he said we were better off without Scout this time around, it felt difficult to disagree with him.

Bishop and I left the apartment into the cool spring evening. It was a beautiful night to talk shop with some vampires. Oh boy, I can't wait.

Chapter 3

When I imagined our confrontation with the Blood Clan of vampires, I imagined busting into some dank, dark cave and getting into it with some bloodthirsty monsters. What I did not expect was to be standing in front of an ordinary office building only a couple of blocks away from the Space Needle.

"Seriously?" I looked up in disbelief. It wasn't a terribly huge building or anything, maybe a half dozen floors or so.

"What did you expect?" Bishop smirked at me.

I decided that my original vision might've sounded silly, so I didn't say anything. Bishop began walking towards the front entrance. As he did so, he made a twisting motion with his wrist. About halfway through, a long wooden staff nearly as tall as he was faded into existence. It wasn't perfectly shaped all the way through, growing wider and thinner along the length. The gnarled wood was carved with runes similar to that of my eskrima.

We entered the building, a small chime echoing as we walked through the sliding doors. The vampires' den continued to defy my expectations. It really was just some sort of plain office building complete with a preppy-looking receptionist sitting behind a large counter. She was a dark-skinned woman with long braids that went past her shoulders. A name tag on her chest read "Tina" and then under that, "Red Moon LLC". Bishop and I walked up to the receptionist's desk.

"Hello, do you have an appointment?" Tina asked cheerfully.

"Yes, I'm here to speak with Mr. Grimaldo." Bishop said.

Tina blinked, though her perfect customer service smile didn't waver one bit. I had a feeling that Mr. Grimaldo was not someone anyone could just ask for.

"Um, name?" Tina stuttered.

"Bishop Leight. Mr. Grimaldo is expecting me." Bishop said plainly.

Something flickered in Tina's expression. Was it recognition? Fear? I couldn't tell exactly, but there was definitely something there.

"Of course, Mr. Leight. One moment please." Tina said, gritted through that permanent smile on her face. It was starting to creep me out just a wee bit.

Tina picked up a phone from a receiver, dialed a number, and after a moment, began speaking quietly. After another couple of minutes, Tina nodded and replaced the phone back on its receiver. A second later, an elevator behind Tina and to her right dinged and groaned open.

Bishop raised an eyebrow and pointed at it questioningly.

Tina nodded. "Just take the elevator, sir. Mr. Grimaldo is waiting for you."

Bishop nodded politely and thanked her for her help. Then he began walking towards the elevator, tapping his staff on the tile floor as he went. I hurried after him, trying not to look nervous. The doors closed and the elevator began moving without any prompt from either of us. To my surprise, instead of heading up, the elevator went down. It wouldn't have been spooky in any other situation, but it creeped me out a bit. It felt like we were being pulled into the den of the beast.

After a few moments, the elevator lurched to a halt and dinged again. The doors opened and we walked out into a large office that took up the entire room. The far wall was made up almost entirely of one large oil painting of a sunset. There were a few small, round tables scattered around the room to fill up the space. In one corner there were a pair of black leather couches with a glass table between them. In another corner, there was a minibar with a mahogany cabinet filled with expensive-looking bottles of alcohol. In front of the ginormous painting was a large mahogany desk. I'm talking obnoxiously large; I'd seen smaller dinner tables.

Sitting at that ego-stroking desk was a man. I wasn't quite sure of his specific lineage, but he was clearly of Hispanic descent. He had long, pitch-black hair that would make a L'Oréal commercial girl jealous. His tailored suit matched the color of his hair, except for the tie, which was the color of blood. Subtle. He had dark brown eyes, nearly black. His pupils seemed a tad too large. His hands were folded in a steeple, the tip of his nose rested on top. I noticed silver cuff links attached to his suit jacket, but I couldn't make out exactly what they were.

"Ah, welcome, Wizard Leight." The man raised his head slightly as he spoke. He spoke with a thick accent that made me realize he'd probably grown up somewhere in Latin America.

"Grimaldo." Bishop responded.

There seemed to be an uneasy familiarity between the two, and it occurred to me this probably wasn't the first time they've met. There was a long moment of silence as the two just stared at each other. I couldn't help but look back and forth between them, waiting for someone to speak up.

After what seemed like an eternity, Grimaldo was the one to break the silence. He unfolded his hands to gesture towards me. "Well, are you going to introduce me to your young companion?"

Bishop was staring daggers at Grimaldo, his grip on his staff tightening. I could hear the wood creak under his hand. "Tobias, this is the Don of the Blood Clan's Seattle chapter, Grimaldo, this is Tobias, my nephew and apprentice."

Grimaldo smiled at me. There was some sort of demented joy in the expression. I felt my feet shuffle uncomfortably under me. To my surprise, there were no pointy teeth to flash sinisterly at me. they were perfectly white, perfectly straight, and perfectly human teeth.

"Tobias Leight, I see." Grimaldo purred. Not like a house cat, but something more like a hungry tiger that was amusing itself with its prey. "I've heard of the business between you and the fallen son, Azazel."

I tried to hide the surprise on my face, but I wasn't too successful. This seemed to further amuse the vampire. He held up a hand in mocking apology. "Don't be shocked, I have many connections in the mystical underworld. I like to keep tabs on all potential players in the game."

My lips moved before I could consult with my brain. "I told those gossip magazines not to spill the beans. I'm going to have to speak with my lawyer." I rolled my eyes dramatically.

Grimaldo's smug expression broke. He blinked and looked back to Bishop for an explanation.

Bishop just shrugged. "He likes to quip. No idea where he gets it from."

Grimaldo relaxed again, folding his hands into a steeple once again. "Well then, my assistant tells me you're here regarding our increased activity in the city?"

Bishop cleared his throat. "If by activity you're referring to the increase in violent shootouts, disappearances, and 'animal attacks', then yes, that is why we're here."

"While I and the rest of the clan appreciate the concern of the Mystic Order, I assure you that it is strictly clan business, and none of yours to worry about." Grimaldo said, his voice smooth and calm.

"But as you know, Grimaldo, the Blood Clan is allowed to operate in Seattle under strict guidelines set by the Mystic Order. So, when you start acting outside those guidelines, we have every right to step in and investigate."

Grimaldo chuckled to himself. He seemed amused at Bishop trying to exercise his authority. I felt a fire spark to life in my belly as I became increasingly more annoyed with the vampire.

“Of course, sir wizard.” Grimaldo drawled, sarcastically. “If you insist, I suppose the talents of a wizard may be useful to resolving our conflict.”

“So, what seems to be the trouble?” My uncle asked. His tone was impatient, but there seemed to be a familiarity. He’d definitely done this dance with Grimaldo once or twice before.

Grimaldo pressed a button on the desk phone and spoke into it. “Tina, could you please bring me the file?” He put a certain emphasis on the word file that made it very clear which file he wanted.

“Right away, sir.” Tina’s voice chirped from the receiver.

We stood there quietly for maybe five minutes. I was keeping track using the tick-tocking coming from the clock on the wall.

Tick, tock.

Tick, tock.

Tick, tock.

God, it felt like an eternity. All the while Grimaldo seemed perfectly content with just staring at my uncle and me. I tapped my foot impatiently and made a poor attempt at whistling casually. I can’t whistle to save my life, so I probably looked like even more of an idiot.

Finally, the elevator dinged once more. Tina walked across the room and over to Grimaldo’s desk. She still had that damn smile plastered across her face. If we weren't staring down a literal vampire lord, she'd be the creepiest thing in the room. In her hands, she held a manila folder. From the looks of it, it could've only contained a few documents. She set it down on the desk, bowed stiffly towards Grimaldo, and then made her way back towards the elevator. It dinged again, and then she was gone. She hadn't even looked in our direction. How rude.

Grimaldo flipped open the folder and spread out the documents within to show us. We approached the desk as he did so we could get a better look. They were mostly stills from a security camera. They were blurry and only in black and white, but with a mild effort, I could make out the form of a young woman and what appeared to be at least two assailants. The assailants had their backs to the camera, so the only thing I could discern from the images was they both appeared to be male.

Bishop tapped one of the photos thoughtfully, "Who's the girl?"

"My daughter, Maria." Grimaldo said simply. "She was taken by the men in the photos and has been missing for three days."

"Which matches up with the start of the increased activity between the vampire clans." Bishop nodded.

I finally spoke up, "So you're assuming that the kidnappers belong to one of the other clans, and you're dishing out punishment until they finally decide to talk with you?"

"More like they're wreaking havoc so that whichever clan has her in custody will consider her too expensive to keep hostage." Bishop corrected. "Am I right?"

"Close enough." Grimaldo nodded.

"And how do you know it was one of the other clans who kidnapped your daughter?" I asked him.

Grimaldo held his hands out in an obvious gesture. "Who else do you propose?"

"Uhh." I said intelligently.

Bishop answered for me. "The other clans have the most motivation. They're rivals in the drug trade and other criminal activity in the city. If anyone has anything to gain by kidnapping the Don's daughter, it'd be one of the other vampire sects."

"Oh, and use her as leverage to get what they want out of the Blood Clan." I nodded. It started to make more sense.

"Precisely, young wizard." Grimaldo nodded. "If the clans don't produce my daughter and return her to me within the next three days, I'm afraid it will be war."

Yikes. That was a scary image. Three rival factions of vampires waging a full-scale war in the middle of Seattle would be major bad news. There'd be hundreds, if not thousands, injured, and even more killed in the crossfire. As a rule, people chose to be ignorant where the magical world was concerned. It was a whole lot easier than recognizing that vampires, demons, and leprechauns are real. Yeah, leprechauns are real, and they're assholes.

"So, I'm going to wager a guess that you want us to find your daughter before the end of the third day?" Bishop asked, for clarity's sake.

"Correct." Grimaldo nodded graciously. "If you can manage this task, I can safely call off any further hostilities, and I'd consider it a favor to be repaid."

"Consider it done." Bishop said. "If you don't mind, I'd like a copy of the case file, and if we can get access to the location Maria was kidnapped from, it would be a great help."

"You can take this copy." Grimaldo waved his hand broadly at the photos in front of him. Bishop flicked his head forward and I stepped forward to gather the pictures into the folder and picked it up. "And I'll have Tina give you the address on your way out."

"Thank you, Don Grimaldo." Bishop inclined his head respectfully. "I assure you; my nephew and I will see the safe return of your daughter."

"See that you do, wizard." Grimaldo's voice became razor sharp. "Because if not, not even you can stop the wrath I will unleash on my enemies, and this city."

On that cheery note, Bishop and I excused ourselves and headed towards the elevator. It dinged, and we walked inside. Grimaldo didn't take his eyes off of us until the doors had slid shut.

"Do you think he's serious?" I asked my uncle. "That he'd really raise hell on the city for the sake of revenge?"

Bishop nodded gravely, looking straight ahead. "Grimaldo is a dangerous man. We've crossed swords before, and I'd hate to see the hell he'd unleash if we don't find his daughter."

"Well, we've dealt with worse, right?" I said, in an attempt to lighten the mood. "Hell, we dealt with the actual devil last year."

"Maybe, maybe not." Bishop explained. "The vampire clans have chapters in every state, and pretty much every country on the planet after that. If the vampires of Seattle start to throw down, their allies across the planet will get drawn into the fray. It may not be as spectacular as the devil trying to conquer the world, but I can assure you, it'll be hell on Earth in its own right."

Gulp. And here I thought things were starting to get simple.

The elevator dinged again. I was starting to get sick of that sound, to be honest. We exited the elevator and walked back into the entrance hall. We stopped by Tina's desk, and she greeted us with a smile before handing us a slip of paper. I took it from her and written on it was an address that I noted wasn't too far from here, it was about half the distance from the office building to our apartment.

I thanked Tina and gave her a polite nod, doing my best not to look at her directly without being rude. That damn smile, man. When I turned to the front door, I noticed Bishop was already waiting for me outside on the sidewalk. Wizards can be spooky quiet and it always freaked me out.

I followed after my uncle and handed him a paper slip. He read it silently and nodded.

"Well, let's get going." Bishop said solemnly.

So, we did, taking off into the night towards our next destination. It was going to be a long night.

Chapter 4

The address that Grimaldo had provided us with led to a rundown apartment building. I was pretty sure it had been scheduled for demolition years ago, but here it stood. There were fences bordering the building and its small yard decorated with signs that discouraged trespassers. We approached the front gate, and further inspection revealed it was chained shut, sealed by a large padlock.

"Keep an eye out." My uncle said, in a voice slightly too loud to be a whisper. He pointed the tip of his staff at the padlock as he spoke.

I turned to face the street. It was starting to get dark, and the temperature had dropped significantly, so there weren't many people out and nobody seemed to be paying attention to us.

Bishop snapped out a word of power. I felt a surge of motion and then the sound of shattering chains. The chains fell limply to the ground with a loud, clattering sound. Bishop nudged the chains away from the gate with the toe of his boot and swung it open. We slipped by and approached the front door. Calling it a door was giving it a bit too much credit. It was nothing more than a few lengths of rotting wood that were broken in several places. The building was old as hell and had become a popular destination for the homeless up until recently. I had a vague memory of an old homeless man who'd put the door together, but that had been a long time ago. Now the homeless folk avoided this place like the plague, and for good reason. It'd become some sort of safe house or something for the Blood Clan.

I pushed on the door and instead of swinging inward, it fell straight forward and shattered into several smaller pieces. Whoops. Honestly, I had been surprised that the Blood Clan hadn't fixed this place up.

"This seems like a pretty crappy safe house." I said.

Bishop shook his head and pointed forward. "Look there."

Immediately down the hall was a reinforced metal door. Or at least, the remains of one. The darkness of the old building had hidden the fallen door from my view at first, but it was hard to miss once you finally noticed it. It'd been ripped off its hinges and forced into the room ahead. There was a big dent in the front of it that made me think of a miniature wrecking ball.

"Jinkies." I knelt down to examine the door, hoping to pick up something with my magical senses, but there was nothing. It had been three days already since the kidnapping had occurred, so if magic had been used, any residual trace would be long gone. It'd been worth a try anyhow.

My uncle had walked past the door and into the room. With a whisper of magic, he called up a beacon of light at the tip of his staff that lit up the entire room. I looked around and started taking down details.

It wasn't a huge room, about the size of your typical bedroom. There were no windows, which was probably the oddest thing about the room. The wall farthest from the door was completely overtaken by a large bookshelf, its contents had been strewn all over the floor. Against the right wall, maybe a foot away from the bookshelf was a work desk that was surprisingly untouched. Opposite it was a twin-sized bed with plain white sheets that looked like they'd been kicked off in a hurry. It took me a moment, but I realized the room matched up to the one depicted in the security camera stills. I turned around and looked up to find the security camera in the corner, its red light still flashing.

"Huh, what the hell happened here?" I wondered aloud.

Bishop tapped his staff on the ground once and let it go. The staff continued to stand straight up, still projecting the light Bishop had called up. With both hands free, he held his hand out to me. I pulled the folder from the inside of my coat and handed it over to him. He began flicking through the pictures, taking only a couple of seconds to examine each still before moving on to the next one.

"Ah, I see." Bishop muttered. He seemed satisfied, judging by his tone. He offered the folder to me. "What's different?"

I took the folder and began examining the pictures. In the first photo, Maria was sleeping soundly on the bed. I flipped to the next photo. The door was being blown in here. I couldn't tell what had wrecked the door. The still was full of static and distortion over where the attacker was. In the next still, Maria was running along the bookshelf. There were two figures, I think, obscured by static, blocking off Maria's escape route. The next photo showed Maria ducking under a burst of static that overtook the bookshelf, which I suspected explained the books now strewn all over the floor. The final photo showed the room as it was now.

I frowned in thought. There was something different about how the room had started and the state it was in now. I flipped between the first photo and then the last one a few times. What the hell was different? It was something that was so obvious that it became proportionally not obvious. I set the folder down and held up the first and last photos from the file, staring at them both at once. That's when my monkey brain finally seemed to put things together. In the first photo, next to the desk, was what appeared to be a large trunk of some kind. In the last photo, it was gone.

"Maria wasn't the only thing taken." I concluded. "Hell, she might not have even been the target, right?" I eyed the section of the room where the trunk should've been.

A proud smile painted itself on Bishop's face. "Very good."

"But Grimaldo didn't even mention the trunk, only that his daughter had been kidnapped." I put the photos down in the folder.

"So, either Grimaldo didn't even notice the trunk was gone, being more worried about his daughter, or maybe he didn't want to let us in on the fact that it was also missing." Bishop pondered.

"But why wouldn't he want to divulge that information?"

"Perhaps, the trunk holds something more valuable to the clan than his daughter, and if we knew about it outright, we'd have thought twice about assisting him."

"But what the hell could be in that trunk that he wouldn't want us to know about?" I asked him.

Bishop threw his hands up. "No clue. But it sure as hell is interesting."

I looked around the room and then pointed towards the mangled door. "What about that? Can either of the other vampire clans do that?"

Bishop knelt down near the warped hunk of steel and studied it closer, tracing his hands along the giant dent. He twitched his head in a motion of understanding, as if he'd put something together.

"Look at the door. Tell me what you see."

I scrunched my eyebrows and looked down at the door again. It was a big slag of metal that looked like it'd been punched in. I'd pictured someone swinging a wrecking ball into it, but perhaps it was something more akin to a cannonball. My eyes widened and I noticed a new detail that I hadn't before in the low light of Bishop's staff. All around the giant dent were these black scuff marks. Correction, they were scorch marks. It wasn't a wrecking ball or a cannonball, but a fireball.

"Someone knocked this down with fire." I said thoughtfully. "Maybe mixed it with some raw force to give it an extra punch?"

Bishop nodded, clearly satisfied. "Very good. Our assailant has an affinity for magic. The bang, boom kind."

"And what does that tell us?" I asked him.

"If this is an attack by one of the other vampire clans, and they're using fire magic, the most likely suspect is the Soul Clan."

"The Soul Clan? What's their shtick?"

Bishop wagged a finger at me and then pointed towards the security camera. "Best not to get too comfortable discussing business under prying eyes."

I looked up at the camera, its red light blinking ominously. Then I nodded towards Bishop. We stood up from the door and prepared to make our way up. Bishop clapped his hands, realizing he'd almost forgotten something. He faced back towards the safe room, where his glowing staff still stood independently. With a flick of his wrist, the light extinguished, and the staff flew through the air and into his grip.

The Grind was a coffee shop just a few blocks away from the abandoned building we'd inspected. It was open twenty-four hours a day, catering to that late night bookworm crowd that just needed a change of scenery from time to time. It also doubled as a library. Instead of advertisements and hollow scenery paintings, the walls were covered in oak shelving lined with books. There were books of all kinds. Fiction, nonfiction, academic, there were even a few tech manuals. Several lights were mounted on the walls, modeled after old-timey candles. Several small tables lined the glass windows that bordered the street-facing wall. In a far corner were worn but comfortable couches complete with a coffee table. There were a few board and card games stacked on the table that were free to use.

We walked in, a small bell mounted over the door signaled our entrance. It was late, but not too late, so there was only one other patron in the coffee shop besides a teenage girl behind the counter. Bishop made his way to the couches and got comfortable.

I approached the counter and was greeted with a small, but polite smile.

"How can I help you?" The girl asked.

I squinted to read her name tag. "Sarah, can I just get two coffees, with two sugars and caramel creamer?"

"Of course, one moment."

Sarah turned to the fresh coffee being brewed and poured two cups to my specifications. Then, she handed me the two steaming cups. I paid her, tipping her well, and took the cups over to where Bishop was sitting.

"Okay," I drawled. "So, what's the deal with the Soul Clan?"

Bishop took one of the cups and sipped on it. He cocked his head to one side, seemingly satisfied with the coffee. He seemed to space out for a second as he gathered his thoughts. After a moment, he finally spoke.

"Alright, so the Soul Clan is an interesting case. They are known as the Jiangshi. They ride a fine line between being a vampire and a zombie. They're corpses, primarily from Eastern Asia, that were reanimated, usually due to improper burial. All the good parts of their spirit, called their *hun*, were able to move on to what comes next. But their *po* is left behind and possesses their corpse. Thus, you have a Jiangshi."

Interesting, I hadn't expected them to be so different from the Sanguine Vampires. I sipped on my coffee and did my best to commit what he was saying to memory.

"The Jiangshi are often referred to as the 'hopping vampire' due to their stiff bodies. Most eyewitness reports describe them hopping along to move around, but this isn't always the case. They are the slowest of the three types of vampires but are just as durable as the Sanguine Vampires and are natural talents when it comes to elemental evocation. They are known to sling around elemental magic, like fire, for example, as their primary form of attack, but that doesn't mean you should let them get too close either, they have a death grip that can only be severed by, well, severing the hand."

I frowned. "Okay, but what makes them vampires?" I asked. "Do they feed on blood, like the Sanguine Vampires?'

"Well, if the Blood Clan feeds on blood, then the Soul Clan probably feeds on..." Bishop trailed off, encouraging me to fill in the blank.

"The soul." I said solemnly.

"Exactly, desperate to fill the void left behind by their hun, they feed on the souls of their victims. If they consume too much of a soul, it can leave the victim as a vegetable at best, but more often than not, it kills the victim outright."

"So, you told me how to lay the hurt on the Blood Clan. What's the Soul Clan's kryptonite?"

"Admittedly, we know the least about the Jiangshi, and what we've learned of their weaknesses is an unproven grab bag of sorts. For one, they don't care for mirrors. Supposedly, their own reflection repulses them and inspires fear. They're weak to wooden weapons as well, it's where the whole 'wooden stake' idea originated, believe it or not. But a weapon carved from a peach tree is said to be especially effective, don't ask me why. There's a certain Taoist talisman that is said to immobilize them completely if placed on their foreheads, but they're expensive as hell to commission from the wizards who can craft them."

Bishop took a deep breath, his voice getting a bit tired. He took another long sip of coffee before continuing.

"They can be distracted by spilled coins, there's some part of their soul that gets greedy and must count the coins. The chime of a handbell can disrupt their soul's attachment to their body, slowing them down for a time. Supposedly, they cannot feed on a person who's holding their breath, simply due to their views of the soul's connection to a person's breath."

Okay, he was right. The Jiangshi really did have some strange and obscure weak points. I'd definitely need Bishop to write these down for me later. Then I asked, "Okay, but none of those are the way to outright kill them, right?"

Bishop nodded affirmatively. "Right, the only way known to kill them for sure is to stab them in the heart with a blade soaked in the blood of a black dog."

"We gotta bleed some poor dog just to kill one of these things?"

"No, of course not. When I say black dog, I'm not referring to man's best friend. No, a black dog in this case is a sort of lesser hellhound. They're servants of the underworld who serve as spies and omens. Very common in the more rural parts of the country. I have a jar of the stuff back home, should it prove necessary."

I breathed a sigh of relief. I was not about to kill puppies, that's where I drew the line.

"Okay, so what now?" I asked my uncle. "Are we just going to knock on the door of the Soul Clan?"

Bishop took a long sip of his coffee and then let out a satisfied sound. "Politely, of course."

Chapter 5

Bishop and I finished our coffees and left The Grind a few minutes after my lesson on Soul Clan vampires. We trekked back out into the night and made our way to our next destination. To my surprise, I realized my uncle was leading us back to Wave Crest Shopping Center. It was about a thirty-minute walk from the coffee shop, and my feet were really starting to hurt now. Would it kill Bishop to invest in an actual car? I was starting to feel like I was making the trek to Mordor.

Back in the far-right corner of the U-shape of shops was a dry-cleaning place that I'd never been to. I was a teenager after all, I had no reason to. Well, I guess I wasn't really a teenager anymore, but that wasn't the point. Given the time, hell it was almost nine o'clock, the dry-cleaning place was closed. But that didn't seem to concern my uncle much.

Bishop aimed the tip of his staff where the door's lock should be and hissed out a word. I felt a whisper of magic rush forth. A moment later, I heard the click of the lock. He swung the door open, and we walked in.

"Wait, couldn't you have done that with the last lock too?" I asked him.

Bishop simply shrugged. "No one's going to care about a shattered lock blocking off an old, abandoned building, but I try not to blow up places of business. Even if they're just a front for supernatural criminals."

I could respect that. Even though we hadn't blown down the front door, the little, old, Chinese lady writing at the counter seemed surprised, and not too pleased, at our entrance.

She began yelling at us and waving her pen in the air angrily. I looked over at my uncle, who didn't seem too phased by her outburst. She just kept screaming and even threw the pen at me. It hit me in the forehead before I could react. Ow. Bishop held up a hand. After a few moments, as if on instinct, the lady seemed to calm down.

"Thank you." Bishop said simply. "We're here to speak with your bosses."

The woman said something in what I assumed was Chinese. It sounded like a question.

Bishop spoke as if he'd understood her. "No, your actual bosses. Not the people who run this business." Then he pointed to the floor. "I'm talking about those guys."

The woman looked at the floor, her face painted with concern. Then she spoke again. She didn't sound so confident.

"Ma'am, I know you're just doing as you're told." Bishop reassured her. "But I know who really works out of this place. And I need to speak with them. If you don't, I have a young apprentice here who has a knack for smashing things. And I'd hate for all of your expensive equipment and client property to get destroyed."

That seemed to click with her, and she replied simply with a few quick nods. She walked into the back of the store where we couldn't see her and disappeared for a few minutes.

I looked over at my uncle. "Were you really going to let me start smashing stuff if she didn't cooperate?"

"Of course not." Bishop shook his head. "But she doesn't know that."

I smiled wickedly. Whether or not the lady realized what we were, she probably had this idea of an American teenager being crazy, unruly, and destructive. In a way, she was right. But she probably imagined I'd just start hitting stuff with other stuff, when in reality I'd probably find a way to blow something up.

A few moments later, she returned and in perfect English said, "This way, please."

She pulled open a small door between the desk and the wall and motioned for us to come through. We did, and she led us past a wall of hanging clothes. We rounded a corner, and she opened up a trap door in the tile floor. There was a staircase that delved into the darkness.

"After you." I said to my uncle.

"Naturally." Bishop said, and then he began carefully descending the staircase. After a moment, I followed him. Of course, I managed to bump my head against the lip of the trap door as I walked down. Freaking ow.

The stairs went deep, surprisingly so. I'd grown up learning of the Seattle Underground. Long lost structures underneath the modern city that were leftover from when the city had sunken into the swampy landscape. I'd taken a couple tours over the years through school field trips and it always fascinated me. But this went even deeper than that.

And as we descended, I realized it was not only deeper, but older as well. Wherever we were going, it was old, ancient even.

There were torches mounted on the wall that illuminated the staircase. The stonework of the walls reminded me of something you might see in old temples. There were strange markings that just looked like a lot of gobbledygook, but when I looked ahead to Bishop, he was studying the carvings with intrigue.

My knees had started to hurt by the time we reached the bottom. Years of martial arts training had taken a toll on my body in certain aspects. It was nothing debilitating, but it was mighty uncomfortable at times. At the bottom of the steps was what appeared to be a temple chamber. There were more torches lining the walls and pillars that held up the ceiling. In the center of it all was a stone chair, not much bigger than you might see sitting at a desk or in a waiting room.

But what was interesting was what sat in the chair. It had been human at one point, but that had been a long time ago. Its features were reminiscent of a man from Eastern Asia but weathered by time immemorial. Its skin was gray, like ashes and pulled taut against its bones. It wore a formal black gi with gold stitching. I noticed it wasn't wearing any shoes, exposing its ashen gray toes. But the strangest detail about the creature was its hair. It was green, and I don't mean a dye job. Its neatly trimmed hair was the color of moss and was a little fuzzy like moss too.

It noticed I'd been taking in its appearance and smiled. In a thick Chinese accent, it spoke, "Welcome, wizards, to my humble abode." It motioned widely with its arms to the room around us. Though, I noted that the motion was unusually stiff.

"Humble, huh?" I muttered, glancing around at the chamber again.

"I don't believe we've had the pleasure of meeting." Bishop said. "My name is Bishop Leight, and this is my apprentice, Tobias."

"Ah, yes, I've heard of you." The creature said. "You may call me Feng Dài. I am the man in charge, as you say, of the Jiangshi here in Seattle."

"And I'm the man in charge of making sure everyone in town cooperates and plays nice." Bishop said. "Lately, that doesn't seem to be the case."

Feng tilted his head, confused. Again, the motion was very stilted. "What do you mean, wizard?"

"Well, recently the Blood Clan were attacked. The Don's daughter was kidnapped. They believe it was one of the other clans who did the deed, and the assailant appears to have used fire magic to break in."

"Ah, I see. And you believe that since the Jiangshi are specialists in elemental magic, that perhaps we might have been the ones to kidnap the girl?" Feng asked. He seemed amused by the accusation.

"It's possible. I have no ill will towards you or your people, Feng Dài." Bishop said, his tone was neutral and polite. "I am simply trying to come to the truth and have this matter resolved."

Feng seemed to consider Bishop's words for a long moment. I took the time to give the room another gander, not only with my eyes, but my magical senses as well. It's hard to describe my magical senses. They don't really parallel any of my other senses, though I suppose touch was the closest. I extend psychic feelers to my surroundings, which allows me to detect ambient magical energies around me.

I wasn't surprised to find that there was a lot of ambient magic flowing through the chamber. The stone bricks that shaped the room were carved with invisible sigils that seemed to be producing the magical energies in the air. I was far from an expert, but if I had to guess, the sigils composed several layers of protective spells. The kind of spells that would protect the integrity of the chamber and hide it from anyone who wasn't specifically looking for it. Otherwise, how else had this chamber been kept hidden from the city? Bishop had said the Jiangshi were good with elemental magic, but it seemed like that wasn't the only thing they could do.

As my arcane senses grazed the back wall, a bolt of lightning ran down my spine. My breath caught in my throat. There was something there. Something more. It felt familiar somehow, but I couldn't place it. The sigils on the wall were mucking with my perception.

Feng finally spoke again. "I wish there was something more I could do to assist you, wizards, but we simply have nothing to do with the attack on the Blood Clan. We have no interest in nursing conflict with the other clans."

Bishop narrowed his eyes. "And you're sure you know nothing about the kidnapping of Grimaldo's daughter?"

Feng smiled again, showing his pointed teeth. "We have no interest in nursing conflict with the other clans, wizard." He repeated the words. His tone was smug and amused. He knew something.

I heard the wood of Bishop's staff creak under his grip, but he returned the smile. It was just as hollow as Feng's. "Well then, we apologize for taking up your valuable time. We'll see ourselves out. Come on, Tobias."

Bishop turned on the spot, tapped his staff against the ground once, and started walking up the stairs. I looked from him, to Feng, and then back to him. Then I hurried after my uncle.

"Happy hunting, wizards." Feng's voice echoed. "And stay safe out there, it would be a shame if your investigation were to lead you to your deaths."

I frowned at those words. What did Feng know? And why was he hiding it? And what the hell was he hiding in this chamber? I had a feeling we'd be back before too long. We made the hike back up the stairs much faster than the way down. My uncle was taking the stairs two at a time and showed no signs of tiring. He didn't want to be here. And if he didn't want to be here, then I sure as hell wanted to get far away. I felt a tickling sensation on the back of my neck, as if we were being watched. The Jiangshi were involved in this somehow, it was just a matter of figuring out how.

We made our way up the stairs and left the store. Only once we had made it back to the open street did Bishop finally stop moving.

"What do you think?" I asked him.

"Feng Dài knows more than he's letting on." Bishop said. "I'm still not sure if he is directly involved, though."

I debated telling him of the familiar magic I'd felt in the chamber, but I didn't want to detract our focus on the current mission. I wanted to figure out if it was relevant first.

"So, what do we do now?" I asked him.

Bishop checked his watch, then frowned at the time. "We've done enough for tonight. We still need to meet with the Emotion Clan, and I'd rather not do it in the dead of night. I'll take another look at everything we know and see if there's anything we missed."

"And what about me?" I asked him.

"Sleep, then school, the usual. After you're done at school, we'll have a meeting with the Emotion Clan."

I groaned. Phenomenal cosmic power, and I still had to report to first period chemistry. At least Harry Potter got to go to wizard school. I was stuck in public high school for another month. What a scam.

Chapter 6

Given we were currently in an active investigation of the supernatural happenings in town, I took Scout with me to school. He was in his service dog disguise. Well, I suppose I can't call it a disguise, since he is legally registered as a service dog. He helped me with the big math problems. It counts, don't judge me.

Scout knew when he had his service vest on that he had to be on his best behavior. He walked alongside me as we made our way down the crowded hallways. The dog really was providing a service. That service being looking out for supernatural bad guys. If there was any trouble afoot, Scout would give me a heads up before the bad guys could have a chance to act. I'd put on my bomber jacket and charms bracelet as well, but school security wasn't a fan of my eskrima sticks, so those got left at home.

The day went off without a hitch. We made our way from class to class, keeping our eyes open and heads low. Nothing happened. Scout took a keen interest in chemistry for some reason, but otherwise, it was an uneventful day. I made it to fifth period English without a single sign of magical baddies to see.

English was the one class that Claire and I shared. We even sat next to each other, so a lot of the time was spent with me passing her notes while she continually tried to get me to focus. Hell, like that was ever going to happen. But today was different. For once in her life, Claire wanted to do nothing but talk to me during class.

"So have you gotten your tux yet?" She whispered to me.

"Uh, well I had one. For about twenty seconds." I shrugged. "There was a problem with it. Had to return it."

Claire frowned, doubt evident on her face. "What do you mean you had one for twenty seconds?"

"Well, someone kinda shot it." I said, matter of factly.

Claire stifled a sound of surprise, quickly slapping her mouth shut with her hand. "Someone shot it?" She said, emphasizing the word 'shot.'

“Yeah.” I said, dragging out the word. “I don’t know all the details yet, but it was more than likely shot up by vampires. Although I’m pretty sure they were aiming for me. I didn’t know the tux long though, so maybe it did something to piss them off.”

“Vampires? Why would a vampire shoot at you?” Claire asked me.

That was a fair question, I supposed. And I’d thought about it too. Why would a vampire shoot at me as opposed to, say, rip me apart and drink my blood? Or soul, or whatever. Simple, because it's effective. A gun would kill me just as easily as any supernatural means, for the most part. I told her as much and she furrowed her brow in a look of concern.

“Don’t worry,” I said, waving away her concern. “Bishop and I are working on a case for one of the vampire leaders. Someone probably was trying to scare us off ahead of time.”

Her frown deepened, and I could tell the information had done nothing to reassure her. “Toby, if you’re going to be in the middle of this vampire mess, then maybe we shouldn’t think about prom.”

Brain don’t fail me now.

I shook my head. “Absolutely not. Nothing’s going to stop me from taking you to our senior prom. Bishop and I will get this settled before then, and then you and I will party the night away. I promise."

Claire's frown became a half-hearted smile. I could tell she still had her doubts. But if I said I was going to do something, I was going to make it happen. There's not a demon, devil, or vampire alive that could stop me.

Suddenly, the building shook and I heard a loud boom. The decorations on the wall clattered against the wall. A performance trophy sitting on the teacher's desk fell to the ground. Another boom. Closer this time. I heard screams fill the school.

Oh no. I looked to Scout, the dog was up and alert, his eyes locked on the classroom door. He was growling. It was a low, almost inaudible sound that I wouldn't have noticed if he hadn't been pressed to my leg. Students were chattering wildly. No one was sure what was going on. But I had a good feeling it wasn't a fire drill. Then I heard gunshots. I could hear the screams of unsuspecting students. Scout's growl rose in volume, and he was braced to move in a moment's notice. From somewhere down the hall, I could hear the sounds of men shouting in a foreign language. Not just any language though, I vaguely recognized it. Whoever was shouting, and presumably firing off guns and setting off explosions, they were speaking in Chinese.

The Jiangshi, it had to be. But why were they attacking the school? I smacked my forehead, mentally cursing at myself. They were here for you, dummy. My classmates were starting to panic now. They were starting to get a grasp of the situation; they'd seen enough news stories to recommend when a threat had arrived on campus. The teacher was trying to shush everyone and instruct them into the corner. I looked from Scout, and then to Claire. I could see the fear in her eyes, but there was also a steady resolve. Hell, she'd been smack dab in the middle of multiple demon attacks.

I grabbed her hand and wrapped Scout's leash around her wrist. She looked from the leash, then at me.

"Toby?" Claire fought to keep her voice steady.

"Just stay here with Scout. He'll keep you safe." I told her, my voice as calm and level as I could make it.

Then I knelt down to Scout. "Listen boy, I need you to keep Claire and the other students here safe. No bad guys get in this room alive; you understand?"

Scout's eyes flickered in understanding. Without any further instruction, he tugged on his leash and led Claire to the back of the classroom where the other students had gathered. Those with clearer heads had already started to form a makeshift barrier with the desks. To the shock of anyone sane, instead of joining the other students, I leapt over the remaining desks and through the door, into the hallway.

When I burst through the door, I had expected a wave of students running to escape. I'd expected Jiangshi gunmen to be firing haphazardly in every direction. But to my surprise, the hallway was empty. There wasn't even any trash or debris scattered across the tile floor. That gave me a moment to breathe and gather my wits.

I turned back to the door and gathered a wisp of magical energy. "*Kagi,*" I whispered.

The door made a loud *ker-chunk* sound as the deadbolt turned and sealed the door shut. I'd whipped up the lockpicking spell to get into my apartment when I'd once forgotten my keys, luckily it worked both ways. It wasn't much, but it was the least I could do.

The shouting picked up again somewhere down the halls, but I didn't hear the screams of frightened teenagers. Hopefully that meant everyone was safely tucked away where they couldn't easily be found. I considered my next action carefully. I could duke it out with the Jiangshi agents here in the halls, but that risked a lot of collateral damage to the student body and faculty. No, the only course of action was to lead them away from the school.

I whipped out my phone and sent a quick text to Bishop. It read simply; 911. I hastily returned it to my pocket and hoped for the best. Bishop could be here within an hour. Less than that if he believed I was in trouble. Failing that, I'd lead them away from the school and find a way to throw them off my scent.

Yeah. Yeah, that was a good plan.

I felt my thoughts rushing through my brain a mile a minute. My breathing was picking up, and it took considerable effort to stop myself from giggling nervously. It had been awhile since I'd been in an honest to God fight for my life without one of my allies at my side. And without my eskrima, I was at a severe disadvantage. High schools frowned upon bringing weapons on campus, even martial ones. I hadn't wanted to get them confiscated or something.

Okay, Tobias, focus. Get moving.

Without another wasted moment, I began sneaking my way down the hall, following the sounds of shouting and gunshots. I peeked my head around a corner and jerked back suddenly. Then I peeked again, more slowly. There were three men in cheap suits and wearing ski masks. If I had to guess, those ski masks hid the gray skin and green hair of the Jiangshi. They were all holding big guns across their chests. I was no expert in firearms, but I had a good feeling the guns they were toting shot really fast and would kill me even faster if I was stupid.

So naturally, I took a deep breath, and stepped out from the corner and stood in the middle of the hallway. “Hey, uglies!” I shouted cleverly.

The men turned around quicker than should’ve been possible, their weapons raised immediately. Without giving me a moment to throw out another quip, they opened fire.

I let out a yelp and dove for the wall opposite from where I’d emerged. Okay, step one, get their attention. Good job, Tobias. Now, what? I heard three pairs of footsteps closing in on me fast. I rose to my knees and prepared for the men to round the corner.

No sooner had the barrel of one of the guns emerged from the corner did I shout, “*Kaze!*”

Wind roared from my outstretched arm. The hitmen never had a chance. They rounded the corner just in time for a huge gust of wind to send them hurtling down the hall from where I came. They flew through the air and hit the ground with not an ounce of grace. They’d barely hit the ground before they were already recovering their footing. The gunmen charged me without a second thought, aiming their weapons at me and opening fire once more. I rolled out of the way of their fire and towards a door.

I attempted to hurl myself through the door but was instead met by its unyielding surface. I heard a cry of terror from within and mentally thumped myself on the forehead. Duh, people were hiding in there. And probably behind nearly every other damn door in the school. Crap.

The gunfire had stopped for a brief moment as my attackers closed in on me. I noticed something strange as they approached. Bishop had told me one of the defining characteristics of the Jiangshi was their bodies were stiff like corpses that had settled into rigor mortis. Yet these guys were moving as if they were spry and healthy. I didn't give myself a moment to dwell on the inconsistency and thrust out my hand toward them.

Again, I screamed. "*Kaze!*"

Another blast of wind, more powerful than the first, roared through me and straight for my assailants. The wind picked them up and sent them flying once more down the hall. They shouted, more in surprise than anything else. But one of the gunmen had kept his cool. Maybe he'd been expecting the counterattack, but as he flew, he steadied his gun and locked onto me.

Bullets ripped through the air, and I barely managed to duck my head behind my arm before they hit. Bullets whizzed past where my head had been a moment before. More struck me in the side and the arm I held in front of my face. They felt a lot like airsoft pellets striking against me, thanks to the defensive spells woven into the fabric of my bomber jacket.

Thank you, Uncle. I made a mental note to give him a thank you card next time I saw him. This must've confused the gunmen, because he said something to his compatriots in broken-sounding Chinese. I was starting to get the feeling that these guys weren't the Jiangshi after all. They moved too fast and couldn't seem to get their Chinese right either. Without giving them another moment to gather their wits, I shot up and bolted down the hallway away from them.

Focus on the plan, Tobias. They may not be who you thought they were, but they were still dangerous. I still had to lure them away from innocent bystanders. I turned to look back at the gunmen to make sure they were following me.

Oh, they were following me, alright. The men had apparently ditched their weapons and were racing after me in a sprint that would've made Usain Bolt shit his pants. In a couple of seconds, they would be on top of me. I wanted them to follow me, but I couldn't afford them catching me. I had to slow them down, even if it was only for a couple of seconds.

So, I tapped into one of the charms hanging from my bracelet. The small, golden charm was in the shape of a comet. I willed my magic through the bracelet and into the charm. With a small inaudible snap, I felt the spell prime itself.

"Alright, chew on this!" I growled.

Still running forward, I aimed my hand back towards my pursuers and snarled, "*Hinote!*"

A fireball the size of a bowling ball suddenly erupted from my palm and streaked towards my attackers. I'd been aiming for the one in the middle, but it wasn't like I'd stopped to take aim. I hit the one to my left instead, but it still had the intended effect. Upon impact, the fireball exploded and filled the section of hallway they'd occupied with flame and smoke.

"Haha! Yeah, suck on that!" I cheered.

An inhuman roar erupted from the flames and the three men leapt through the flames and continued their pursuit. Small patches of flame had burned holes in their clothes, but they seemed otherwise unbothered by the fireball I'd just chucked at them.

"Oh, come on!" I complained.

The men had recovered the distance they'd lost in a moment's notice and were once again closing in. I mean seriously, it's not even fair. I burst through a set of doors and found myself in the entrance hall. I looked to my right and found the front doors of the school.

One of the men leapt at me and I managed to duck under him out of pure reflex. But that didn't save me from the other two, who tackled me to the floor. We hit the ground in a discombobulated heap. I shouted and struck at them, but they didn't seem to even notice the blows. One struck me in the gut and completely knocked the wind out of me. If it hadn't been for my jacket, I was pretty sure my ribs would've been broken, or worse. The other was trying to rip my arm out of its socket.

I screamed and punched and kicked, but it was no use. They had a hold on me and weren't going to be dispatched by my feeble teenage strength. I let out a defiant shout and unleashed whatever magic I could muster. "*Kaze!*"

Without my eskrima to use as a focus, there was only so much I could do to control how my wind spell behaved. I could only aim it at a given direction without much control. But I didn't need control for this. I let the magic run wild. Wind roared and rushed outwards in every direction, with me at the center. The men were suddenly ripped away from me. I felt an explosion of pain in my right shoulder. Evidently the man who'd been trying to rip my arm off had a strong grip. The winds had hit him so suddenly and with such force that he must've ripped my arm out of socket as he went. I screamed in pain as the spell roared and ripped around the room. The men had been unceremoniously flung away from me. One of them hit the ceiling. Another went through the doors we'd come through. And the last hit the wall where a bulletin board was mounted.

As the winds died down, I managed to pull myself to my feet. I held my dislocated arm with my remaining good hand and ran for the exit.

I stumbled through the double doors and damn near fell down the stairs. I took them two at a time, a shock of pain running through my shoulder with each step. It wouldn't be long before the...

The three men burst through the door and leaped clear of the stairs and onto the sidewalk below. I cursed and stopped about halfway down the steps. Lucky for me, they hadn't dislocated the arm wearing the bracelet. I took aim, focused my power on the comet-shaped charm again and shouted, "*Hinote!*"

Another bowling ball-sized ball of flame burst from my outstretched hand and surged towards the men. They were ready this time. A moment before the comet hit, they jumped out of the way with inhuman speed and grace. The fireball struck the concrete, and the impact shattered the slab, sending shards of stone flying in every direction. I held up my arm, shielding my face from the debris, and it bounced harmlessly off of my jacket.

One of the men had flanked my left side and was charging again. Supernatural bad guys were used to dealing with wizards slinging spells and doing some gnarly shit with their power. What they weren't used to was getting popped in the schnoz.

"*Duro!*" I shouted. My skin hardened into something like steel and with one swift motion I threw an elbow back towards the leaping attacker. My attack struck home, and I felt his nose crunch under my elbow. I couldn't see the blood spilling from his nose, due to the mask, but I caught the distinct, metallic smell in the air. The man fell to the ground and collapsed in an unconscious heap.

One down, two to go.

Apparently the second man had been a whole lot smarter than the first. He'd flanked my right side, where my dislocated arm hung loosely. Crap. Before he could close in, I twisted and swung my good arm towards his face, hoping to replicate the result from the first guy. Again, the second man proved to be a lot smarter. He'd been expecting the attack, and swiftly ducked under it. He tackled me to the ground, and I fell against two steps awkwardly. The man got on top of me and started raining down blows at my head. If it hadn't been for my durability spell, I'd probably have been pounded to a pulp. It still hurt like hell though, and the spell wouldn't last much longer.

I'd trained for years in a mixed martial art that was prepared for any sort of fight. Stand up, on the ground, I was ready for it. I bucked my hips and twisted, sending us both into a tumble down the stairs. We hit the bottom and rolled off of each other. I breathed heavily as I dragged myself to my feet, my arm still dangling uselessly. I extended my hand out, preparing to unleash another fireball spell. The charm had three charges before it would have to recharge. It usually took about a day or so to refill all three, so I'd have to make this last one count.

I focused my magic on the charm. I could feel the durability spell fall away as I turned my focus on the fire magic. I was about to unleash the spell when the third man struck me from behind.

I let out a startled sound of pain as I fell to the ground, landing on my bad shoulder. Of course. Any magic I'd gathered up dissipated instantly. The second man recovered, and they both started hitting and kicking me with surprising strength. All I could do was curl up into a ball to protect the most vulnerable areas of my body.

I'd given it my best effort, but these guys had the jump on me, and I hadn't been prepared for such a sudden attack. I felt myself lose sense of my surroundings and my vision became a mix of blurry images and flashing lights.

"*Igni*!" I heard a man shout. Then there was a wave of heat and the screams of the two remaining gunmen. I felt a surge of motion as they were flung through the air and away from me.

I rolled onto my back in time to see the blurry image of a man holding a staff standing over me in a wide, defensive stance. I didn't need my full vision to recognize the shape of my uncle standing over me.

I coughed. "About time you showed up."

Bishop twirled his staff and aimed one end where the men must've fallen. The men must've recognized the sudden shift in the battle, because they said something I couldn't understand through the haze. A moment later, I heard the sounds of retreating footsteps. Bishop muttered a curse, then he twirled his staff in the air, and it disappeared. He adjusted himself and knelt down to help me sit up.

"Are you alright?" His voice became clearer as I regained my focus.

I nodded drunkenly.

Bishop took a look at my arm and frowned. "I need to reset it before there's any permanent damage."

I nodded again and braced myself. Bishop grabbed my arm, gingerly extending it out in front of me.

"One, two..."

Before he'd even finished counting, my uncle yanked on my arm. Fire erupted from my shoulder as it popped back into place. I gritted my teeth and let out a pained grunt.

"Three." Bishop finished.

"Thanks, I thought they'd gotten me." I told him.

"Any idea who they were?" He asked me.

"I was hoping you would know." I shook my head. "At first, I had assumed they were Jiangshi. They were speaking Chinese, I think, and I heard explosions that I thought were coming from fire magic. But they moved too fast and once I'd confronted them, they relied on guns and their sheer strength alone."

Bishop mulled on that for a moment. "Anything else?"

I thought for a moment. "They practically shrugged off my fire spells. Ran right through the first one, in fact."

Bishop nodded, but he looked more concerned than satisfied. "That almost certainly rules out Sanguine Vampires then."

"So, what does that mean?" I asked.

"If this is related to the vampire conflict, then they may well have been agents of the Emotion Clan." Bishop said.

"The Emotion Clan? What's their deal?" I asked.

Bishop shook his head. "Not here. We'll discuss it at home. Where's Scout?"

"He's with Claire. I wanted to make sure she and the other kids from my class were safe."

"Probably a good call. He can stay with her for now, we'll get him back later. For now, let's get out of here. Authorities will be here shortly."

Bishop helped me to my feet, and we made our way back to the apartment. In the distance I could hear sirens. Man, we'd really gotten ourselves into trouble this time.

Chapter 7

Bishop had called the school to assure them I was safe. Sure, it hadn't been the first time I'd been in the middle of an attack at the school since I'd been thrust into the world of magic, but it was better safe than sorry. After we'd finally got home, the first thing I did was call Claire to make sure she was okay.

"I'm fine." She said, though I could hear the shakiness in her words. "What about you? What happened?"

"Some bad guys were posing as some other bad guys and were attacking the school to draw me out." I told her. "I fought them off for a while, but if Bishop hadn't shown up when he did, I'm not sure what would've happened."

"Are you hurt?" Claire asked me.

"A little banged up, but not as bad as I could be. How's Scout?" I asked.

"He seems a little antsy, but he won't leave my side."

I smiled. The dog desperately wanted to come back, but I knew he'd stay with Claire until he was given the okay to return. "Good. Keep him with you, he'll make sure nothing happens to you."

"And what are you going to do?" Claire asked.

"Well, Bishop thinks he has a pretty good idea of who sent those men. So, we're going to kick down their door and start asking questions." I said in my best cool, gruff action hero voice.

I heard her giggle and smiled. It was good she hadn't gotten too shaken up by the events. Then her voice leveled again as she said, "Just be careful, Toby. I can't have anything happening to you."

"Don't worry, I'll be just fine." I reassured her. "Compared to Azazel, these guys are like cheesy Saturday morning cartoon villains."

"Okay, talk to you soon."

"Yeah. See ya." I said with a smile before hanging up.

Bishop came back from the kitchen and tossed me an ice pack wrapped in a towel. I caught it with one hand and pressed it gently against my shoulder. It was still sore after being dislocated, and a mild shock of pain twinged at the touch of the ice pack. I winced, but it wasn't too bad. It wasn't the first time I'd dislocated an arm, but I'd never had it ripped out of socket by some supernaturally strong monster before.

"How are ya feeling?" Bishop asked me.

"Sore as hell, but I'll be alright." I told him.

"You did good, leading them away from the innocent bystanders." Bishop said. "Hell, you even got quite a few good licks in."

"Yeah, I guess, but if you hadn't shown up, I would've been screwed." I said. "You said they may have been from the Emotion Clan of vampires? What are they like?"

Bishop sat down in his recliner across from me and seemed to be searching for the right words. "The Emotion Clan are made up of the Motus Vampires, and if you can guess by the name, feed on emotions. They're half-humans that descend from the original incubus and succubus, Lilu and Lilith.

"Wait, incubus? Succubus?" I said, somewhat stunned. "You mean, like sex demons?"

"Well, yes. Though the Motus Vampires are more than that. Sure, they can feed on human lust. But they've also been known to feed on sadness, anger, greed, fear, and pretty much any other negative emotion humans have." Bishop explained. "It fuels their powers of strength, speed, and durability, much like the Blood Clan. Though the Emotion Clan is not nearly as powerful in that regard. Where they excel though, is in their illusory abilities. They're experts in veils and illusions, which they use in their attempts to deceive. It makes them very dangerous."

Interesting. It certainly made them unique amongst the vampire clans. For one, they had a much wider assortment of food to choose from, but more importantly, they had a wider array of weapons to choose from. The Blood Clan, the Sanguine Vampires could only feed on blood that fueled their superhuman abilities. The Soul Clan, the Jiangshi, could only feed on souls, and while they were also very strong and durable, their stiff bodies prevented them from employing much of that strength. They made up for it with their abilities to cast elemental magic. The Motus Vampires had a bit of both worlds at their disposal.

Bishop continued speaking, "But one of their most dangerous abilities is their demon form. If a Motus Vampire is cornered, with no other options, they can assume a demonic form that is even more powerful than that of the Sanguine Vampires."

"What do I do if that happens?" I asked him. I'd thrown down with demons before, but I wanted to be sure of any details that might be useful.

"Well, whether or not that happens, there are weaknesses you can exploit." Bishop explained. "Motus Vampires are severely vulnerable to symbols of Christian faith, and other blessed objects, due to their demonic heritage. Think holy water, crucifixes, rosaries, and the like. It repels and burns them, though it won't stop them outright if they're determined enough."

That was simple enough, and holy objects like that were easy enough to come across. Though I felt conflicted about the use of religious paraphernalia. I didn't hate religion or anything, but I'd steered clear of it ever since I could remember. I didn't know much of my religious background since my parents had died. For that matter, I didn't remember much of anything before they had died. But for as long as I could remember, I'd focused on myself as a person and the positive force I could be on my own merit. I didn't need religion to be a good person, and any religion I'd come across was tainted by its own dark side, one way or another. But for the sake of not dying at the hands of psychic demon vampires, I think I could make an exception this time.

"You detailed ways to kill the other two kinds of vampires, so I'm assuming you know of a way to kill Motus Vampires, if it comes to it." I said, hopefully leading him to the information.

"Yes, of course." Bishop nodded. "If it comes to it, the only way currently known to kill a Motus Vampire is to pierce their wrists with nails soaked in holy water."

My eyes widened slightly. It didn't take a genius to draw the parallel there.

"Alright then." I said, committing the information to memory. With that done, I'd learned the basics of the three known types of vampires. Hopefully, I wouldn't need to employ such information, but having it available to me was a comfort.

"So now what do we do?" I asked him.

"For now, you should get some rest. We have a meeting with the duchess of the Emotion Clan in two hours. I need you fresh and ready for when we leave." Bishop said.

I nodded. "Okay, sounds good."

So, for once, I did as I was told. I stretched out on the couch and closed my eyes to take a nap. I'd exhausted myself in the confrontation with the unknown gunmen who'd attacked the school.

No sooner had I closed my eyes did I feel myself jostled awake. I opened my eyes to see Bishop kneeling over me, his hand on my shoulder. A brief glance out the window showed that the sun had begun to set. I groaned, feeling jipped by the lack of rest. I moved to rise, and Bishop held his hand to my back to support me.

"Easy." Bishop said. "You're still pretty banged up. We're going to be headed out for our meeting with the duchess in fifteen minutes. Are you still okay to go?"

I rolled my injured shoulder a couple of times, testing it. It was still sore and tender, but it was usable. "I'll live."

"Good, then get ready." Bishop clapped me lightly on the back before standing up and heading to his room upstairs.

I sat up and took a moment to think. The three clans were in semi-open conflict throughout the city. Point one, the Blood Clan had informed us that they felt wronged due to the kidnapping of Maria Grimaldo, the Don's daughter. But that missing trunk gave me reason to believe that there was more to the story. Whoever had kidnapped Maria, they'd also stolen something of value to the Blood Clan. Yet, Grimaldo had chosen to omit any mention of the missing trunk, and I doubted they hadn't noticed its absence. It made me think that whatever was in the missing trunk, Grimaldo didn't want us to know he possessed it.

Point two, the kidnappers had used fire magic to break into the Blood Clan's safe house. Simple deduction pointed towards their rivals in the Soul Clan. But we hadn't been able to get anything out of Feng Dài, not even one little inkling of a clue. He hadn't been the least bit nervous when Bishop and I had shown up on his doorstep to question him. We'd have to find another means of extracting that information.

Point three, someone was very keen on getting in our way of figuring this whole mess out. I'd been attacked at the school. No doubt I was perceived as an easy target they could use to motivate Bishop to cease his investigation. And I'd hazard a guess that whoever had shot at me yesterday was involved somehow. No way in hell had that been a coincidence.

I cursed. I didn't have enough information. All these separate points of information but no connective tissue in which to link them. I had a feeling this meeting with the Emotion Clan's duchess wouldn't yield much fruit. If the vampires all had anything in common, besides being vampires of course, it was that they all seemed secretive as hell. They were all playing things close to the chest, and it was making things more difficult. Even the Blood Clan, whose best interests were to aid us in our investigation, were giving us only tidbits of the information we needed. I decided that I didn't care much for vampires. They were proving to be a royal pain in the ass.

Oh, and I couldn't forget point four. Prom was in less than three days, and I'd made no progress in procuring the proper attire or a ride. Hell, I wasn't sure that prom was still on at this point, considering the recent attack at the school. They might cancel it due to poor timing. That made me worried. I had fostered an image in my mind of Claire and I, dancing close under fluorescent lights, moving in rhythm to slow music, leaning in closer and...

I shook my head, getting my mind back on track. There'd be plenty of time to fantasize about that later. Right now, I had to focus on resolving the issue at hand.

Bishop came down the stairs, wearing a fresh flannel shirt, a fur-lined leather jacket, and a pair of old jeans. He wasn't holding his staff, but I knew it was something he could make appear with a twist of his wrist.

"Are you ready?" He asked me.

"Uh, yeah. One sec." I walked over to the door, where my eskrima lay in their holster on top of my gym bag that held all my martial arts gear. I strapped the holster to my right leg, then looked up at my uncle and nodded.

"Alright, how do you feel about strip clubs?" Bishop asked me, a small smirk creasing his face.

I never understood the appeal of strip clubs. I mean, yeah sure, a bunch of naked girls, or guys, dancing around provocatively was certainly enticing, initially. But it's not like it was going to go anywhere. The dancers were paid to act like they like you. They weren't going to go home with you, and they sure as hell weren't going to call you back the next day. Plus, the clubs were just plain dirty. The couches and chairs were suspiciously sticky or crusted over, and it was just plain gross.

Bishop and I arrived at Heaven's Door just as it began to open for the night. From what I'd heard, it was the most popular high-end strip club in all of Seattle. The building was shaped like a pristine white box with a large logo written in golden, cursive letters. The doors themselves had a strange design that made them look like golden gates. If nothing else, they certainly had their presentation down pat. The parking lot was already full, and there was a line stretching down the length of the building.

I whistled, impressed by the sight. "How the hell are we supposed to get in? That line's ginormous, it'll take us hours to get through."

Bishop held his hand up and flicked two fingers upward toward the sky. I looked up to what he was holding. It was a simple metallic white card with a single gold strip stretched across it.

"What is that?" I asked him, my voice full of a mix of concern and doubt.

"A membership." Bishop said wryly. "VIP status."

"Bishop, you dog." I let out a laugh.

"It was a gift from the duchess a few years back." Bishop explained. "I've never really used it for recreational purposes. Just during times when I need to bypass this line whenever I have business here."

"Ah, is that right?" I said slyly.

"Yes, and that is all." Bishop said. His tone had a sense of polite finality to it.

I shrugged. "Alright then."

We walked up to the golden gates, passed all the other people in line. They looked mighty peeved that we strolled right past them. A mountain of a man was guarding the door. He was damn near seven feet tall with a recently shaved head. His features were brutish, like a troll. Though I hadn't met a troll yet, I couldn't be sure of the comparison. The man's neck was so thick, I had to wonder if he could turn his head at all.

His arms and chest were thick with an absurd amount of muscle.

"You blind or something, mister?" Thick Neck asked. He cocked his head towards the line. "The end of the line is down somewhere that way."

Bishop flicked his VIP pass as he'd done a moment before, flashing it to the man. Thick Neck snatched it from his hand and brought it close to his face, squinting at it. Then he tossed it back to Bishop, who caught it effortlessly. Thick Neck didn't look too pleased that we'd had it, but he seemed to respect it. He unhooked a red rope and waved us through.

Past the rope was another man who looked like he could've been Thick Neck's brother. Without saying anything, he motioned for Bishop to hold up his arms so he could be patted down. Bishop did as he was instructed. The man patted him down, looking for any paraphernalia, but he didn't find anything. Then he did the same with me. It didn't take long for him to notice my eskrima.

"I'm gonna need you to take those off." The man said.

"Listen, Tiny—" I started to protest.

"Tobias." Bishop's voice snapped. "Do as he says."

I glared at Bishop, and then back at the second security guard. Without breaking eye contact, I unstrapped my eskrima from my leg. I rolled up the straps around the holster and turned it over.

"I expect those back, Tiny." I growled.

Tiny grunted and smirked down at me. I resisted the urge to knock his teeth in and followed after my uncle.

We made our way into Heaven's Door through a dark hallway. As we progressed, the distinct sound of club music started getting louder and louder. Oh yeah, another thing I hate about clubs, strip or otherwise, the music is so damn loud. We emerged through a curtain and were immediately assaulted by light, sound, and the smell of alcohol. I shielded my eyes for a moment while my sight adjusted, but Bishop just kept moving forward.

I'd heard a lot about Heaven's Door, only the most beautiful men and women worked here. There were multiple stages scattered around, all populated with multiple dancers each. The men and women were all wearing various amounts of clothing, all with clearly different tastes in mind. Off to my right, I noticed several patrons cutting lines of a white powder. It didn't take a genius to figure out what they were partaking in. There were customers being guided into back rooms for private shows, others were indulging their desires with each other, surprisingly, while seemingly pleased dancers watched them with a sensual gaze.

I cleared my throat and adjusted my pants for reasons. Look, I'm young alright? These things get to me easily. Bishop didn't seem too concerned, though. He just continued straight forward, like a man on a mission, and I hurried to keep up with him.

I noticed Bishop seemed to be making a beeline towards a round couch near the far wall of the large room. It was illuminated by several spotlights. There were five people sitting around the couch. Two men sat at either end of the couch, hunched over the table in the center. They were indulging in the unknown white powder. Sitting between them in the middle of the couch were three unbelievably beautiful women. On either side of the woman in the middle lounged twin raven-haired women with long, alluring legs, curvy hips, and a perfectly sculpted chest.

Their skimpy clothing left almost nothing to the imagination. Only two pieces of long, white cloth draped across their breasts and their waists retained any sense of modesty. The cloth garments were held in place by small gold chains that hung from their shoulders and waist. They draped themselves provocatively over the woman in the center, stroking her and placing the occasional kiss on various parts of her body.

The blonde lounging in the center was a long-legged woman who'd probably tower over my uncle, even without the three-inch black heels she wore on her feet. Her skin was the color of fresh cream and was absent of even the slightest imperfection. Her blonde hair fell past her shoulders and disappeared behind the back of the couch. There wasn't a single ounce of excess fat on her body. Quite the opposite, actually. Her nearly pure white skin was shaped by the muscle of a gymnast who spent her spare time deadlifting dump trucks for fun. Speaking of dump trucks, I couldn't tell, seeing as she was sitting between two exceptionally beautiful women, but I hazard a guess that her rear was uh...quite pleasant. Her breasts were held back by twin black bands of silk that extended from behind her back, up her chest, and around her neck. Her black silk shorts, though I could hardly call them that, covered nothing but her waist and pelvic area, and were bound by a simple band of silver. Though considering how tight they seemed, I doubted she needed to wear it.

"Well, well, well," the middle woman purred. Her voice, like her clothes, was silken, smooth, and sultry. "If it isn't my favorite wizard? How are you, Bishop?"

Bishop smiled politely, though I knew him well enough to tell it wasn't genuine. "Hello, Duchess. It's been quite awhile."

The Duchess made an amused giggling sound. It was interrupted by an abrupt, but pleasurable gasp, her mouth opening wide in surprise and ecstasy as she did. I realized one of the women at her side had gotten exceptionally eager and bitten at her earlobe.

I tried to clear my throat and realized my mouth was hanging open. I tapped my chin with my hand to close it.

"Well, Mr. Bishop, aren't you going to introduce me to this young morsel?" The Duchess mused, gesturing delicately to me with the fingers of one hand.

"Right. Duchess, this is my nephew and apprentice, Tobias" Bishop said, I could hear the displeasure in his tone. "Tobias, this is the Duchess of the Emotion Clan, Oliviana Wight."

Chapter 8

I stuttered for several seconds as I tried to find the appropriate words. But instead, all that came out was something along the lines of, “Uh, duh, gah...”

Oliviana giggled, clearly amused by my oh so clever response. “It’s okay, little boy. Many young men and women have similar reactions upon their first meeting with a Motus Vampire, especially myself.”

I smacked myself across the face lightly and managed to gather my thoughts. “Uh yes, hi. Nice to meet you.” I adjusted myself discreetly.

Bishop shook his head, but I could tell he’d still expected the reaction. “Oliviana, I trust you know why we’re here.”

“Mmm, yes.” Oliviana twirled the hair of one of the girls at her side thoughtfully. “You’re here regarding the plights of the Blood Clan. The very same plights that have started this unprovoked war between the clans, yes?"

"You consider the war to be unprovoked?" Bishop asked.

"But of course, Bishop dear." Oliviana held her hands up obviously. "The Emotion Clan has no interest in stirring conflict within the city, and I doubt the same of the Soul. It's simply a waste of resources."

I cocked an eyebrow at that. "Then explain the superhuman goons who attacked me earlier today?"

Bishop whipped his head around to me, his face full of disapproval.

Oliviana's expression didn't waver from the amused, sensual mask she'd been wearing when we'd first arrived. "And why do you assume they were my subordinates, child?"

"Superhuman strength, yadda yadda yadda, they weren't hurt by sunlight, and shrugged off my fire spells like they were a stiff breeze." I noted.

Oliviana let out a low, amused laugh. "Silly boy, they could've been a number of things."

"A number of things who coincidentally decide to jump me at the same time as all this nonsense we've been thrust into?" I proposed.

Her expression didn't falter, not one bit. "I suppose that is a fair criticism. But again, why assume it was my people?"

Bishop took a half step forward. "They don't fall under the qualifiers for either of the other clans. And while we are not directly accusing you, we are just trying to figure out what is going on here. The Mystic Order has ordered us to investigate the situation, and Don Grimaldo has directly requested our assistance in the matter."

"Well, I assure you, wizards, the Emotion Clan and I are fully willing to cooperate in your investigation." Oliviana said. "Whatever you need from me, you have it."

"Okay then, I'll make this simple." Bishop said. "What can you tell us about the current situation between the clans?"

"Skip passed the pleasure and straight to business, I see." Oliviana pouted. "I never could get you to indulge in your base desires." Her mouth curved down into a childish frown.

"Oliviana." Bishop's voice was steady and rigid.

"Right, yes dear." Oliviana waved her hand. "It started with the attacks on the Blood Clan. An unknown third, no, fourth party has been hitting their safe houses methodically throughout the city. The

Sanguine Vampires on duty were killed and the safe houses were ransacked. But, and here's the kicker, nothing had been taken."

"Until..." I began.

Oliviana pointed a finger at me, approvingly. "Until they hit the safe house where Maria happened to be. There hasn't been an attack on a Blood Clan safe house since Maria's disappearance. Yet there has been no ransom, no demands, so what changed?"

"The trunk." I said. Some of the dots were starting to connect.

Again, she flicked a finger at me. "Very good, young wizard."

"So, what's in the trunk, Oliviana?" Bishop asked.

Oliviana shrugged, jostling the twins slightly. "No idea. But how curious is it that both the trunk and the Don's daughter would be at the same place at the same time? Especially when the Don knows his safe houses are getting hit."

The Duchess had a point. That was quite a coincidence. There was no way they'd just happened to be at the same place at the same time, right? Not if they were both so important enough to snatch away in the middle of the night. There was a connection, but I couldn't figure out what.

"Maria's safe house was blown in by fire magic." Bishop said. "We first thought that meant the involvement of the Soul Clan, but we don't have enough evidence to peg them for it. Is there anything you can tell us about that?"

Oliviana pursed her lips in brief thought. "I'm not quite sure it was them who perpetrated the attack. Fire magic is quite the easy thing to mimic, yet you are so sure that was the kidnappers' weapon of choice."

"We detected traces of residual magic where the door was blasted in." Bishop said. "It didn't take a rocket scientist to put two and two together."

"No, but it doesn't take a rocket scientist to point your suspicious gaze at an easy frame either." Oliviana pointed out. "If the Jiangshi are not the culprits who cast this fire magic, who is the next most likely suspect?"

A flicker of realization crossed over my face. "A wizard?"

Oliviana nodded slowly. "Very good, young wizard. There have been whispers that a rogue wizard, a warlock, has been making rounds through the clans. My own associates have reported attacks. Someone is searching for something that the clans have."

"And what do the clans have, Oliviana?" Bishop asked her. His voice had gotten low and gravelly. It was hard to hear amongst the noise of club music and excited cheers.

Oliviana shook her head. "Genuinely I do not know, Bishop. I may be high up on the ladder, but even I am not told everything. Contraband is transported amongst the clans' chapters all the time without the local leaders knowing what they're storing."

"I don't believe that, Oliviana. Not for a second." Bishop glared at her. "You're far too smart to let unknown contraband pass through your possession without learning something about it."

Oliviana frowned. Unlike before, it was a much more genuine expression. "All I know is that the clans have gotten into their possession extremely powerful and ancient artifacts. Like the Blood Clan, my clan too has a trunk in our possession. But it's been warded by a powerful magic, we cannot open it."

"So, each clan has a trunk." I said. "And now someone's gunning for them. A warlock is tracking them down one by one and stealing them. But for what?"

"We can't know for sure without knowing what exactly is inside." Oliviana purred.

"So, let me take a look at your trunk, Oliviana." Bishop suggested. "I assure you; I can crack the wards."

Oliviana let out a laugh. A bona fide, deep, throaty laugh. "Come now, Bishop. Do you really think I'd just let you peruse my storage facilities, examining extremely important assets? Especially when there's a warlock on the loose? For all I know, it's you and your apprentice who are the ones searching for these trunks."

Bishop's eyes lit up in a furious blaze of purple light, brighter than any spotlight in the building. "You dare accuse me?" He barked.

"Oh, there's that righteous fury I so deeply admire." Oliviana wagged a finger at my uncle. She didn't seem the least bit intimidated by my uncle's anger. "Listen, Bishop, honey. I am not at liberty to allow an outsider into our vaults. But I assure you, the artifact is safe. One lone warlock is not strong enough to blast their way through our defenses. Maybe you should worry less about what's inside the trunks, and more about recovering Maria and the trunk that's already been stolen."

I grimaced. In a way, I suppose she had a point. Oliviana was not going to reveal what was in her clan's possession without a fight, anyhow. Our mission was to find Maria. And if we find her, maybe we'd find the trunk too. Then we could figure out what was inside all on our own.

"Bishop, we've learned something, but I don't think we're going to get any further wasting our time here." I told him, my voice was low and calm, but I was close enough for him to hear.

Bishop's eyes were still glowing with that violet rage. But he set his jaw, swallowed once, and nodded. "Thank you for your time, Oliviana. We may be back."

Oliviana nodded. "I look forward to your next visit."

Then she turned her attention to the women beside her. For the sake of modesty and keeping my head clear, I won't share what kind of activities they started to perform. The whole time, the two men sat on either end of the couch never looked up or took their attention away from their drugs.

Bishop and I turned around and walked back the way we came.

Before we'd gotten ten feet away, Oliviana made an excited sound before hushing one of the girls.

"Oh, and Bishop?" Oliviana said through an aroused laugh.

Bishop stopped and turned halfway to look over his shoulder back at the Motus Vampire. I followed suit. Neither Bishop nor I said anything.

"You mentioned that you had reason to believe your nephew's attackers were of the Emotion Clan, yes?" she asked, her voice more level, but laced with a hint of sensual pleasure.

Bishop nodded, not speaking.

"Well, if you find them," Oliviana's voice called. When she continued, it became something less aroused and something more deadly serious. "Take care of them for me. I don't appreciate traitors amongst my race."

Bishop didn't even twitch his head. He simply turned away and kept walking. I looked from Oliviana to my uncle, I'm not so sure I had the stomach for what she was skiing. I hurried after my uncle in silence.

Thick Neck returned my eskrima to me as we left. He had a smug look on his face as we left. I didn't much care for it, and any other day I'd be tempted to knock his block off, but there were more pressing issues to take care of.

"Well now what do we do?" I asked. We'd pretty much reached a dead end. Both the Soul Clan and

Emotion Clan hadn't turned up anything we could act on.

"I'm not sure yet. Give me a moment to think." Bishop grumbled, crossing his arms.

I thrust my hands in my pockets in a fit of frustration. Something clinked against my fingers. It was a misshapen lump of metal. I fiddled with it in my pocket for a second before surrendering to curiosity and pulling it out.

My eyes widened. It was one of the bullets I'd recovered from the drive-by. In my rush to get to class this morning I must've put on the same jeans.

"What's that?" Bishop asked, raising an eyebrow.

An idea came to mind. "I think...it's our next lead."

We made our way away from Heaven's Gate and found a nearby convenience store. Instead of going inside, however, we went around to the back, away from prying eyes.

"You got chalk, right?" I asked my uncle.

Bishop dug in his pocket for a moment and pulled out a lump of white chalk. He tossed it to me underhand. I fumbled with it in the air for a second before managing to catch it.

"You're going to perform a tracking spell on the bullet then?" Bishop asked me.

"Yeah, if I shape it right, it should lead right back to the gun it was fired from." I looked at my uncle in a moment of doubt. "Uh, right?"

Bishop nodded. "A simple tracking spell only requires one object to create the link. In this case, the bullet should lead you to the gun it was fired from. But links like this don't last forever. If you'd waited another day, maybe two, any metaphysical link would've faded away."

"Noted." I said. I took the chalk and drew a circle on the asphalt. I was careful to make it as perfectly round as I could.

For a simple tracking spell like this, I only needed a magic circle. Tracking the gun didn't require the use of a full tracking spell, one that took several magical foci and a pull magic pentacle. Those were reserved for tracking things you didn't necessarily have a direct link to. But the misshapen bullet was still fresh enough that it was directly linked to the gun that fired it.

I placed the bullet in the center of the circle, and then focused on my magic. Circles were a tool of ritual magic. Unlike combat magic, which could afford to be quick and messy for the most part, ritual magic needed more care and attention. Wizards had been using magic circles for hundreds of years as a way to keep a ritual spell isolated from outside forces that could potentially interfere with it.

With a small breath, I willed an inkling of my magic into the circle. I felt a thrum of energy in the air as the circle sealed itself. It hummed with energy that manifested as a static charge in the air. If I'd be standing inside the circle my hair would've probably stood on end.

I began chanting quietly in nonsense syllables, inspired by Japanese, Latin, and a little Spanish for good measure. I gathered magical energies in a swirling vortex around the circle, charging it with power. I could feel the energies seeping into the bullet itself.

"*Semitas.*" I chanted.

With the final word, the spell coalesced and snapped tightly around the bullet. Before I'd had the chance to dissipate the magic circle, the bullet was already sliding slowly across the ground. It was being pulled towards the gun it'd been linked to.

"Yes, it worked!" I cheered. I was still getting used to the more delicate side of magic, so I hadn't been entirely sure I was able to get it to work, but it did.

I smudged the circle, releasing any leftover magic that it might've sealed, and picked up the bullet. I could feel it tugging at me lightly. It was pulling me to the west.

"Alright, so we have our bloodhound." Bishop nodded approvingly. "Now let's see what we can sniff out."

"Sounds like a plan." I smiled.

We made our way back onto the main road and followed the bullet to wherever it was taking us.

Chapter 9

My tracking spell had been the work of a novice. Bishop only allowed me to be the one to perform it for the sake of practice. According to him, I was progressing phenomenally. I had a natural talent for shaping spells on the fly, even if they weren't the cleanest workings he'd seen.

The tracking spell was less of a GPS and more like a compass. It only pulled me in the general direction of the weapon I'd drawn a link to. The spell had very little regard for tiny annoyances like entire buildings or cross streets. So, there was a lot of wandering back to and fro in order to get a better fix on where we were going. Not to mention, the sun had all but set at this point and cloud cover had started to set in for the evening. Thank God for the human obsession of placing lights absolutely everywhere.

We wandered the city for over an hour. My body had taken quite a bit of punishment over the last day or so and I was feeling the effects of it now. My legs and shoulders ached to hell and back, and my feet were starting to hurt on top of it. But after an eternity of searching for our next stop, I was pretty sure we'd finally made it.

The tracking spell placed on the bullet had led us to the outskirts of the city, to the industrial district. Lots of boring gray, rectangular buildings were lined up in neat rows. For the most part, they all seemed to basically be the same, save for a few details here and there. I was pretty sure I'd locked onto the building we were after. Just to be sure, I ran from one end of the building and then to another, feeling the pull of the spell shifting accordingly. No matter where I moved, the spell was locked onto something within the building, presumably the weapon in question.

"We're here, I think." I said, my voice uncertain.

Bishop nodded. "Good work, nephew."

His eyes glowed with that same purple light that usually flashed when he was angry, and he seemed to take in every detail of the warehouse building as he did so. After a moment, the light died down and he nodded to himself.

"I can't be sure on specifics, but I'm detecting quite a few supernatural auras." Bishop stated. "I'm not sure who or what they are, but safe to say, I think we're onto something. We'll have to go in under a veil, to be safe."

"Right." I said.

I shook my wrist once, and my charms bracelet adjusted to a more comfortable position. It had two charms attached to it. One was the fire spell charm in the shape of a comet, currently still with one charm. But the second charm was of a different nature entirely. It was in the shape of a twisting wisp of smoke.

I reached for the charm with my power, and I felt the magical energies seeping into the small runes carved into the metal of the bracelet and down to the wisp charm.

I let out a slow breath, and whispered, "*Decivus.*"

I felt the magic rush from the charm and swirl around me, wrapping around me like a thick blanket. The world became...duller somehow. Color seemed to drain from my surroundings, and the outer edges of my vision seemed to blur. The stealth spell was something I'd whipped together last year, but it had been sloppy work. Anyone who was paying attention to their surroundings may have been able to notice it as a disturbance in the air. I'd worked hard to improve it and attach it to the charm. Veiling magic was not something I was particularly good at either, it was something delicate like the tracking spell. But that's what the charm was for, I only had to get it working pretty good once to attach it to the charm. And now I could perform it any time I wanted to. The only downside was, like the comet charm, it had a limited charge. In this case, instead of three uses, it lasted for about thirty minutes at a time. After that, it would take about a day to recharge.

My uncle had years upon years of practice. Veils weren't his specialty either, but you wouldn't know that just by looking at his. Or rather, not looking at it. My spell had taken me a few seconds to whip up, even with the help of the charm. I looked over at my uncle. Before I'd stopped turning my head, he'd whispered a word, and then, he was just gone. There was a very faint shimmer in the air, like the distortion caused by heat, but it was hardly noticeable in the dark.

"Come on." My uncle's voice spoke from thin air. Even though he was right next to me, the words sounded distant and modulated someway. Like he was speaking through the spinning blades of a fan.

So, I did my best to follow him. It was a pain in the ass, I'll tell you that much. We approached the front door, and I saw it wiggle slightly as he tried to open it. But it bumped against its hinges, probably locked by a deadbolt.

I sensed a motion from Bishop, but I couldn't tell what exactly he was doing. Then I felt a surge of energy as he called for his magic, and suddenly the hinges of the door exploded. The door fell awkwardly to the ground in front of us as it fell out of the frame. My uncle must've moved, because it fell where he was standing only a moment before.

No alarms went off, and if anyone had noticed our little B&E, they weren't making a loud ruckus about it. I did my best to follow my uncle through the doorway. Inside was a small reception area. It was probably only really for whoever worked here, because I couldn't imagine this place being a public business of any kind. Passed the desk was a door off to the right. I tried the door and found it unlocked. Sweet.

"Bishop?" I whispered, though loud enough to be heard by my uncle.

"I'm right behind you." He said.

I took his word for it, and we proceeded through.

We'd entered the warehouse proper. The ceiling was at least thirty feet high. Metal shelving full of giant storage containers reached up to just under the ceiling. I noticed several forklifts off to one side, as well as one of those industrial golf cart things that workers often used to move around these places quickly. I strained my ears to listen through the veiling spell. I didn't hear any voices or footsteps, nothing that would signal that we weren't alone.

I considered dropping the veil. I thank God everyday that I didn't because just as I was about to make the effort necessary, two figures walked out past the shelving on our left. They were speaking in hushed tones, making it impossible for me to understand. And they moved completely silently. From what I could tell they were wearing heavy work boots, but they didn't make a sound. That seemed unfair. I felt a tug on my shoulder pull me back behind one of the storage containers. I almost cried out in surprise, but a hand clapped itself over my mouth.

I looked up to see my uncle, sans the veil he'd been using a moment before. His eyes were glowing purple, unaffected by the color draining effects of my spell. They saw right through my veil. He held one finger up to his lips in a shushing gesture.

"Motus Vampires." Bishop whispered. "Hiding ourselves via magical means won't do much here. They're well skilled in stealth-based magic and know what to look for."

Given that information, I sighed and willed my spell to dissipate. The world came back into normal view a second later. Though given how dark it was in here, it was hard to tell the difference.

"So, the Emotion Clan were the ones who shot at me yesterday." I said, careful to keep my voice pitched low so that even my uncle could barely hear me.

"Seems so. Though I have a feeling that these are rogue agents. I think if Oliviana had been gunning for us, we wouldn't have made it away from Heaven's Door alive." Bishop surmised.

I tapped his shoulder and pointed down to the opposite end of the row, from where we'd walked in. Two figures hopped forward stiffly from the door that led to the reception. If I wasn't nervous as hell, it would've made me laugh. It was a funny sight, to say the least.

"Jiangshi?" I guessed.

"Interesting." Bishop said, seemingly confirming my guess.

"What are they doing here though?" I asked.

"Not sure, not yet." Bishop shook his head. "But if they're here too, then there's even more to this than I realized."

"Rogue Motus Vampires and Jiangshi working together, you think?" I wondered.

"You might be onto something." Bishop said. "But working together for what? The vampire clans have a wary respect for each other on the best of days. Most days, they despise each other and actively avoid interaction wherever they can."

"Oliviana said that there may be a warlock at play." I said. "Could he or she have brought them together?"

"It would take a hell of a lot of motivation." Bishop scratched his chin in thought.

The Jiangshi hopped forward, surprisingly quick considering how stiff there bodies supposedly were. Bishop and I crouched low, hiding in the shadows of the storage container. From the other end, the two Motus Vampires approached. They met in the middle just passed our field of view, obscured by the same storage container that hid us. I was careful to breathe as quietly as possible. It wouldn't do us any good to get caught at this point.

"How goes the recovery of the next artifact fragment?" A feminine voice said, presumably one of the Motus Vampires.

"The Soul Clan's fragment is well protected. Defended by tight quarters and magically enhanced architecture, as well as armed guards. Procuring it won't be as easy as the one recovered from the egotistic Blood Clan." A Jiangshi said through a thick accent.

"You call that easy?" A second Motus Vampire said, this voice being masculine. "We had to call in the boss to bust the damn door down."

"One door compared to the numerous defenses laid out by our kind?" The Jiangshi said, somewhat sarcastically. "It would take a carefully crafted operation to breach the Soul Clan's defenses and retrieve the fragment."

"We'll have to consult the boss on how to move forward." The female Motus Vampire said. "She will know what to do."

Aha, interesting. Whoever the mastermind behind this uneasy alliance was, it was a woman. It wasn't much to go on, but it was new information regardless.

"What about the Emotion Clan's fragment?" A second Jiangshi asked.

"Its whereabouts are still unknown. Oliviana's best have hidden it. Even for one of us, it will be hard to find." The female Motus Vampire said.

One of the Jiangshi grunted disapprovingly. "And what of the wizards?"

"The boy has escaped both attempts on his life so far," the male Motus Vampire explained. "As for the other one, we've yet to make an attempt against him. He's not one to attack lightly. He's been in the business for a few hundred years now. Time and experience like that make for an exceptionally powerful wizard. If we're not careful, he alone could tear this whole operation apart."

Holy crap. I'd known my uncle was older than he seemed, but hundreds of years older? That didn't seem possible. But I suppose for a wizard, it very well could be.

My leg was starting to cramp from being crouched so awkwardly, and I had to fight the urge to shift my position. One wrong move and we'd be caught. Even with my uncle here, I didn't think getting into a fight would do us any good. We were here to learn what we could and get out without being noticed.

"They are asking too many questions." The first Jiangshi said. "If your kind was the least bit capable, perhaps we wouldn't have to worry about their interference."

"I haven't seen your lot doing much to help, in that regard." The male Motus Vampire countered. "Hell, I heard they marched up to your boss' secret chamber uninvited and walked off scot free. Hardly what I'd expect from the *revered* Jiangshi." He said with a heavy dose of sarcasm.

"And you've had two chances to kill the young one and failed. So perhaps neither of us has proven to be very capable." The second Jiangshi pointed out.

"We'll have to consider alternative methods, then." The female Motus Vampire said. "What of the boy's associates?"

"The golem is well occupied with his responsibilities elsewhere." The male Motus Vampire said. "But the girl, she is here in Seattle, and ripe for the picking."

A surge of anger threw me forward at the vampires. If it wasn't for my uncle, I'd probably have picked a fight I couldn't win. He held me back, keeping me out of sight. Luckily for us, it seemed the vampires were too caught up in their own conversation to hear my movement.

They had just threatened Claire. I could feel a low, inaudible growl of anger rise up from my chest. If they touched her, I would kill them. Simple as that.

"We will see to her capture," one of the Jiangshi said.

"With her, we can lure in the boy easily." The second added. "Through our observations, we've seen he has quite the affection for her. It makes her prime bait."

"That's it." I growled, not even bothering to keep my voice down.

"Tobias, wait-!" My uncle tried to grab me, but I shrugged him off before he had the chance to get a good grip.

I pulled out my eskrima and emerged in full view. I emerged from behind the storage container. The Jiangshi had their back to me, but I was in full view of the Motus Vampires. They had bleach blonde hair, were wearing biker leathers, and were sculpted like contestants on The Bachelor. The Jiangshi were almost identical to each other, from what I could tell. Same purple robes, pale skin, and mossy hair. I didn't really care though.

"Hey, True Blood!" I growled, raising my eskrima towards the group. "*Kaze!*"

A roaring gale of wind rushed forward from the rod. I'd managed to catch them off guard, and they were sent hurtling down the walkway. They let out startled cries as they flew through the air.

Bishop cursed and emerged from our hiding place. "Damn it, Tobias!"

He had his staff in hand, held defensively.

I didn't pay him any mind. I would kill these things for threatening Claire. I thrust my eskrima forward again, screaming, "*Hinote!*"

I drew on the final charge in the comet charm and channeled the fire spell into the eskrima. A lance of fire roared and rushed at the downed vampires. It consumed them in the blaze, and I saw their bodies go up in flames. They hadn't been expecting the attack. I grinned, smug pleasure consuming my thoughts.

"One more oughta do it." I growled.

A screech rose up from the burning forms. Rather than pain, it was full of rage. One of the Jiangshi rose, despite the flames and snapped a word in Chinese. A moment later, a gust of wind erupted from its body and snuffed out the flames consuming him and his compatriots.

The other vampires rose, looking more annoyed than hurt. I grimaced. That hadn't been what I was going for.

"We need to leave, now!" Bishop growled "*Magnus*!"

Bishop swept his staff from left to right. I felt a surge of energy rush forth as he did. The shipping containers on the first three levels of shelves between us and the vampires suddenly screeched and flew from where they rested and crashed down on the vampires.

With his free hand, Bishop grabbed my wrist and took off towards the exit. I heard angry roars erupt from the piles of containers. Oh, come on, that wasn't fair in the slightest. How much punishment could these guys take? I'd made a dangerous mistake. If Bishop hadn't been here, I probably would've gotten myself killed. These guys were stronger than I realized. We emerged outside once more. Bishop turned back towards the industrial building. The screams of the vampires could be heard distantly inside.

My uncle aimed his staff at the doors and growled, "*Igni!*"

A gout of purple flames erupted from his staff and completely consumed the reception area. It must've hit a gas line or something, because an explosion of orange flame erupted from the purple flames. The explosion shook the building, and I saw the ceiling crumble in on the entryway.

"That should slow them down enough." Bishop said, his voice tight. "Come on, we need to get somewhere safe."

So, we ran. Running was something I knew I could do fairly well. Thank you, invincibility of youth. Though given my rash action just now, maybe I gave it too much credit. I'd let my anger and protectiveness over my friends cloud my judgment. That would be something I'd have to learn to keep in check if I wanted to be in this business for any length of time.

But hey, we learned a couple things. At the very least, rogue Motus Vampires and Jiangshi were working together, under the coordination of some big bad. Maybe that warlock that Oliviana had theorized? This was getting more and more dangerous by the second.

I guess it's true what they say. When it rains, it freaking pours.

Chapter 10

"Are you dense?" My uncle yelled. His voice was rough and gravelly.

We were back at The Grind. It was the closest safe haven we could get to in a timely fashion. It was unlikely anyone would attack us here. Too public and too close to the Blood Clan's territory to risk an attack. At least, that's what we'd hoped.

"Bishop I'm—" I stammered.

"I don't want to hear that you're sorry!" My uncle barked.

The barista behind the counter looked a bit nervous but she kept to herself, polishing one of those fancy beaker-style pots they brewed their original blend in. I'm not sure what you called it.

"Your reckless behavior could've gotten us killed, Tobias!" Bishop's voice had lowered in volume, but only increased in severity.

"They were threatening Claire! And hell, if Jacob was in town, they would've considered going after him too!" I said, my voice slightly more confident.

"Think, Tobias!" Bishop tapped his temple with his finger. "Jacob is safely out of town, and Claire is with Scout. If the vampires made a move on her, Scout would literally raise hell against them."

Bishop rubbed his forehead, clearly frustrated.

I sipped on my espresso, sighing. "Look, I'm sorry. But at least we learned something. We know for a fact that the Motus Vampires and the Jiangshi are working together to find and steal some kind of artifacts from the clans."

"And what of Maria, Grimaldo's daughter?" Bishop raised an eyebrow. "The whole reason we've gotten involved in this mess in the first place."

I frowned. Again, we'd learned nothing about the whereabouts of Maria. We had not heard even a whisper in reference to her. Everyone was worried about these super secret artifacts.

"I'm starting to think this has nothing to do with her." I said. "She could've just been in the wrong place at the wrong time."

"I agree, but regardless, Maria is still our main focus." Bishop said.

"These artifacts sound dangerous as hell though." I countered. "Hell, do you remember what kind of chaos the Holy Grail caused last year?"

"True enough." Bishop nodded in agreement, though he still looked tense and upset. "Either way, we need to work on your control. You let your emotions dictate your actions far too often."

I scoffed, as if his accusation was completely off base. It probably wasn't. There had been several occasions, even before learning about magic, where my anger and loyalty to my friends and family had gotten me into compromising situations with bullies, both of the supernatural variety and otherwise.

"I know, I know..." I sighed. "I've just been stressed. First with going to prom last minute and now with this vampire drama."

Bishop held up a hand, halting the conversation. "Prom? You're going to prom? When?"

I sighed. "Saturday." I rubbed my face, pulling and stretching it in a way that was surprisingly therapeutic. "I don't know how at this point though, given this nonsense going on."

Bishop seemed to consider this. He let out a sigh, scrunched up his face, and then nodded in reservation.

"Alright then," Bishop rubbed at the back of his neck. The stress and anger visibly dwindled away. "We'll need to take another look at that storage facility soon. Perhaps there's more to learn there. But I fear we've learned all we can there tonight."

I nodded. "You think we'll get it all figured out by the end of tomorrow?"

Bishop rubbed his chin, thoughtfully. "I'm not sure. There's still a lot going on here that we do not understand."

I sighed and nodded again. "Okay then."

I chugged down the rest of my coffee, tossing the empty cup skillfully into the trash can a few feet away. I rolled my injured shoulder once, wincing, and then rose.

We both left for home. It was another long, cold walk. I was getting real sick and tired of long, cold walks. Bishop leaned his staff against the wall near the door. I followed suit with my eskrima, placing them on a large duffel bag I kept there.

Bishop turned to me and smiled. "Get some rest, Tobias. You're going to need it." Then he turned towards the stairs and made the trek up to his bedroom.

A moment later, I heard his bedroom door close. I decided he was probably right and headed upstairs as well. I made it up to my room down the hall, just past my uncle's. I stripped and left my clothes in a pile near the foot of my bed. Then I unceremoniously flopped onto my bed.

I woke up only a moment later, or at least, that's what it felt like. But when I sat up to look around, it was clear that time had passed. That assumption was further proven by the clock on my nightstand reading 3A.M. The witching hour, how appropriate. For whatever reason, I felt wide awake.

I decided that there was no point in trying to fall back asleep and rolled out of bed. I stood and found a stray pair of sweatpants to throw on. I headed downstairs and into the kitchen.

I raided the pantry, grabbing a pack of Pop-Tarts, some cheese crackers, and one of those chocolate and cream cupcakes. Juggling my spoils awkwardly, I made my way past the kitchen and into a door that led into the apartment's small garage.

As a kid, I'd never been allowed in the garage. Bishop had installed a knob that locked from both sides. Once I'd come into my magic, Bishop revealed the contents of the garage to me. It was a laboratory of sorts. Here, Bishop had tools to create magical foci, potions, and other magical trinkets. It was here he had modified my eskrima sticks to channel magic. I hadn't spent a ton of time in the garage, but Bishop had shown me a couple of things.

Like how to make potions. I didn't know a lot about making potions just yet. But I'd learned just enough to get myself into trouble. In the center of the garage was a large wooden table, littered with documents, tools, and ingredients. I set my snacks down on top of some important looking documents on magical theory and took a look around the room.

The motor that opened the garage door had been completely removed, and the door itself had been sealed with air tight strips. On the wall to the right of the door had multiple shelves mounted onto it. These too were stacked high with books and boxes that held more tools and magical components. Since I knew I'd be awake for a while, I figured I might as well get some practice in on my technical magic skills.

Potions were a type of magic focus that stored some sort of spell within the contents of the liquid. There were all kinds of spells one could chug down, like invisibility, flight, and teleportation. But all of those were way outside of my wheelhouse where skill and knowledge were concerned. The potion I had in mind was a simple one, a rejuvenation potion.

As a young wizard, my reserves crapped out pretty quick. Especially when it came to throwing around extremely taxing spells often used in combat. Given how often we were butting heads with these rogue vampires, a rejuvenation potion or two might just come in handy.

I searched through the boxes and totes scattered around the room and on the shelves, until I found the ingredients necessary. Potions were a lot like any other kind of magic, the specific ingredients didn't matter as much as the wizard's intention did. While eye of newt and frog tongue were still perfectly viable ingredients for the appropriate potions, those weren't always as readily available.

My version of a rejuvenation potion was quite simple. I set down the gathered ingredients on the large table. A Monster energy drink, a small bottle of liquid bandage, and some aspirin. Believe it or not, that's all it took. In the center of the table was a large mixing pot that I filled in a sink that Bishop had installed on the wall opposite of the shelving. I filled it about halfway and placed it on a portable stovetop that Bishop kept under the table. I flicked it on and waited patiently for the water to begin boiling.

I munched on one of the Pop-Tarts thoughtfully in the meantime. The world had become a much scarier place in the last year. I'd learned about magic, demons, and monsters. Hell, I'd slugged it out with the devil himself.

Last year, when my whole world changed, a fellow wizard turned renegade named Kat had tricked me into trusting her and because of it, I'd almost been possessed by the devil himself, Azazel. Supposedly, my family had been manipulated for centuries into merging two powerful wizard bloodlines, that of Merlin and Nicolas Flamel, to create the perfect vessel for Azazel, so he may one day return to this world. We'd managed to thwart Kat's plans, and she'd disappeared in the aftermath. Even though I hadn't known Kat for very long, I still felt a stabbing pain in my soul where my trust for her had been obliterated. She'd understood my frustration when seemingly no one else had, or so I thought. Even though I knew the pain I felt was irrational, it persisted just the same.

The sound of boiling water brought me back to focus, and I realized I'd finished my Pop-Tart and was now nervously biting at my nails. I shook my head and wiped off my fingers on my pants. No more time for reminiscing, it was time to do some magic. I gathered the ingredients and lurked over the boiling pot like some kind of mad scientist.

"Mwahahaha..." I laughed sinisterly for my own amusement.

I popped open the can of Monster and took a swig. The sweet nectar of carbonation and sugar passed over my tongue and down my throat. Satisfied,

I turned over the can and emptied its contents into the pot. The boiling water wavered only for a second before resuming its normal intensity as it changed into a yellowish green color, mixing with the energy drink.

After that, I used some scissors to cut open the small tube of liquid bandage. I held it over the pot and squeezed out the adhesive. It dribbled in chunks into the pot, sinking to the bottom. Though I could barely make out it slowly dissolving in the water. Finally, I grabbed the aspirin bottle. I pushed down the lid and turned it, disabling the safety lock and removing the lid. I dumped out about half of the bottle into a small bowl. Then I took a small stone masher, the kind used to mash up herbs and stuff, and grinder it against the pills.

Just for the record, I don't recommend ever adding half a bottle of aspirin to any concoction normally. That kinda thing will kill ya, but when you add a bit of magic, it makes it mostly safe to consume.

After grinding the pills into a fine powder, I carefully tipped the bowl over the boiling pot. The powder dissolved quickly into the water, and soon there was no sign of it.

"And now, for a little magic." I took a deep, slow breath as I focused my mind. I held my hands above the pot and began muttering my usual chant of nonsense syllables derived from Japanese, Latin, and Spanish.

Energies began to coalesce around the pot, manifesting as eerie green wisps of smoke. The liquid itself began to glow in the same light, dousing the garage around me with a sickly green tinge. The pot began to rumble, and the boiling became more intense. The green smoke grew thicker and larger around me, completely obscuring my view of the room around me.

Finally, I shouted, "*Barista*!"

The green smoke rushed into the pot all at once, a rush of wind almost knocking me off balance. The neon concoction stopped boiling suddenly before letting out one last puff of green smoke that erupted from the pot. I jumped back in surprise. But nearly as fast as it had appeared, it was gone.

The wind and smoke had snuffed out the burner's flames and I could hear the faint hiss of gas being released. No reason to have the room full of flammable gas when there were countless things in this garage that could trigger it easily.

I pulled out a couple of shaker bottles from one of the storage bins, the kind often seen used by gym rats to drink protein drinks. Then I carefully dumped the contents of the pot into the two shaker bottles before twisting the caps on.

Satisfied, I cleaned up my mess in a utility sink that Bishop had installed, making sure to clean off any remaining residue with the running water. Running water was an almost universal anti-magic. Or at least, that's what Bishop said. It supposedly diluted the magical energies and made it hard for mortals and magical creatures alike from using their abilities.

With that done, I grabbed my remaining snacks and the two bottles and made my way back to my room. I made sure to lock up the garage behind me before returning upstairs.

Once safely back in my room, I stored the bottles in my backpack and sat down on my bed. I munched on my snacks absentmindedly. Today was going to be another busy day for sure. I'd be at school for most of the day and then after that it was right back to dealing with all this vampire nonsense. We had to figure this thing out before tomorrow otherwise there was no way in hell I'd make it to prom. And I'd miss out on my chance to have an amazing night with Claire.

I set my jaw. That wasn't going to happen. We'd wrap this whole mess up by the end of the day and I'd have just enough time to gather everything I needed for prom. There was no way in hell I was going to let Claire down.

Chapter 11

I lay in bed as the sun cast rays of light through my blinds. My eyes stung. As I figured, I hadn't been able to fall back to sleep and I was starting to feel the consequences. The sunlight burned my already irritated eyes and I pulled my blankets up over my head. I groaned in annoyance.

I heard a small knock on my door a moment before I heard it open. What the hell was the point of knocking if you were just going to welcome yourself in anyways?

"Tobias, wake up." Bishop's voice came from beyond the shelter of my blankets.

I made an affirmative groaning sound.

"Good. I just got a call from your school." Bishop said. "Classes are cancelled today, in light of yesterday's events."

I bolted upright, flinging the blankets away in the process. "What about prom?" I asked him, my voice urgent.

Bishop waved a hand at me in a calming gesture. "Seeing as how prom isn't on campus, it seem they saw no reason to cancel it. It's still on for tomorrow."

I let out a sigh of relief. That was probably the only ounce of good news I'd heard in the last couple of days.

"Now, with school cancelled for the day, I'd say we use the extra time as an opportunity to get a leg up on our enemies." Bishop said. "We need to learn more about Maria and where she may be."

"Any idea where to start looking?" I asked.

Bishop shook his head. "Not yet, but I'm going to chase down some leads. In the meantime, I want you to take it easy for a few more hours. I'll return when I have something more concrete to act on."

"Uh, okay." I shrugged. My mind felt a little foggy, from the lack of sleep and all.

Bishop nodded once, then stepped out of my room. He closed the door quietly behind him. I laid back down, pulling my sheets up to my neck. Alright then, so I had a day off from school, and a few hours before I'd need to concern myself with any of the vampire weirdness. I could snooze for a few hours, rid myself of some of the weariness I was feeling. As appealing as the thought sounded, and as comfortable as the embrace of my sheets felt, I knew that wasn't the best option. I could go gallivanting and blow some stuff up hoping to turn up a lead, but I'd already tangoed with the vamps once and it didn't exactly go my way. So there was really only one other option I could think of.

I called Claire.

She didn't answer the first call. Figures, it was still pretty early. But I tried again. On the third ring, she answered.

"Mmph, hello?" Claire said through a thick slur that one only gets when they've just been woken up.

"Morning, Claire." I said, making an effort to make my voice sound extra bright-eyed and bushy-tailed

"Ugh, good morning." She groaned, taking a breath. "What's up?"

"Well with school cancelled and all, I had a few free hours before I have to get back on the vampire hunt." I explained. "So I was thinking we should grab some breakfast."

"Oh, is that right?" She giggled. I could practically see the small smile spread across her face.

"Uh, yeah." I said. Any trace of confidence I had a moment before seemed to wither away at the sound of her laugh. "I mean, if you want. I know it's early and all, but I wanted to spend some time with you before I had to get back to this nonsense with the vampire clans."

Claire made a sound like she was considering that for a moment. I swear it felt like an eternity. Then she said, "Okay, meet me in an hour? Sunnyside Cafe?"

I nodded. "Sure, see you in an hour."

We hung up and I dropped my phone back onto the bed at my side. I lay there for a moment more, fighting the urge to stay there and fall to sleep. It was tempting as hell. My body hurt. I'd somehow managed to get my ass handed to me more than last year when I was fighting Azazel's demon goons. Vampires were deadly as all hell. And if I didn't stop them, then more people would suffer than just me. The city would devolve into chaos and violence as the vampire clans took each other out. Before long, their allies in the other states and beyond would hear about it, and they too would go to war. It wouldn't be long before the world was consumed in the three-sided war. I smacked my head lightly in frustration. I felt helpless. I still had nothing actually useful that I could act on.

Okay, so rogue vampires of the different clans were forming an alliance of some sort. They were supposedly doing this to gather three artifacts that the clans had gathered over the years. What those artifacts were, however, I had no idea. What those artifacts did, I also had no idea. How dangerous were those artifacts? I had to assume extremely so. At the head of this alliance was a warlock, a wizard gone rogue. They had to be exceptionally powerful as well, or how else could they be at the head of an alliance between the Motus Vampires and the Jiangshi? But what did the vampires themselves have to gain from his alliance? Power, money, status? Did they plan to betray the warlock and take the artifacts for themselves? And there was still the matter of Maria. She was probably just a victim of circumstance. Wrong place at the wrong time. But what was she doing at the safe house that apparently housed one of these artifacts? There was something important there that I just couldn't figure out.

I shook my head. Take a break, Tobias. Enjoy a nice breakfast out with Claire. Don't think about the madness for a couple hours. There'd be plenty of time to be stressed out about that later. So with a sigh of resignation, I rose from my bed and hurried to get ready.

I went through the usual routine, enjoying a warm but brief shower, hurriedly brushing my teeth, and shimmying into clothes that didn't smell too bad. My hair was a rat's nest but that was nothing new. Overall I looked passable. I headed for the stairs, but before I'd even gotten halfway down I stopped and ran back to my room. I found my bomber jacket draped over the end of my bed and pulled it on. I found my charms bracelet and eskrima close by as well and put them on too.

Sure I was just going out for a nice breakfast with a friend, but I wasn't about to risk getting caught with my pants down again. If the bad guys were gunning for me or those I cared about, they'd have to contend with a fully armed gung-ho teen wizard.

After I felt comfortably prepared, I headed down the stairs, taking them two at a time and slipped out the door, locking it behind me. The morning air hit me immediately. It was pretty cold out, and I was thankful that I'd grabbed my jacket. The clouds were covered in a sea of gray clouds. Man, I loved this weather. Nice, cool, and cozy. Perfect day for an early morning breakfast.

I headed out, walking out the gate of our apartment complex and into the open street. I made my way for Seattle proper, walking at a brisk pace. If I keep it up, I should make it to the Sunnyside Cafe on time. I didn't want to keep Claire waiting.

I made it to the small cafe with a few minutes to spare. It was tucked between two much larger buildings and looked like every small, quaint cafe you might see on TV. It had a small patio corralled by a wrought-iron fence. There were a half dozen tables that matched the fencing. The patio was protected by a large overhead awning. Inside the cafe itself were a few more tables, but it was mostly dominated by the kitchen.

Claire hadn't arrived yet, but I decided to get a head start while I waited. I approached the host stand and requested a table for two. It didn't take long for the hostess to get me a table. I sat down and began perusing the menu while I waited. I grimaced, I forgot how expensive this place could be. I had money for it, sure, but it would all but drain my reserves.

After about ten minutes of waiting, I heard the excited bark of my personal hellhound. I recognized it anywhere. I looked up from the menu to see Claire and Scout approaching from the opposite way I had come. She was dressed in a baggy sweater and a pair of skinny jeans. Her hair was tied up in a messy bun, though a few stray strands of hair hung delicately over her face.

"Hey, Toby!" Claire called as she closed the distance.

I rose from where I was seated. Scout rushed over to meet me. He did so excitedly, but politely, so as not to disturb the other guests. I kneeled and petted him furiously, making sure to scratch behind his ears and under his chin. After he was satisfied, I rose and embraced Claire in a deep hug. It was a nice feeling, having her close to me. Her modest, feminine form pressed against my body was a comfortable, familiar sensation.

"How are you doing?" Claire asked, looking up at me after we released the hug.

"I'm okay." I tilted my head once. "You? Has Scout been giving you any trouble?"

"Not at all. He's been keeping me company while I study for my precalc exam. Heck, I think he might understand the material better than I do," she said.

I raised an eyebrow at that. I couldn't tell if she was kidding. I pulled out a chair for her and she sat down. I helped her scoot in, and then returned to my seat. Scout curled up under the table, taking great care to make sure he was clear of the walkway.

"What happened after I left the classroom yesterday?" I asked her.

"Well, we heard yelling...and explosions." Claire said, looking down to one side. I could tell that recalling the events wasn't easy for her. "Maybe fifteen minutes after you bolted out the door, the police arrived and said it was safe to come out. Then we waited for our parents to pick us up. Nothing too crazy." She let out a small laugh.

"Right, nothing too crazy." I chuckled nervously.

"So who were they?"

"I'm pretty sure they were Motus Vampires." I said. I noted her confused look, then I added, "Oh, uh, basically they're vampires, but instead of blood, they feed on emotions. Super strong, super fast, can take a magical haymaker like it's nobody's business."

"Okay," Claire said slowly, "But why did they attack the school?"

"Why else?" I said. "To get to me."

"Wow, ego much?" Claire smiled coyly.

"Trust me, I wish they weren't gunning for me." I put up my hands. "But I heard it from them myself. In theory, I'm a much easier target than Bishop is."

"But seems like you gave them a run for their money."

"Almost." I nodded. "If I hadn't given Bishop the heads up, I don't think I would've beaten them.

They're stronger than the demon mooks I fought last year. A lot stronger."

A server came by. She wasn't much older than us. We ordered food and drinks, keeping the interaction pleasant but brief. The young lady nodded to us and then hurried off to punch our order in.

"Since they've had no luck with me so far, I have a feeling they're going to try after even easier targets." I said grimly.

Claire's face froze for half a second. Scout perked his head up, looking from me to Claire. He let out a soft whine.

"So you're saying I'm in danger?" Claire asked me. Her voice didn't quite shake, but I could hear the apprehension in her tone.

"Maybe." I nodded. I wasn't going to lie to her. "Which is why I want you to hold onto Scout for a little while longer. With him around as a deterrent, I don't think anyone will come for you lightly."

Claire frowned. "So, what does this mean for prom?"

I shook my head, with a little more energy than I had meant to. "No, I'm going to get this wrapped up before they get a chance to ruin prom for us."

Claire smiled. It was weak, but it was there.

"I just don't get how all these pieces fit together." I muttered.

"What do you mean?" She asked.

I caught her up to everything else I'd learned. The alliance between the rogue vampires. The artifacts they seemed to be after. The mysterious warlock who seemed to be in charge. And Maria, the piece that fit least of all. Hell, if I didn't know better, I'd say it was from a different puzzle entirely.

"Any idea what's actually in these trunks?" Claire asked.

"Not a damn clue. Hell, they could be concert tickets for all I know." I shrugged. "I'm pretty sure I know where the trunk that the Jiangshi have is kept."

Claire raised an eyebrow at that. "And you haven't gone to check it out yet? I'm surprised, knowing you."

I didn't exactly glare at her, but I stared at her nonetheless. "What do you mean?"

Claire put a hand up. "I'm not saying to do that or anything. I've just noticed you're playing this a lot more carefully than you did last year."

"Last year I almost got you killed." I said quietly.

She shook her head. "No you didn't. I chose to be there. I had plenty of opportunities to steer clear but..." She paused for half a moment. "They hurt my dad. I had to help you get them."

I winced. Her father had been injured in my defense when a demon named Leonard came knocking. He didn't remember much of the event. I'd explained that some 'roided up burglars had come and tried to break in. He'd gotten hurt but I managed to scare them off. It wasn't my best lie, but it was way more believable than a giant scaly demon man had come to eat my face. Now, Mr. Williams could only walk with the help of a cane. A pang of guilt stabbed me in the gut.

I sighed. "Look, these rogues are already considering going after you. I just don't want to piss them off any more than I have to."

Claire smiled sweetly. "Toby, you can't tiptoe around this stuff just because you're worried about me." She leaned down and patted Scout twice on his side. The dog panted happily. "Plus, I have my faithful protector."

The waitress appeared with our food and drinks on a large, circular tray. She placed the items down on our table and told us to enjoy. So we held off our conversation on and started eating. I slipped Scout a strip of bacon. He scarfed it down enthusiastically. We ate in relative silence, only speaking up occasionally to comment on the quality of the food. For the record, it was heavenly. This was one of the few restaurants I knew that served fresh food. Eggs were taken fresh from the chicken coop. Bacon was picked up from the butcher's earlier this morning. They prided themselves on the freshness of their ingredients.

Something tickled at the back of my neck. A cold, sickly feeling. My head shot up and I started looking around, scanning my surroundings.

"Toby, what is it?" Claire asked.

I held up a finger to my lips, keeping my eyes on everything else around us. Then I saw it, standing on the opposite side of the street. A shadow. It stood in the middle of all the passersby, who seemed completely unaware of its presence. There were no details to its form, but somehow I could tell it was staring right at me. It stared at me with...it wasn't malice. I couldn't tell what it was. But it was something dangerous. This wasn't the first time I'd seen something like this.

My mind flashed back to last year. It'd been doing a lot of that lately.

I shot up, knocking my seat over. "Stay here." I said, my voice rough.

I threw my wallet onto the table so Claire could pay and took off towards the shadow. I damn near got hit by a car as I ran across the street. Right before I hit the sidewalk, the shadow suddenly shifted, bolting down the sidewalk and around the corner.

"Oh son of a...!" I snarled.

I ran after the thing, despite the protests that my battered body screamed. The shadow had the luxury of not having to worry about all the other people on the sidewalk. It just phased right through them. Every John and Jane I ran past managed to jam a shoulder into mine. My bad one, of course.

"Come on!" I growled, shoving passed the crowd. I could just barely see the shadow up ahead. That was strange, the thing was clearly faster than me. It could've gotten away by now.

Which means, it's leading you, or luring you, ding dong. That figured. I pulled my eskrima out of the harness on my leg without slowing down. This thing wasn't about to catch me off guard. When I finally caught up it was gonna get a face full of kablooey magic.

I rounded another corner after the thing just in time to see it go down an alley. Every movie and tv show ever told me that that's where I'd be facing off with the shadow thing. I gripped my eskrima tighter and preemptively gathered up my magic.

"Showtime, baby." I muttered under my breath.

I skidded around the corner and swung my arm to point my eskrima down the alley. “Freeze, this is the police!” I said in my best manly cop voice.

To my surprise, there was no shadow thing. The only thing standing there was a girl, a young woman. She wore stylishly ripped goth clothing with a fishnet bodysuit under the band t-shirt and black denim shorts. She wore combat boots that looked like they'd kicked in a few teeth now and then. Her hair was cut short in a punk rock kinda look and dyed a snowy white color.

“Hello, Tobias.” She said in an amused tone.

I swallowed. “Hello, Kat.”

Chapter 12

I was at a loss for words. I hadn't seen Kat in a little over a year, not since that whole fiasco with Azazel. I'd never figured out exactly what had happened to her. Evidently she'd managed to escape.

"What are you doing here?" I said. My voice was low and hard. It took a monumental effort not to snap and fling her into the wall. She'd abused my trust and taken advantage of me when I'd been disoriented by the new world I'd become a part of. I thought she'd been a friend, one who understood my frustrations but in reality she'd just been another tool of the Devil himself. She'd tried to have me possessed and turned into a monster.

Kat smiled at me. It was genuine, in a backhanded sort of way. I had the feeling she was actually happy to see me. "What, Toby? Not happy to see little old me? I thought we had something special. But seems like you already replaced me with the girl next door back at the diner."

"Why would I be?" I growled, ignoring her comment about Claire. I still had my eskrima pointed right at her chest. The energy I'd preemptively gathered was starting to give me a headache, but I didn't let up.

"Well after everything we'd been through last year." She suggested.

"You mean everything you put me through," I corrected her. "I'll ask again. What are you doing here?"

Kat ignored me. She pointed a finger at me and did a little waving motion, gesturing at me. "Look at you, all geared up with magical implements." She said, amusement in her tone. "You've come along quite well since I last saw you."

"Cut the crap." I snapped. The tip of my eskrima began to glow with a reddish light, parallel to my growing anger and annoyance. "What. Are. You. Doing. Here?"

"Feisty as always." Kat smiled. "I was just in the neighborhood. I heard you're causing quite the ruckus with the vampire clans."

A flicker of realization crossed my mind. "The warlock that the vamps have mentioned, that's you isn't it?"

She flashed me a knowing smile, but didn't outright confirm my suspicions. But there was no way it was a coincidence that she was in town at the same time as a warlock riling up the vamps.

"What's the endgame then? What's in those trunks?" I asked her.

"Tobias, come on now. Do you really think I would divulge any information that could make you more of a pain?" Kat asked. "From what I've been told, you've already proven that you're a major thorn in the vampires' side."

"Who, me?" I said, in a mock bashful tone. Then I flattened it out. "You made the mistake of luring me here for what? To taunt me? Gloat? You got some vampire buddies who are gonna jump me in a second? What's the deal?"

"I couldn't help it. I missed you, Toby." Kat sighed, there was a pleasured undertone in her voice. Then her voice leveled out again. "No one's going to jump you, love. I just wanted to say hello, and give you an idea of just how deep this rabbit hole goes."

She had a point. If Kat was in town, the stakes were higher than I realized. What the hell was in those trunks? They had to be big, bad magical artifacts if Kat was involved. Hell, she'd been after the Holy Grail itself last year, and that was a pretty big deal.

"I don't understand." I said. "I don't understand why you'd reveal yourself like this. And I sure as hell don't understand what your end goal is here."

Kat laughed. "And you never will, Tobias. By the time you figure it out, I'll have already succeeded. When my work is done here, the vampire clans will kick off a war the likes mankind has ever seen."

"Like that's going to happen." I growled. "I'm putting an end to this, now!"

I took a step forward, swinging my eskrima overhead. As I did so, I focused on the tip of the stick, gathering kinetic energy there in a vague mallet shape. When it was level with Kat, I unleashed the force with a shout of anger. The mallet of force surged forward, straight for Kat's abdomen.

Evidently, she'd been expecting me to attack. Kat crossed her arms across her chest in a defensive gesture. As she did, a disc of red light fizzled into being. As my kinetic mallet hit her shield, it exploded into a display of color and sound. The shockwave caused me to stumble back. There was a ringing in my ears that lasted only a couple of seconds. After a moment, I shook off the daze. Just in time to see Kat sprinting towards me. Lightning arced up and down her right arm as she swung it towards me. I raised my eskrima to block the attack. Her arm swept towards me in a chopping motion and I just barely managed to catch the strike between my eskrima.

The enchanted wood of my foci grounded out most of the electricity she'd called up, but several smaller bolts erupted from the discharge and hit me in the chest. My body locked up for a second and I felt the electricity race up my arms and down my spine. I worked through the shock and used my eskrima's loose grip on her hand to swing her arm over and across her body, leaving her wide open.

I thrust one of the sticks forward at her belly and hissed, "*Kaze!*"

A cyclone of wind erupted forth and sucker punched Kat in the stomach. She made a choking sound as the blast of wind hit right before she was flung down the alley. I had to give Kat credit, she recovered well. She hit the ground in a backwards roll, managing to get her feet on the ground and skid to a stop. Kat looked at her hand and made a disgusted face before shaking it. She'd probably put her hand in a questionable substance.

"I don't want to fight you, Tobias." Kat said quietly.

"Huh, weird. Because I really want to fight you!" I rushed forward, preparing my eskrima for an attack.

Kat extended her arm forward, fingers spread out. "*Raiko!*"

An arc of lightning lit up the alley way and hit me directly in the center of my chest. The strike sent me flying back and into an overfilled trash can. My head hit the brick wall hard, filling my vision with stars.

Okay, ow. Pro tip: lightning hurts. So do brick walls.

I tried to focus my vision but it was nothing but blurry shapes and bright lights. But I could just barely make out Kat approaching. She knelt down close to me and her face came into focus more as she did.

"This is your one chance to steer clear, Tobias." Kat said. Her voice sounded distant and distorted somehow. It echoed strangely. "I'm letting you off with a warning. Stay out of the way of this vampire business. Next time we cross paths, I'll kill you."

I tried to say something witty and smart-sounding but all that came out was, "Blergh..."

Kat slapped my face lightly, almost affectionately. Then she leaned down, kissed my cheek, and whispered in my ear. "Good seeing you again, love."

She rose again, once more becoming a blurry mess and walked passed me. After a few moments, my head cleared and I realized I was alone in the alleyway. I sat up, rubbing the back of my head where I'd hit the wall. It was tender to the touch, but I wasn't bleeding. I looked down to see my shirt had been scorched. There was a burned hole about the size of my fist through my shirt where the lightning had struck.

I heard the distant sound of a dog barking. I spun on my ass to where the alley met the street. A second later, Scout came bounding around the corner, barking urgently. A second after that, Claire rounded the corner too and they both ran over to meet me.

"Toby! Are you okay?" Claire fell to her knees and looked me up and down. "What happened to your shirt?"

"Uh, had a disagreement with a Pikachu." I rasped. My voice was hoarse, as if that lightning blast had evaporated every ounce of spit that coated my mouth. I wasn't sure if it worked like that, but that's how it felt.

"What?" Claire raised an eyebrow.

I shook my head. "Had a friendly reunion with Kat. She was here."

Claire's eyes widened. I was sure memories from last year were flooding her mind. Kat had tried to use my friends against me. She'd damn near succeeded. So the fact that she was back probably scared Claire more than it did me. I held an arm out to Claire. She draped it over her shoulders and helped me stand. My legs felt like jelly and I slumped drunkenly against the wall.

"The vampires mentioned a warlock was in town coordinating their efforts." I reminded Claire. "I have a feeling I just met her."

"Kat's working for the vampires?" Claire asked.

"No." I said. "It's the other way around. These vampires hate each other too much to work together of their own accord. No, I'm pretty sure Kat's the one in charge. Whatever's in those trunks that the vampires have acquired, Kat wants it."

"So what do we do now?"

I sighed. "I need to learn more about whatever's in these trunks. I think it's high time we confront the vampire clans about what's inside."

I walked Claire home. Though my legs were still a bit shaky, it was more like she walked me to her house. Scout stuck close to my legs, offering what little support he could. Her house was in a neighborhood close to mine, but I didn't feel comfortable leaving her to walk home alone, so I decided to stick with her until I heard from my uncle. Claire's home was the epitome of American suburbia. White picket fence, a rose garden, and the like. She helped inside and I immediately collapsed on her couch.

The house was strangely quiet. Usually her mom would be cooking up a storm or her dad would be watching a recording of some sportsball game on TV. No one seemed to be home. To be honest, I was thankful. I still got a pang of guilt in my stomach whenever I saw her father hobble around on his cane. Claire disappeared down a hallway, leaving me and Scout alone in the living room. I sighed. Man, this truly sucked ass.

One more fight like that and I was worried I'd be down for the count. I was young but there was only so much punishment that I could take. My legs hurt, my shoulder hurt, and now I had a migraine the size of New Jersey. What was next?

A moment later, Claire came back with a bottle of aspirin and one of her dad's old t-shirts. The bottle of aspirin reminded me of the rejuvenation potions I'd crafted and oh so wisely left at home. I literally ached for one of those potions right about now. But the aspirin would have to do.

Claire handed me the bottle and ran to the kitchen to get a glass of water. A moment later she came back and handed me a plastic red glass filled to the brim with water. I poured out three small pills from the aspirin bottle and threw them into my mouth and then took a big swig from the water cup. It spilled a bit passed my mouth and down my ruined shirt. I was a bit messy, I'll admit.

Then I sat up to shed my jacket, and then my ruined t-shirt. Claire handed me her dad's shirt and I slipped into it. It was a slow, careful effort as I worked around my sore muscles and bones. There was a strange reddish spider-web pattern across my chest where the lightning had struck. I wondered if it would be a permanent scar. If it hadn't hurt so much, I would think it looked pretty cool. Her dad's shirt was a bit too big for me so I tied it off so that it didn't fit so loosely towards my waistline.

"How are you feeling?" Claire asked.

"Like I got struck by a bolt of lightning." I said matter of factly.

Claire puffed her cheeks disapprovingly and I responded with a cocky smile.

"Sorry. Just trying to keep the mood light." I admitted. "Anyways, in a few I'll call Bishop and update him on my end of things. Hopefully he's found something helpful. Until then, I think I'm gonna take a nap."

I hadn't slept all night and the unexpected but short lived fight with Kat had worn me out further. A few Z's would do wonders for me. I'd need every ounce of strength I had to confront the trouble the rest of the day was sure to yield.

"Okay, lie down." Claire nodded towards the couch I was sitting on. "I'll keep an eye on things. I'll wake you if I need to."

I was grateful for that and smiled. Then with no sense of grace, I fell onto my side and stretched out onto the couch, hoping some sleep would bring me a few hours of peace.

Chapter 13

The insistent vibrations coming from my pocket woke me up. It felt like only a few moments had passed and I didn't feel even the least bit rested. I could feel Scout snuffling at my hand, trying to wake me up. I fussed with my pocket while my phone continued to buzz. Eventually, I managed to wrestle my phone free. Without bothering to look at the screen, I answered.

"Hello?" I groaned. My voice came out slow and groggy.

"Tobias, where are you?" A man's voice said. It took me a moment to realize it was my uncle, Bishop.

"Ugh, Claire's place." I mumbled. I did my best to sit up. My body still ached but it didn't feel so tingly now. The scarring on my chest from the lightning bolt burned and itched.

"You sound...tired. Did something happen?" Bishop asked. His voice sounded like that of a parent who knew his child got into something he shouldn't have.

"Uh, sort of." I said. "I ran into Kat."

I could practically hear Bishop's eyebrows climb his forehead. "Katherine is in town? No one's seen hide nor hair from her since she disappeared from Fachnan's castle."

"Well she's back." I muttered. "And she all but confirmed that she's involved in all of this. I think we found our mystery warlock."

"I concur." Bishop said. "Did she give you anything useful?"

"Not really. But judging from her attitude, whatever's in those trunks is bad news. Could it be something like the Holy Grail?" I wondered.

Bishop paused for a moment to think that over. "There are many biblical artifacts unaccounted for. The idea that the vampires have their dirty claws on one, possibly three, of them, is disturbing to be sure."

"We need to know what's in those trunks, uncle." I told him.

"Well there's only a couple of ways we're going to figure that out," my uncle said. He didn't sound too pleased.

I sighed. "Let's go stir up some trouble with the vampires."

"Meet me at the Blood Clan's office building." Bishop said, then he hung up abruptly.

I knit my eyebrows and looked at the phone, somewhat disgusted. "Rude."

Claire entered the room a moment later. A towel was wrapped around her body, and her hair was done up in a towel as well. She must've just gotten out of the shower. I cleared my throat awkwardly, as I felt my cheeks heat up. I did my best not to look directly at her. Scout's mouth hung in a grin as he looked between us. Cheeky dog, I swear.

"I heard you talking so I uh," Claire hesitated only for a moment. "Uh, I came to check on you."

"Uh, yeah. I'm alright." I said. My throat felt dry. I raised my phone. "Uh, Bishop called. It's time to get back to work."

"Oh, right." Claire said. "I guess you'll be going then."

She seemed somewhat disappointed by that. I tried not to imagine why. Keep your head in the game, Tobias. No time to get distracted now.

"If I don't see you before tomorrow. Be safe, and kick some vampire butt for me." Claire said, forcing a smile.

I nodded. "Thanks. I will." I rose from the couch, somewhat stiffly, but I managed. Scout rose to follow me. I shook my head at him. "No, boy. I need you here with Claire. I don't trust the bad guys to keep away from her. I'd feel a lot better if you stuck close by."

Scout glared up at me and sneezed. He was not pleased to be sidelined. But he padded over to Claire and sat down next to her, looking back towards me.

I smiled awkwardly. "I'd uh, hug you goodbye, but..." I gestured up and down towards her.

Claire blushed, holding the towel a little tighter against herself. "Uh, right." She waved slowly and awkwardly.

"I'll see you soon." I said, and made my way out of the living room and through the front door. I closed the door and a moment later, heard the lock click behind me.

Alright, now with that awkward moment out of the way, it was time to go meet up with my uncle and start putting pressure on the super pissed off, super dangerous, Blood Clan vampires. What could possibly go wrong?

After a long walk back into the city, God I needed to get my license, I found my way to the office building where I'd first been introduced to the Sanguine Vampires. My uncle was waiting for me across the street from their lair, doing his best to look inconspicuous. He was wearing a thick flannel shirt and jeans, as well as his steel-toed boots. Bishop's wardrobe was two things: consistent and functional. He noticed me once I was only a few feet away.

"Wow, you look like crap." Bishop said, he seemed slightly amused.

"Yeah, yeah." I rolled my eyes. "Crazy how you never seem to be roughed up."

"Crazy how you always seem to run into danger without thinking first." Bishop pointed out. "What a weird correlation that seems to be."

"Hardy har har." I mocked a laugh. Then my face straightened. "Let's just do this."

We turned toward the office building and walked across the street to the front door. We were greeted by one of the office assistants who seemed oblivious that she was working for bloodthirsty vampires. It was the same girl as before. What was her name again? Tiffany? No, Tina. Tina, that's right.

"Hi, Tina." I said politely. "Door duty, today?"

"Hello." Tina said stiffly through a freakishly stretched smile. There was an awkward pause as we passed her and into the building. She said nothing else. I was starting to not like Tina.

I found it strange that she was standing outside by the front door, since the doors were automatic and during our previous visit, she'd been sitting at the front desk. I chalked it up to the idea that what made sense to her vampiric employers might not make sense to me. Still, her behavior on both visits was odd. Her face seemed permanently contorted into a smile that was way too perfect and she didn't seem to have much of a personality of her own. I realized Bishop had gotten ahead of me and did a quick couple of jogging steps to catch up to him. If he'd noticed Tina's behavior, he didn't see a reason to acknowledge it. I supposed that was good enough for me. I noticed the place didn't seem as busy as it had during our last visit. Probably because it was an early morning.

Or maybe because the tension between the clans had begun to grow, and both patrons and employees of Red Moon LLC were smart enough to keep their heads down. Who was to say?

There was no one at the front desk, and I gave Bishop a quizzical look.

"Stay on your guard." Bishop said. "I have a feeling things may get dicey."

I nodded to him. My mind flashed briefly to the image of the pick-me-up potions still in my backpack at home. It had been a foolish mistake to leave them behind. Though I'd made it worse, and it was still early enough in this misadventure to stop those mistakes too.

The elevator we'd used before dinged and opened up, seemingly on its own. It seems that Grimaldo and friends were expecting guests. Bishop and I stepped cautiously into the elevator without saying a word. I prayed we weren't walking straight to our untimely deaths. The elevator dinged as it closed and after a brief pause, it began to descend. I shifted my balance from one foot to another nervously. I didn't like this. Not one bit.

The elevator slowed to a stop and dinged happily as it opened its doors, revealing Grimaldo's large office space. The curtains lining the large windows were drawn down, the only light in the room coming from the fluorescent bulbs overhead. The room was bathed in an artificial white light, and silent save for the distant humming sound that the bulbs made.

Sitting in his chair as I'd seen him before was Grimaldo. He leaned back in his big, fancy chair with his hands folded in a steeple. He didn't seem to be surprised that we were here.

"Grimaldo." Bishop said.

"Wizards, it is good to see you." Grimaldo said. "I trust you bring news regarding the disappearance of my daughter."

Bishop frowned, and shook his head. "No, I had some questions for you."

Grimaldo's expression flattened. He didn't seem too pleased. "Questions?"

Bishop nodded. "Yes, it may help us with locating your daughter."

Grimaldo nodded, showing no emotion. "Okay then, wizard. Ask your questions."

"First and foremost, why didn't you tell us that something else was taken when your daughter was kidnapped?" Bishop asked. He wasted no time getting down to business.

Grimaldo's eye twitched. And for a moment, they seemed to change. For only a second, his eyes seemed to be consumed by darkness. Was that surprise? Maybe anger?

"What do you mean?" Grimaldo said, though I'd told enough of my own half-baked lies to know he knew more than he was letting on.

"When we investigated the safe house, we noticed something else was missing from the room, based on the photos you gave us." Bishop said. "A trunk, about four feet long, two feet wide and tall, ring any bells?"

Grimaldo was a smart man. He knew when the jig was up. He let out a sigh and sat up straight. "Yes, it rings a bell or two."

"So I ask again, why did you not mention it when you told us about your missing daughter?" Bishop asked, his voice firmer and more critical than it had been a moment before. It was a sign his anger was on the rise.

"Well, because I was more concerned about my daughter, of course." Grimaldo explained.

"Forgive me if I don't buy that." Bishop said dryly. "We've overheard rogue agents discussing similar trunks that are in the possession of the other two clans. They seem very important. Hardly something you wouldn't bother mentioning, unless you'd hoped I wouldn't notice it."

Grimaldo glared daggers at my uncle. "You are treading on dangerous ground, wizard."

"So are you, if you think you can deceive me and get away with it." Bishop growled. "If I get even an inkling that you're trying to manipulate a wizard of the

Mystic order for your own nefarious reasons, I'll strike you down myself. To hell with the politics."

Grimaldo's eyes went entirely black, I was sure of it this time. "You dare threaten me, wizard?"

I stared back and forth. I was feeling uneasy. It felt like a fight was going to break out any second. I inched my hand towards the harness that held my eskrima, an unconscious action. The twin sticks were starting to feel like a security blanket. I wanted to say something, I don't know what, but I decided it was best to keep my mouth shut.

"It's hardly a threat. Just a statement of fact." Bishop retorted. "Now tell me, what's in the box?"

"None of your concern, wizard." Grimaldo growled, his voice was tight.

"You know, it's funny, because it kinda feel like it is our concern." I said before I realized the words had even escaped my mouth. I mentally kicked myself for saying anything at all.

Both Bishop and Grimaldo shifted their gaze to me, both of them glaring daggers, but for completely different reasons. I looked back and forth between them. I gulped.

Grimaldo's eyes suddenly flashed back to normal, and he laughed. It was a genuine, hearty laugh. I let out a nervous little laugh to accompany his. My uncle kept quiet.

"I will admit, boy, that I like your attitude." Grimaldo smiled, seeming to relax. But I could see a subtle tension in his posture. He was far from relaxed. Then again, his eyes flashed into something less than human. "But if you speak out of turn again, I will take it as a personal insult to me, my clan, and my house of power. Understood?"

Gulp. "Uh, yeah. Sure."

"Good." Grimaldo nodded, his eyes already fading to normal once more.

"My nephew does have a point, Grimaldo." Bishop said, turning his attention back to the vampire. "Whatever is in those trunks is connected somehow to your daughter's disappearance. If we knew more about what was inside, it may help us in finding her."

Grimaldo's face contorted, his expression a mixture of confusion and anger. His back was against the wall, a feeling he didn't seem too familiar with and he didn't like it much.

"Very well." Grimaldo sighed. "I cannot give you specifics, because to be quite honest, even I don't know what exactly is inside."

"How could you not know what's inside?" I asked.

Bishop gave me a disapproving glance, but no one seemed to want to blast me, so I guess I hadn't spoken out of turn that time. My uncle nodded to Grimaldo, signaling he'd had the same question too.

"The Blood Clan makes purchases and trades of all kinds that rarely need my direct attention." Grimaldo explained. "I have investors who buy, sell, and trade in all sorts of valuables. Stocks, works of art, weapons, drugs, and historical artifacts. Artifacts that may or may not have varying levels of magical significance. Given the experience of these investors, I rarely ask questions. Only that these transactions are written down for the record, should it ever come up."

"So you have a receipt for this trunk?" Bishop asked.

Grimaldo nodded. "Yes, if you give me a few moments, I should be able to pull up the exact file that will detail what's inside that trunk."

Grimaldo picked up his desk phone, dialed a number, and then waited. Bishop and I traded another glance, then we turned our attention back to Grimaldo, waiting patiently. After a few moments, he spoke quietly into the receiver. I couldn't make out what exactly he was saying, but it didn't sound like English to me. Grimaldo tilted his head in a nod, and then hung up the phone.

"My associates are bringing up the file regarding the trunk and should be here shortly. It will only be a moment." Grimaldo stated.

Sure enough, less than a minute later the elevator dinged and opened up. A man with a vacant expression appeared from within. He wore simple clothing, a white t-shirt and jeans. I narrowed my eyes when I noticed he wasn't wearing any shoes. His feet were dirty and scarred. The man seemed to move robotically from the elevator and straight over to Grimaldo's desk. He didn't even seem to notice us, going as far as to bump into Bishop's shoulder without slowing down. The man walked around Grimaldo's desk and leaned down to whisper into his ear.

Before the man had even finished speaking, Grimaldo's eyes went black. His face seemed to distort somewhat, becoming longer and strangely bat-like. "What?" he bellowed.

Grimaldo swung his arm in a wide arc and hit the man hard on the chest. The vacant man let out an unintelligent sound of pain as he was flung into the wall. I heard a sickening crunch as the man collided with the wall. He fell limply to the floor, leaving behind a sizable crater in the spot where he'd hit the wall.

The man didn't get up. My eyes were wide in horror and I felt my hand grip the eskrima harness strapped to my leg. Grimaldo had killed that man out of sheer frustration, without a second thought. My instincts screamed at me to blast this guy to kingdom come, but I noticed Bishop hadn't moved an inch. I could tell he was angry, but he made no move to avenge the fallen man's death. I had to wonder why?

Grimaldo made a visible effort to slow his breathing and control himself. As he did, his facial features seemed to return to normal and he slumped back into his chair. I kept quiet, I didn't care to be on the receiving end of Grimaldo's wrath.

"What is it?" Bishop finally said.

"According to my associates, there does not seem to be any record of purchase of the trunk or its contents. No seller, no money transfer, nothing of the sort." Grimaldo said.

"So that means-" Bishop began.

"It means I have traitors in my midst." Grimaldo interrupted. "Someone seeking to undermine my seat of power and authority."

"So there's no way of gathering any clues on the trunk's contents through your financial channels." Bishop said. He sounded disappointed.

That was interesting. Grimaldo hadn't known a damn thing about this trunk, only that it existed, and was kept in one of his safe houses. Hell, I wasn't sure he'd even known it was all that important. He'd never mentioned it before; he truly had not seen it as relevant to the situation at hand. But the fact that there was no record of the trunk's acquisition in his records, anywhere, had scared him, made him angry.

"It would seem not." Grimaldo's voice came out low and gravelly. "I wish I could be of more help, wizards, for the sake of my daughter."

Bishop nodded. "Us too. We should be going, I believe we have more work to do."

Grimaldo tilted his head. "Thank you for your assistance, wizards. It seems there is much for me to do concerning this traitor. If I learn anything, I will be sure to contact you."

Bishop turned to leave. "Come on, Tobias." Then he began walking towards the elevator.

I followed him. It seemed as though the rabbit hole kept growing deeper and deeper. I had to wonder though, what would happen when we finally reach the bottom?

Chapter 14

It had started to rain. Of course. I loved Seattle and the weather that came with it. I really did. I'd grown up here for most of my life after all. But sometimes it felt like it was purposely trying to bring me down. This was one of those times.

"Don't you think it's weird that Grimaldo doesn't know a thing about whatever that trunk is? Or what's inside it?" I asked Bishop as we ran across the street to the shelter of a large oak tree. Well, I ran. My uncle seemed content walking slowly through the rain. He didn't reply until he too had reached the tree.

"I do. For the lord of a clan as large and formidable as his, it's a bit strange that such important contraband would come into his possession without his noticing." Bishop said.

"So he's lying, right?" I asked.

To my surprise, Bishop shook his head. "No, I don't believe he's lying."

"And why the hell not?" I wondered.

"Because Grimaldo is nothing if not practical." Bishop said. "When he realized that there was no record of the trunk or its contents, he was angry. So angry he blindly killed one of his thralls in a fit of rage."

"I meant to ask you about that, by the way." I said. "Bishop, he killed a man. Right in front of us, and you didn't so much as flinch. I get they're vampires and all, and yeah, they're going to kill people. But that guy was an innocent, hell, he didn't even drink his blood or anything. He swatted him away like a fly. But you did nothing. What gives?"

Bishop sighed, a sad expression painting his face. "That was a thrall. A mind slave. The venom of a Sanguine Vampire is a toxin of sorts that addicts those who are fed upon. It makes them impressionable, deteriorates their sense of self, their will. Feed on one particular victim enough times, and they become nothing but a walking husk. That man has long since been dead, his body just never got the memo. As unfortunate as it is, Grimaldo killing that man was an act of mercy, whether or not it was intended as such."

A flash of anger came over me, and I had to fight the urge to punch the tree we stood under. That was just...wrong. Grimaldo, or one of his subordinates, had stripped a man of his humanity. Robbing him of all that made him a man. Did that man have a family? One he'd probably hadn't seen in ages? Who loved and missed him? Who worried that he probably hadn't come home in so long? That man probably had goals, aspirations, hopes and dreams that he would never get to live out. I decided that I didn't care much for Sanguine Vampires, or vampires of any kind for that matter. And if it weren't our obligation by the stupid Mystic Order to help them work out this squabble, I'd probably blast the bastard where he sat smugly in his big, fancy chair in his big, fancy office.

I took a deep breath. Calm down, Tobias. Save the anger and blasting for the bad guys you're after at this very moment. There will be a time and a place for Grimaldo to get his comeuppance.

"Well, that's stupid." I said, after careful consideration of my words.

Bishop nodded in agreement. "Indeed it is."

An idea popped into my head, and I was surprised it hadn't occurred to me sooner.

"Wait a gosh darn second. We've met with all three clan leaders at this point. And only one of them has mentioned any knowledge of these trunks." I said, speculatively as I put the thoughts together.

A small smile spread across Bishop's face. Was that pride I saw in his face? Nah, couldn't be. "I was beginning to think the same thing. Interesting, isn't it?"

"So what do we do with that information?" I asked.

"We head to our next stop." Bishop said. Then his smile turned into something more smug. Or maybe it was mischievous. "And we knock. Loud."

My mouth curved up into a wicked grin and we headed down the street.

By the time we'd made our way to Heaven's Door, my phone chimed happily, letting me know I'd reached my step count for the day. That was a bittersweet revelation, considering it was barely past noon. Given how early in the day it was, I wasn't surprised that Heaven's Door was currently closed. There was no line at the door or a security guard to man it. Hell, the fluorescent sign and lights weren't even on yet.

We walked up to the front door of the establishment unimpeded. I wondered for a second if anyone would even be home. But Bishop didn't hesitate for a second. He angled his staff towards the door at a forty-five degree angle.

I felt a surge of energy rush through the air as he barked, "*Vitum!*"

A cannonball of kinetic energy rocketed from the tip of his staff and struck the double doors with a thunderclap of sound. The doors were ripped clear from their hinges and flew into the front room, twisting and ricocheting off the walls dangerously fast.

Not a second later, two men brandishing machine guns rushed from the side hall that led to the club. Without a second's hesitation, they started firing. For those who don't know, gunfire is loud and scary as hell. The movies don't do it a lick of justice. I flinched and immediately crouched into a ball so that the enchantments on my jacket would hopefully protect me. To my pleasant surprise, no bullets came whizzing by, let alone struck my jacket. The sound of the gunfire had dulled, as if I was hearing it through a thick wall. I looked up, and noticed a translucent barrier of purple light stood between my uncle and I and the gunmen. The tip of Bishop's staff glowed with the same light, and I realized he'd called up a shield of energy to protect us.

Okay, now that was pretty cool. I stood up, doing my best to look serious and dignified. As if the gunfire hadn't sent me into a cowering crouch a second before. The guns clicked as they expended their last round, and the men moved to reload their weapons with clips strapped to their waist.

Bishop didn't give them a chance. He collapsed the shield and shouted, "*Vitum!*"

Another blast of kinetic force like the one he'd called up before rushed forth. Though I could feel that it had been shaped differently than when he'd used it on the doors. Instead, the blast was shaped like a curtain, not as solid but much wider. It blew the gunmen away and firmly on their asses. Their loose clips clattered uselessly out of reach.

Bishop took two steps further into the building. The gunmen scrambled for the clips that had fallen away and with another whispered word of magic, a gust of wind pushed the ammunition further away. The gunmen turned back to Bishop. They looked terrified, justifiably so. I had to wonder if they had any idea who they were actually working for. Either they had no idea what they'd just witnessed, or they had seen something like it before and were feeling an all too familiar sense of fear.

"Gentlemen, I don't wish to frighten or harm you further." Bishop said in a perfectly calm, reasonable tone. "We just want to speak with your boss, Miss Wight. Let her know we're here and I assure you we will behave appropriately as guests."

"And if we don't?" One of the gunmen, whom I realized was Thick Neck, said. He did his best to keep his voice from shaking, but I could still hear it in his voice.

"Well, if you choose to escalate this confrontation, then I may just let my young apprentice here cut loose. He's got a lot of pent up energy, teenage angst and all, you understand?" Bishop spoke, diverting his glance to look over at me.

It took me a moment to get the hint. I picked out a nearby light fixture attached to the wall and flicked my wrist, putting only a hint of my power into the motion. A rocket of kinetic energy about the size of a tennis ball flew through the air and smashed the fancy light. The room darkened slightly. I let out a sigh as I felt the relatively simple spell tax me far more than it would normally. Damn, I needed a good night's sleep. I really hope they'd get the message after that one, because I wasn't sure I could pull another off without looking visibly tired.

Thick Neck was smarter than he looked. "Alright, alright. Just uh, wait right here." He scrambled to his feet and hurried down the side hall, presumably to retrieve Oliviana.

I whistled while we waited, doing my best to look at anything except the remaining cowering man, who looked like he was about three seconds from pissing himself.

A moment later, Thick Neck peeked out from the hall. “Uh, Miss Wight will see you now.” He said.

“Lovely.” Bishop said, his voice positively chipper. He tapped his staff twice on the ground and a strong gust of wind lifted the remaining gunmen to his feet. “Lead the way.” He tilted his staff to Thick Neck in a polite gesture.

We followed Thick Neck to the club floor. It was fully lit up, so I could see all the imperfections that the dark, strobing lights usually hid from view. It was strange to see a club like this fully lit and so empty. It felt wrong that no one was here. It was just one of those places you expected a lot of people to be. The back of my neck itched and I glanced around slowly. I noticed men and women peering out at us from side rooms and hallways that presumably led to their dressing rooms. That was strange enough, but what really put me off was their eyes. They were cloudy, as if they were blind, but something told me they could see me just fine. Could this be the gaze of a Motus Vampire lying in wait? I adjusted my jacket nervously, making sure it was lifted high to protect my neck against any surprise attacks. Though if what Bishop said about the Emotion Clan was true, my neck was the least of my worries.

The couch where I'd met Oliviana Wight last time was empty, and noticeably cleaner than any other seat in the place. I had a feeling that's where she spent most of her time. But it was empty, and Thick Neck walked right by it. Instead he led us to a door tucked into a corner. On the door was a sign that read "Employees Only."

Thick Neck unclipped a ring of keys from his belt. It jingled noisily as he fumbled for the correct key and slid it into the lock on the door. Had he been so nervous that'd he run to this door, unlocked it, spoke to Oliviana, came back out, locked the door again, and then come back to retrieve us? Or was that just standard procedure here? Who was to say?

The door clicked and opened up into yet another hallway that stretched maybe fifty feet down before rounding the corner. Oh great, more walking. Boy was my pedometer gonna be so proud of me after today.

We followed Thick Neck down the pristine halls that distantly reminded me of the endless hallways of Light Haven, the headquarters of the Mystic Order. But that was a story for another time.

Eventually he led us to a door that stood out from the perfectly white hallway. It was quite the opposite, a perfectly matte black color. I noticed there was no door knob. I'd be intrigued if it weren't for the fact I'd seen plenty of stranger sights in my time as a wizard's apprentice. Thick Neck began rapping his knuckles against the door in a long and complicated series of knocks that would be nearly impossible to replicate unless someone was paying an absurd amount of attention.

Finally, Thick Neck finished his secret handshake with the door and after a couple seconds' pause, something in the door clicked. There was a mechanical whirring and a circular knob protruded from the door. It was no magic, just fancy mortal technology.

If it wasn't particularly impressive, it was pretty neat, at least. Thick Neck turned the knob, and opened the door inwards without moving from where he stood, allowing for us to see into the room and enter it without bumping into him. I looked to Bishop, who didn't take his eyes off the doorway. Instead, he just stepped forward and through the door. That was all I needed. I followed my uncle through the doorway.

The office inside was impossibly pristine, white tile floor and perfectly white paneled walls and ceiling. The furniture matched the door, perfectly black and free of any imperfections. It was all very square and modern-looking. The kinda thing you saw at IKEA with no hopes of affording, but even nicer than that. I wouldn't be surprised if the furniture was all custom-ordered.

Sitting in a relatively modest office chair behind the desk was Oliviana. She wore what appeared to be a pantsuit that was the exact same color as the furniture, save for a white dress shirt she wore under the jacket. Her blonde hair looked like it might have been freshly dyed and straightened, but the color was just a little too perfect. Could it have something to do with her abilities as a Motus Vampire?

“Well, I can’t say I’m not a fan of the decor,” I said, letting out an impressed whistle.

Oliviana let out a pleased laugh. The sound sent a tingle throughout my entire body. It was like being bathed in the light of Heaven itself. Which was disturbing, considering if what Bishop told me was true, Oliviana and her kind were the farthest thing from heavenly.

“I’m glad you appreciate it. I wasn’t quite sure how I felt about it yet, myself.” Oliviana purred. “Hello wizards, it’s a pleasure to see you again. Though I must say, if you wanted to speak with me, you hardly had to toss around the help. All you had to do was call.”

“In my experience, the last thing anyone wants to do is let a Motus Vampire lord such as yourself know that they’re on their way.” Bishop said.

Oliviana's mouth curved up at one side in a smirk. "You always were quite the smart man, Bishop."

Bishop shrugged one shoulder and brandished a half-smile of his own. "I know just enough to keep me alive."

Oliviana nodded, she seemed to like the answer.

I looked back and forth between them and gagged loudly. "Blegh, get a room, you two."

Oliviana's eyes narrowed, her eyes trailing from Bishop, then to me, and then back to Bishop. "Wouldn't be a half bad idea. What do you say, Bishop?"

Bishop let out an exasperated sigh. "You know that's not gonna fly. We're here on business, Oliviana. Business I'm not too sure you're going to like."

Oliviana frowned, and sat up a little straighter, no longer as calm, cool, and collected as she had been a moment before. "Go on, then."

"Over the last few days, we've been pinballing back and forth, meeting with the different leaders of the vampire clans. During that time, we've learned bits and pieces regarding this whole mess. But one thing that's been consistent, is whispers regarding these trunks, which contain some mysterious MacGuffins that have the vamps' feathers ruffled quite a bit." Bishop explained, recapping our ordeal so far.

I waited patiently for the ball to drop, my body tense with uncertainty. There was a very good chance this could go bad very quickly. Honestly, I didn't see how this could go over well at all. I tried not to show the apprehension in my stance, but I doubt I was very successful. My hand hovered over my eskrima like a cowboy's over his gun right before someone called out "Draw!"

"But what's interesting is that neither Grimaldo nor Feng Dài demonstrated any knowledge regarding these trunks. Hell, Grimaldo was outright furious when he learned that a subordinate of his obtained the chest right under his nose." Bishop continued.

"What's your point?" Oliviana asked, her tone urging him to get to the point.

"My point being that there are in fact, two factions, who seem to have knowledge of these trunks." Bishop held up two fingers, I assumed for dramatic effect. "First, these rogue vampires, who seem to have an alliance to undermine the authority of the individual clans, and the second, is you, Oliviana."

Something flickered in Oliviana's expression. Anger? Surprise? I wasn't sure.

"When we came in here and started questioning you, you helped us conclude that this rogue faction was after the trunk." I said. "But you made a mistake, not realizing that Grimaldo had no knowledge of the trunks. So gotta wonder, what gives?"

Oliviana was silent for a few seconds, just staring at us. She stared at us, not even blinking. Bishop returned the stare. I did my best, but I'm not too good in these kind of standoffs. I teetered back and forth between the balls of my feet nervously, just waiting for someone to speak up.

Finally, Oliviana broke the silence. "Quite the theory that you two have crafted. But for the sake of being thorough, I have to ask, what does Feng Dài think of your theory?"

Oops.

I guess in our hurry to wrap this up nicely and pin the conspiracy on Oliviana, we'd sort of forgotten about Feng Dài and the Soul Clan. Sure, they hadn't expressed any knowledge about the trunks. But there was no proof that they didn't know about the trunks either. That was an incredibly dangerous oversight, and I suspected that Bishop felt similarly. I had inferred that there was some sort of bad blood between Bishop and Oliviana after our last visit. Had the underlying discourse between them led to a hasty conclusion to our investigation? I'd have to ask Bishop what the hell happened between the two of them after we got out of our present predicament.

Bishop cleared his throat. “Ahem, uh. We actually have not spoken to Feng Dài since our first meeting with him.”

Oliviana raised an eyebrow. “Oh, and instead, you just immediately assumed it was I who was behind this conspiracy?”

I looked awkwardly between the two. It was like the Cold War. Everyone was suddenly on edge, just waiting for the other to shoot first. Bishop once told me these old magical types made a pretty big deal out of respect. And I wasn't too good with respecting douchey types like these vampires, but even I knew that by accusing her without sufficient evidence was a major blow of disrespect. If she decided to take offense to the remark, I had a feeling we'd just be another homicide statistic in the vicinity of a strip club.

Gulp.

But finally, the tension broke. Oliviana chuckled to herself, shedding the mask of anger and disdain she'd worn a moment before. “Oh, Bishop. If you were anyone else, I'd devour you and your apprentice where you stood. But you are who you are, and I feel inclined to give you some leeway.”

The room seemed to release its held breath. The tension in my muscles seemed to recede and I stood a little straighter. I didn't let my guard down, necessarily, but I relaxed just a bit.

Bishop performed a slight tilt of his head that seemed reminiscent of a bow. A gesture of thanks and respect. I felt inclined to mimic it, but it felt awkward, coming so late after him.

"Thank you, Duchess." Bishop said. His voice had become straight and more respectful.

"Uh, yeah." I stumbled on my words a bit. "Thank you."

The Duchess inclined her head in a returned gesture of respect. "I understand that this matter is complicated. So some confusion can lead to hasty decisions at times." For a brief moment, her voice returned to that terse, dangerous tone. "Just don't let it happen again."

"Understood." Bishop nodded.

Oliviana seemed to loosen up again. "Now, if that is all, I have to prepare for our work tonight."

"Very well." Bishop said. "With any luck, we won't have to return."

Then Bishop turned back to the door and began walking out. I looked back and forth with a hint of nervous energy. Then I spedwalked after my uncle and we made our way out and towards the exit.

And just when I'd thought we'd have this all figured out. But I should've known. When it comes to magic and monsters, nothing is ever simple.

Chapter 15

"And I thought high school was stressful." I muttered. I pointed back towards Heaven's Door as we walked parallel to the main road. "But th—that gave me a few gray hairs. I thought she was gonna tank us both for a second there."

It was still raining. In fact, it had started to pour. And my jacket did not come with a hood. I felt miserable and probably looked worse. The last few days had not been kind to me, and it still wasn't over yet.

"I'm sorry for jumping the gun on that." Bishop sighed. "For a moment, I thought we'd figured this whole thing out, I was eager to grab her and put her away, or down, for good."

I arched an eyebrow at him. "Yeah, I meant to ask. Something has obviously happened between you and Oliviana before. What's the deal there? You're usually pretty calculating and level-headed. Sure, I'm an amateur and probably would've walked right into that road block head on, but you're smarter than that, uncle, so what's going on?"

We approached a bus stop. The kind that had an overhang that kept people out of bad weather, mostly. No one else was around, so I took a seat. I needed a second where I wasn't being pelted by cats and dogs. There'd be plenty of time for that. Bishop took shelter under the metal structure as well, though he did not sit.

My uncle leaned against his staff, staring down at the ground near my feet. His face scrunched up as he seemed to get lost in his thoughts. It was rare that I saw him like this. There was no confidence or dignity in his expression. For a second, I didn't think he was going to say anything at all. I thought he would clam back up, reclaim the mask of old confidence and mystic wisdom.

"I was a young up and coming wizard, a few years older than you. I'd just finished my apprenticeship and moved to Seattle, back when it'd barely been recognized as a city." Bishop began.

Before Seattle had been recognized as a city? That was well over a hundred years ago. Sometimes I forget that wizards can get old. Very old. I'd never asked my uncle how old he was, I didn't think it was polite to ask, after all. But that would make Bishop nearly two-hundred years old. I wondered what it would be like to live to be that old. I guess I'd find out, one day.

Bishop continued speaking. "One of my first missions here was to disrupt the drug trade ran by the Emotion Clan. Psychedelics, magically enhanced. But they were dangerous, and bodies were turning up. The Mystic Order feared if the local constable got too interested, there'd be a massacre. I was dispatched to cause some trouble, convince the Morts to take it down a notch."

"So what'd you do?" I asked.

"What else? I did some convincing." Bishop said. "Busted up a few of their production sites. But cause enough trouble in a vampire-run drug ring, eventually you catch the attention of folks higher up the ladder. Long story short, I came face to face with Oliviana."

I swallowed. I had a bad feeling about what was coming next.

"Instead of killing me, like I'd expected. Oliviana took a liking to me. She saw something in me. My younger self had perceived it as genuine attraction. In reality, she saw a tool to be held, a weapon to be wielded. She used her abilities in mind magic to manipulate me, shape me, and so on. I never even realized it was happening. Soon enough, I was pulling double duty. I was busting heads not only for the M.O., but for Oliviana as well. The Order saw it simply as me working extra hard to keep the city safe. Which in a way, I was."

"How long did this go on for?" I asked.

"Years." Bishop said. He refused to make eye contact with me. "For years, Oliviana had a grip on me. To her credit, it helped me to shape and perfect my magic even further. I grew at a phenomenal pace."

"Maybe don't give her so much credit." I said critically.

Bishop cocked his head in recognition to that remark. "But one day, Oliviana sent me out to do a job. At first, it seemed like any other job. Off some Sanguine Vampire thugs who'd been encroaching on her territory. But when I arrived at their safe house..."

I looked up at him. He'd gone silent, his eyes staring off into the middle distance. I arched an eyebrow. "Yeah?" I said, urging him to continue.

Bishop cleared his throat and continued speaking. He spoke each word with purpose, pausing a fraction of a second between each one as he spoke. "I arrived at the safe house. I busted in. I killed the vampires, but not before they... Not before they'd had lunch."

My eyes widened when I realized what he was about to say. "They had..."

"Kids." Bishop said, with a disturbing finality.

Neither of us said anything for a moment. It was a long, painful silence, disturbed only by the rain pattering down on the metal overhang above us. I didn't say anything. No way in hell was I going to be the first one to speak up.

"It hit me hard. Brought me back to reality. No matter of mind magic or supernatural sex could blind me to the fact that that right there, is what I was supposed to be fighting for. I was not supposed to be the hitman of some supernatural predator. Hell, I wasn't even supposed to fight because the Mystic Order told me to. No, I was supposed to fight because it was the right thing to do. I turned away from Oliviana from that point. She's never forgiven me for it. And she's never stopped chasing me, hoping she can get me back under her thumb again one day. But I never forgot that moment, when I saw those kids. It's what keeps me centered, reminds me why I have to keep fighting."

I let the words marinate for a moment, giving myself some time to process them. Bishop had been tricked, or coerced rather, into working for one of the bad guys. Something that he was probably incredibly bitter about for years, decades even. No wonder he had such a blind spot when it came to Oliviana. There was probably a deep well of resentment inside of him that had been stewing since he'd broken free. No doubt he was looking for the perfect opportunity to take her down for good.

I had a sneaking suspicion myself that Oliviana was playing her cards close to the chest. She knew more than she let on. But we wouldn't get anywhere with her without more proof.

"So what do we do now?" I asked him.

Bishop continued to stare into space for a moment longer, before snapping back to reality all at once. "We go knock on another door."

My mouth spread into a grin at that remark, and we made our way to our next destination.

We made our way back to the dry cleaning shop that was one of the secret hideouts for the Soul Clan. Despite it being the middle of the day, the storefront was strangely closed. The lights were off, the inside only being lit from the faint light of the cloud-cloaked sunlight. That was weird to be sure. Bishop and I approached the front door of the shop. My uncle didn't hesitate to point the tip of his staff towards the door's lock.

Bishop hissed an incantation. Nothing flashy happened, the lock simply clicked and the door drifted free of its frame. Bishop and I escorted ourselves inside of the empty store. There was a pinging sound from an alarm system that we'd tripped. Once again, Bishop didn't hesitate. He pointed his staff to the approximate location of the pinging and hissed another word. I felt a movement in the air, a small surge of disruptive magic. A second later, sparks flew from a panel on the wall and the pinging died down to a dull whine that eventually faded into silence.

Sometimes, it was the smaller feats of magic that impressed me the most. Without another word, Bishop and I made our way to the back of the store, where we knew the hidden entrance to Feng Dài's lair was. We found the latch on the floor and I tugged on it, lifting it up and away from us. The dank staircase we'd been down once before loomed sinisterly below us, disappearing into darkness.

"After you." Bishop said, mildly amused.

"Ha ha," I grumbled. I'd made him go down the stairs first last time. It only made sense he'd make me go first this go around. But I didn't offer any further complaint. Though the distinct voice of Arnold from the Magic School Bus cartoons echoed in my mind.

"I knew I should've stayed home today." The phrase plastered itself to my thoughts.

The stairwell was dark, smelly, and spooky, to say the least. And so far it had been my least favorite of the scenery my uncle had shown me. I couldn't help but imagine a grotesque, monstrous beast emerging from the depths to chew my face off.

But no such beast made its presence known, and after a long descent, we'd reached the underground chamber where I'd first come face to face with the leader of the Jiangshi. The torches were out, so the only light came from a faint purple glow from the tip of Bishop's staff. It did not lend itself well to easing my worry. The purple light cast strange shadows that seemed to move sinisterly as the light bobbed in accordance with our movements. I had a bad feeling nagging at the back of my mind.

"Looks like no one's home." Bishop noted.

I tilted my head. "Yeah, isn't that strange?"

Bishop shook his head. "Not necessarily. You think Feng Dài spends all his time down here? He's probably somewhere else, at one of their other facilities. That being said, we shouldn't stay too long. Let's have a quick look around, see if there are any clues to find."

So we did. The room wasn't large, so it didn't take us very long to comb every inch of the place. There was nothing, save for the modest throne, stone walls, and torches. As I traced my hand along the back wall, a lightning bolt of sensation ran down my spine. This wall. This was the wall that I sensed that strange power emanating from last time.

"Bishop." I said.

Bishop turned his attention to me, and I hooked my thumb at the wall.

"There's something here. Something with some major magical power." I explained.

Bishop nodded. "Move." He leveled the tip of his staff at the spot I'd pointed out.

My eyes widened and I scrambled to get out of the way. "Vitum!"

Raw kinetic force whipped outwards from Bishop's staff, through the air, and struck the wall with incredible power. The wall exploded outwards and I had to duck close to the ground to avoid the rock fragments. A thick blanket of dust enveloped the room, and despite my best efforts, a chalky film coated the inside of my mouth. Gross.

Bishop shouted another word of power, and a gust of wind quickly dispersed the dust, sending it up the stairwell and out of our way. Once the winds had died down, I managed to rise to my feet.

The center of the far wall had been completely destroyed. Bishop's spell had revealed a small alcove previously hidden by the stone wall. Sitting in the alcove was a simple leather-bound trunk, appearing identical to the one in the security footage from the Blood Clan's safe house.

I approached the trunk cautiously, giving it a brief once over without touching it. I extended my magical senses towards it, and sure enough, I could feel that same, overwhelming power emanating from deep within the chest.

"What is this thing?" I wondered, though I hadn't meant to say it aloud.

"No idea, but we're sure as hell going to find out." Bishop said. "Grab the trunk, we're taking it with us."

I looked over to him, my eyes widening as I saw what was lurking just behind him. I pointed past him. "Uh, I think they might have a problem with that."

Bishop whirled around and cursed as his eyes crossed paths with three human figures. In the dim light it was hard to tell who they were. But one detail was evident, even in the poor lighting conditions. They all had mossy, green hair.

The lead Jiangshi shouted something in a language I didn't understand. And then they attacked.

The Jiangshi were supposed to be stiff and slow moving. That's what Bishop told me at least. He failed to mention that they moved slowly for vampires, not people. I only had a split second to react as the pale-skinned vampires came at us. I let out an undignified yelp of surprise as I let go of the trunk and dove to one side. I hit the floor hard and felt the stone tile rip a layer of skin from my elbows as I tumbled. The Jiangshi that had come for my throat missed me by inches and instead made an example out of the stone wall behind me. It dug its fingers into the stone with startling strength, sending shards and bits of stone flying around.

I scrambled onto my back, turning to face the monster. Luckily enough, its strike had worked a little too well. I watched it strain to dislodge itself from the wall. I grinned and managed to pull myself to my feet and unholster my eskrima, holding one in each hand. Not a moment later, the Jiangshi wrenched its hand free with a grunt of effort, sending more stone debris rattling across the room.

The vampire's eyes had lost the battle to cataracts a long time ago, they were covered in a foggy gray film.

But that didn't stop the monster from giving me a look of deep, predatory hatred.

"Aww come on, little buddy." I chided. "We can work this out, can't we? No reason I gotta splatter your brains, right?"

The Jiangshi stretched its mouth open with an inhuman roar. Inside its maw, I made note of a full set of serrated, shark-like teeth. My overactive imagination granted me a lovely image of those teeth digging into the flesh of my arm. I felt an involuntary shudder travel up and down my spine.

"I'll take that as a no, then. Fine." I extended my arm out, aiming the tip of my eskrima for its ugly mug and shouted. "*Kaze!*"

A miniature spear-shaped cyclone erupted from the rod and flew straight at the creature's stupid face. It struck home, whipping its head back to the side as if I'd slugged it.

It slowly turned its head back to face me. I heard a creaking sound coming from its jaw as it did. With a sudden jolt of movement, its jaw shifted and I realized it had just reset it into place. Snap, crackle, pop, and its like my last blow hadn't even happened.

"Well that's just unfair." I moaned.

The Jiangshi rushed me again in a burst of speed. I didn't have enough time to move. And if I didn't do something fast, the thing would skewer me and serve me up on shish kabobs.

I hissed out a panicked spell. "*Duro!*"

The soul-sucking vampire hit me a second later, driving me into the wall directly behind me. I let out a grunt of pain. Under normal circumstances, that blow would've killed me three times over. But my spell had kicked in just in time. My skin had become as tough as steel, taking on a texture similar to tough rock. The durability spell had saved my skin on more than one occasion, and I thanked the Heavens above that I'd remembered to use it.

The Jiangshi had a confused expression painted on its face. Normally, things it struck like that usually died, I assumed. So the fact that I'd come out of the attack without so much as a scratch was probably baffling to the thing.

That's not to say though, that the strike hadn't absolutely rocked my world. The durability spell had kept me from turning into a pancake, but I still felt the impact. It had been like getting hit by a semi. Stars danced in my vision as the Jiangshi backed away, stunned at my survival. I slumped for a moment, but the Jiangshi was already getting ready to swing at me again. I saw its arm raise and light seemed to coalesce in its open hand. I couldn't tell what exactly it was conjuring, but I knew it couldn't be good.

Even with my thoughts as blurry as they were, I managed to raise up my own hand to match the Jiangshi's. I reached into the spell formula that was bound to the metal comet charm on my wrist and hissed out a word, "*Hinote!*"

A fireball the size of one of those bouncy exercise balls burst forth from my outstretched hand and impacted immediately against the Jiangshi's torso. It exploded immediately, and I felt the heat wash over me and a wave of concussive force pin me against the wall again. In retrospect, it hadn't been the smartest move. I'd rocked my head against the wall as a result and earned myself a renewed fireworks show in my vision. It was hard to see, but I'm pretty sure the Jiangshi had flown back into the stairwell from where we'd entered. That gave me a second to get my head on straight.

I shook my head, blinking the stars out of my eyes. I turned to my right, where Bishop was currently engaged with the remaining two Jiangshi. I had to give my uncle credit, the old man could scrap with the best of them. He wielded his wizard's staff like a bo, successfully parrying attacks from both Jiangshi simultaneously. Every time one of them went to throw fire or lightning at him, he effortlessly deflected their aim towards the wall or the ceiling. Neither of his assailants seemed to be able to get a handle on him.

But it was a losing battle. Bishop was forced to stay on the defensive or else risk getting roasted. The Jiangshi left him no room to take the offensive. But I could see he was slowing down. The vampires' spells and strikes were getting closer, bit by bit, to hitting their intended target. If I didn't do something...

I had a fraction of a second to register the sound of footsteps rushing towards me. I turned back towards the stairwell just in time to see the Jiangshi stab at me with its nails, which were rippling with freaking lightning. Of course.

My shoulder erupted into a wildfire of pain and static as the Jiangshi's razor sharp nails sunk into my shoulder, sending pain and lightning throughout my entire body. I won't lie, I screamed. It wasn't a pretty sound. Hell, I couldn't even call it dignified. That shit hurt.

It didn't take long for that good ol' fight or flight response to kick back in. The pain turned into fury and I glared daggers at the monster, clenching my teeth to hold back any further screams. With every ounce of strength I could muster, I did something I don't think the Jiangshi was expecting. I slugged it in the face.

And I'm pretty sure I broke my hand in the process. The electricity ceased but was replaced with crackling, red hot pain emanating from my right hand. The Jiangshi stumbled back, gripping its nose and grumbling in pain. I slid against the wall onto the ground, gripping my shoulder. Small muscle spasms caused my arms and legs to jerk slightly as I tried to gather myself. The wound freaking hurt, and it was definitely going to need stitches. Add that to the bruises on my back, the skinned shin, and the nearly broken nose I'd earned myself thus far.

Man, if I even made it to prom at this point, there were gonna be some interesting pictures.

I cursed as I tried to get myself up without putting too much pressure on my wounded shoulder. That punch must've stunned the vampire more than I thought, because by the time I'd managed to stand up, it was still holding its face in pain.

"Alright, time for the sucker punch." I muttered. "*Kaze!*"

I aimed one of my eskrima at the Jiangshi and pictured the result I wanted. It wasn't perfect but I was impressed with the maneuver. A cyclone erupted from the end of the rod and roared towards my assailant. It struck the monster straight in the chest and with a flick of my wrist, the cyclone picked up the Jiangshi and slammed it into the stone ceiling with bone-crunching force. I know, because I heard the Jiangshi's stiff, brittle bones crack. It was a sound eerily similar to crunching leaves, but dialed up to eleven.

As the cyclone died out, the Jiangshi crashed limply to the ground. It twitched and let out choking sounds as it did. I noted that there wasn't a drop of blood to be seen. That was interesting. Did Jiangshi not have blood? I made a mental note of that, I'd want to add it to my supernatural study guide on vampires.

"One down," I turned to see Bishop still locked in combat with the other Jiangshi. "Two to go."

Which was a fairly optimistic attitude, all things considered. Bishop was holding his own against the remaining two Jiangshi, but I could see he was getting tired. He was keeping his use of magic limited, probably because the combat magic he could dish out at his level was pretty dangerous in close quarters, far more so than my own.

I took a step forward to assist him when I heard something jingle in my pocket. My brain raced as information came surging to the forefront of my mind. Of course, one of the Jiangshi's biggest vices was...

I dug my hand into my pocket and pulled out half a dozen coins I'd received only a couple of days before. With a mischievous grin and a flourish of my wrist, I chucked the change towards Bishop and his opponents. The coins clattered noisily to the ground and there was a brief yet eternal moment where the fight simply stopped. I could see the Jiangshi's bodies twitching involuntarily as they struggled to fight their basic instincts. But before long, the two vampires scrambled to the floor in order to gather and count the coins.

Lucky for us, the instinct to count the spilled coins was so strong, they were fighting over whatever coins they'd managed to gather. I looked up at Bishop and silently came to the same conclusion. It was time to get the hell out of here. Bishop hopped over the occupied Jiangshi and helped me lift the trunk. With a Herculean effort, we booked it up the stairs and ran out of the laundromat until we couldn't run anymore.

We ended up in an old abandoned lot. I remember dropping my side of the trunk and falling to the ground, completely winded.

It seemed like hours had gone by since we'd escaped the Jiangshi lair and I'd collapsed in the lot, but in reality it had only been a few minutes. Bishop woke me up, warning of the dangers of being out in the open after assaulting and pillaging an enemy base. I suppose he was right, but damn it the gravel lot had felt as comfy and inviting as a bed made of unicorn hair and fluffy clouds.

I barely remember the trek home. After taking only a few minutes to get our wits about us, Bishop insisted on hurrying home. Ugh, I mean come on. Can't I take a quick nap in this gravel lot like some kind of drunk hobo? Was that too much to ask?

But through sheer, teenage stubbornness, I did as I was told. Despite my aching back, nose, legs, hand, and probably half a dozen other minor injuries I'd accrued in just a couple of days, I persisted. I felt like a zombie though, and the walk home seemed more like a dream than anything else. We each held one of the trunk's handles, walking awkwardly with it between us. Carrying heavy ass stuff like that with someone else is always awkward. You're both half stumbling the entire time, bumping each other with the shared load.

It was a fight to ignore the trunk continually bumping my leg. My knee felt like it would buckle and I'd fall flat on my face. I'm not sure how much time had passed since we'd started walking. The cloudy weather did nothing to help with my perception of time. We'd arrived at Heaven's Door around noon, right? How long had it been since then?

Our apartment was a sight for sore eyes. It had only been a few hours since we'd been home, but I'd managed to get myself into not one, but two brawls with the supernatural. Images of my short-lived fight with Kat flashed across my eyes. Her proximity to this both confused and concerned me. What did she have to gain by throwing in with the vampires?

After awkwardly struggling to open the front door with the trunk in hand, we made our way inside and made a point to lock the door. I vaguely remember

Bishop saying something about getting some rest, and who was I to argue with him?

I dropped my side of the trunk and it made a loud thumping noise against the carpet. I wasn't sure what my uncle had planned for the trunk now that we had it in our possession, but that would be a concern that Future Tobias would have to worry about. I drunkenly made my way up to my room and flopped onto my bed.

It felt like Heaven.

Chapter 16

I was jolted awake by a loud bang. I sat up groggily in bed, trying to make sense of where I was or why everything hurt so much. As the abstract weight of sleep faded away, I managed to recall just what had happened before I passed out in my room. Kat. Heaven's Door. The Jiangshi. The trunk.

Judging by the gray light coming through my window, it had to still be daytime. Or had a day passed? Shit, I hoped not. There wasn't time to lose. It certainly didn't feel like I'd slept that long.

Wait, what the hell had that loud bang been? Could be trouble. I found my hand pressed to my eskrima harness on my leg. Seems like I hadn't removed it before I passed out. Good, because there was a very good chance I'd need them. Maybe the

Jiangshi had followed us in an attempt to retrieve their stolen property. I removed one of the fighting sticks from its harness as I rose out of bed and quietly made my way to the door and down the stairs.

There was no sign of forced entry. The door was still intact and on its hinges. The windows hadn't been broken.

BOOM!

Another loud bang, no, more like the sounds of an explosion, filled the apartment. Deductive reasoning suggested it had to be coming from the small garage turned wizard's study. Still gripping my eskrima, I made my way to the door that led to the garage.

My hand shook slightly as I reached for the door knob. Was it nerves, exhaustion, or a not so healthy mix of both? I gripped the door knob, but paused for a moment to listen. I didn't hear any signs of commotion coming from the other side. But my anxiety persisted that there may be trouble. Slowly, I turned the door knob all the way.

With one fluid motion I swung the door open and leapt into the garage with my eskrima raised, ready to fire off some kind of offensive magic. I let out a less than dignified battle cry as I did.

Imagine my embarrassment when all I found was my uncle with his back to the door, staring at the trunk in the garage. He held his staff in hand, and I could see wisps of smoke coming from its tip. My gaze shifted from Bishop to the trunk, which sat on the opposite side of the garage, farthest from the door. Wisps of smoke traced its edges. Now it made sense.

"You trying to wake up the neighbors with all that racket?" I asked him. My voice came out a bit raspy, and I had to clear my throat to rectify it.

Bishop turned towards me. "Oh, you're awake already. I'd expected you to be comatose for at least a couple hours."

My face scrunched up to form a puzzled look. "Yeah well, hard to sleep when you're apparently blasting that damn box. How long was I out?"

Bishop looked down at his bare wrist, then back to me. "About half an hour or so, give or take."

That tracked, given how tired I still felt. "Ugh, so why exactly are you fighting the mystery box?"

"I was trying to get it open. I can't seem to pick the lock. And trying to cut the lock cost me a nice set of bolt-cutters." Bishop explained. "So I figured it was magically warded and sealed. Lobbing magic at is the quickest way I can get a feel for its defenses."

"And?" I asked, inviting him to explain further.

"Whoever sealed this trunk, they're good. Like really good."

"How good is really good, exactly?"

"So good that I'm not sure a wizard alive could've put these wards together." Bishop said, his voice grave and low. "I've never seen anything like it. Not even the wards that protect Light Haven are this powerful. I've been hitting it as hard as I can without tearing the whole apartment complex down and there's not a scratch on it. It's like I never even tried."

Now that was scary. Bishop hadn't taught me a whole lot about setting up long term magical defenses yet, but I could still appreciate the scale the trunk seemed to operate on. Whomever had built the trunk and sealed it, was, or perhaps had been, a major player. Whatever was inside must've been seriously important to go through all that effort to make sure no one opened it.

"I suppose there is some good news to be had there. If we can't get it open, perhaps the vampires are out of luck too." I offered, trying to look on the bright side.

Bishop nodded his head, but he didn't seem too confident. He rested both hands on top of his staff, resting his chin there, as if in thought. "For now, but I don't think Kat and her rogue vamps would've gone to the trouble of finding these trunks if they didn't believe they could eventually get them open."

"So what happens now?" I asked him.

Bishop sighed. "We need help on this. We'll have to take the trunk to Light Haven so we can get more eyes and minds on it. Figure out how to open it and find out what's inside. We need to know what we're dealing with here."

I rubbed my eyes blearily as I holstered my eskrima. Wonderful. And here I had been hoping we'd be able to avoid involving the Mystic Order directly in this whole ordeal. They weren't devils or anything. Trust me, been there, done that. But they weren't exactly my favorite bunch of people either, and I was pretty sure they didn't care much for me. Y'know, given the whole vessel for the Anti-Christ thing. You get possessed by the devil one time and suddenly everyone keeps a suspicious eye on you.

My face must've expressed those exact feelings because Bishop's mouth stretched in an amused smile.

"Tobias, I know you're generally wary of the Mystic Order, and with good reason as I share the sentiment." Bishop said. "They may be a bunch of paranoid bureaucrats but on most days they're reasonable. And occasionally even helpful. But it could take me ages to figure out what's in this trunk or even how to open it. Plus, as strong as the magical defenses are in this apartment, there aren't many places in the universe more secure than Light Haven."

I sighed, knowing that I had no chance at winning this battle. And after all, he was right as much as I hated to admit it. "Alright, when do we leave?"

"Well, I say we get freshened up. Get some ice on your bruises while I shower. How's the hand?" Bishop asked.

I flexed my hand as a twinge of pain went through it. I remembered punching one of the Jiangshi right in the schnoz. Felt like punching a brick wall.

"Everything still works and moves. Hurts like hell though."

"Yeah you gotta be careful hitting the Jiangshi. Their bones are practically petrified. It's what makes them so stiff most of the time. They can only manage quick bursts of movement." Bishop explained.

I scoffed. "Could've fooled me."

Bishop barked out a laugh. "Yeah, despite that, they can still give your average mortal a run for their money. Anyways, I'm gonna hit the showers. Ice up! Wheel's up in ten."

Bishop headed back inside and the door closed behind him. Leaving me alone in the wizard's lab with the mystical mystery box. I chuckled to myself. When the hell had my life gotten so weird?

As the thought crossed my mind, something strange happened. And I know strange, but this was a new one. I heard...whispers? No, not just whispers. Voices, singing voices. It was a faint sound, just on the edge of my senses. I turned my attention to the trunk, sitting on the far side of the garage. As I turned my eyes on it, as if like a trick of the light or an optical illusion, an aura of white light seemed to surround the trunk. The singing voices grew louder as I focused my vision on the chest. It was almost as if it were calling to me. The trunk yearned to be opened.

Without so much as a second, or even a first thought, I felt myself moving towards the trunk, my hand reaching towards it. The voices grew louder and I realized it sounded much like a choir at church, singing wordlessly in prayer to...

A sharp tug on my shoulder pulled me out of the trance. The singing and light faded in an instant. I was whipped around and found myself face to face with Bishop. The look on his face was that of someone who'd just witnessed a horrific car accident.

"What were you doing?" Bishop asked me.

I looked him up and down. He'd showered and changed into a fresh flannel and cargo pants. His beard had been cleaned up a bit and he smelled like an ocean's breeze.

I babbled for a second, trying to get my mouth to work properly. "The uh, the trunk, it was..." I struggled to articulate the sensation into words. "It was calling to me."

Bishop's face settled into something hard. He was trying not to show his concern or fear, but I knew him too well by now. Whatever had just happened, it scared the hell out of him. Whatever was in that trunk must've scared him too. And that had me rightfully concerned too.

"We need to get that trunk to Light Haven. Now." Bishop said.

The local entrance to Light Haven was located in one of the strangest tourist attractions in Seattle. The Market Theater Gum Wall was a relic of Seattle's past that just wouldn't quit. One account claimed patrons would stick coins to the wall with gum to tip performers. Others claimed it was a sign of protest as gum wasn't allowed in the venue. I couldn't tell you the whole truth behind it, but I'd come to learn that was the least remarkable thing about the wall.

You see, for wizards, the Gum Wall acted as a doorway into Light Haven. It was one of countless entry ways into the wizards' headquarters. I hadn't visited any of these other entrances, but I had to hope they were at least a little bit more sanitary. Bishop pressed a combination of gum wads as if they were buttons on a keypad. The specific pieces of gum had a faint glow to them that only a wizard could see.

After he had done so, the wall seemed to melt away into a passage of pure light. Any passerby around us seemed to be completely oblivious to this. We hefted the trunk once more and walked through into the light.

A brief moment went by where we were surrounded by nothing but blinding white light. Then, just as quickly as it had appeared, the light melted away like a curtain as we stepped into Light Haven's Portal Nexus. The Portal Nexus, like the rest of Light Haven, was characterized by white tile floors, white paneled walls, and white tile ceilings. Though I could never pin down a light source, the room was lit as if the sun itself were shining in the room. The place had been quite a marvel upon my first visit, and even after visiting this place a dozen times since then, it still took effort not to leave my jaw hanging open at the wonder of the place. Mortal wizards, elves, dwarves, and pixies all milled about as if they had to be to the most important meeting in the world. I recognized a few faces but none of them by name. And they were far too busy with whatever they had going on to recognize the presence of two more wizards carrying a large, awkward trunk. As far as they were concerned, it was just another day at the office.

I wasn't surprised that our colleagues didn't really care to make way for us, and trying to shuffle through the crowd while carrying the trunk between Bishop and I was a slog to say the least. Bishop took the lead, and I did my best to scurry along behind him without bashing my knees into the trunk too much. I thought back to when I had been alone with the trunk. As soon as my uncle had left the room, it seemed to come to life. It spoke to me, no, called to me, like a living, breathing thing. Did whatever was inside the trunk possess some sort of intelligence? Only time would tell.

Eventually we were able to break through the crowd and make our way into the halls. This place continued to feel like a maze to me, and I swore the halls and rooms changed all the time. But Bishop moved along as if he knew exactly where he was going. I guess when you spend enough time here, you get to know all its habits and quirks. Huh, that was weird to think about. For a facility like this to have such things as habits and quirks. But could it be true? Something to consider later, I suppose.

We made our way into the surprisingly plain office space where many of the desk monkeys handled the day-to-day stuff that any large company might have to deal with. The only remarkable thing about the large room was the ever-changing scenery in the background. Last time I'd been here it depicted the rolling hills and beautiful forests of Alfheim. Now, it depicted snowy mountaintops plagued by a blizzard.

"Where's that?" I asked.

Bishop shrugged. "Not sure, could be a few places. Jotunheim? Or perhaps the realms of the Winter fae? Hard to be sure."

We made our way past a couple dozen rows of cubicles and into a corner office where the face of the Mystic Order was lounging in his office chair. Roland Braun was a tall, well-built man with dark skin and long, graying dreads. He had amber colored eyes that seemed to stare right into your soul. Who knows, maybe they did? Magic and all. When it came to magic, I made no assumptions as to what was possible.

"Ah, Bishop and Tobias Leight, a pleasure to see you again." His deep voice was sprinkled with a hint of a German accent. He eyed the trunk between us. "What have we here?"

"High Elder Braun, in our efforts to investigate the brewing conflict between the vampire conflicts, we found something...interesting." Bishop said, hefting the trunk up for a moment to adjust his grip.

Braun's eyes seemed to glow for a second as he focused on the trunk. His face contorted as he processed whatever it was he saw. Concern, amusement, and fear all flashed across his face in a single moment. "Well, well, well, you've found something interesting. Quite interesting, indeed."

I think that scared me more than anything. From what I was told, Braun was pretty much the cream of the crop when it came to wizards. I'd yet to see him show any of his power, which only added to the mystery of it. And I prayed I was never in such a bad spot that he had to come in and save the day.

"Maybe we should take this somewhere a bit more spacious." Bishop said. "This thing has a bit of an attitude."

"Pfft, yeah that's one way to put it." I laughed.

"Very well, let's take this to the training court then." Braun nodded as he rose from his chair.

"Might want to call Fachnan in." Bishop suggested. "His expertise in the dark arts may be helpful here."

Fachnan, oh boy. He'd been mind-whammied last year by Kat and her hellish friend. He'd been helping them along and acting as a scapegoat to keep us distracted while their plan unfolded. He and I had come to an understanding after that whole ordeal, but our friendship, if you could call it that, was shaky at best.

We arrived at the training court shortly thereafter. Braun led the way as Bishop and I lugged the trunk between us awkwardly down the halls. Fachnan had already arrived and was busy drawing with chalk on the hardwood floor. I tried to rack my brain to recall if chalk would actually work on hardwood. I chalked it up-haha-to magic nonsense.

Fachnan was a tall, skinny man with neat, red hair that formed nicely around his head. His face seemed to be constantly stuck in an expression of disinterest, or perhaps disdain when he saw me. He looked up from his work for a moment to acknowledge our presence, narrowing his eyes as we approached.

"You can place the trunk in the center of the circle." Fachnan said, pointing towards the circle's center, where a five-pointed star within a smaller circle was drawn. The pentacle. Bishop had once explained to me it was a symbol of mortal magic.

Bishop walked forward, almost dragging me along to the center of the circle as specified. With a heavy thump, we set the trunk down.

"What are you planning to do, Fachnan?" Bishop asked.

"A sort of investigative magic," Fachnan explained, even as he shooed us out of the large circle's boundaries. His Irish accent seemed to add an extra layer of impatience to his tone of voice.

"Maybe a bit more explanation for those of us who might not know what the heck you're talking about?" I asked, very politely, I assure you.

Fachnan's face twinged as he raised an eyebrow. He looked directly at me for the first time since we'd arrived. "The circle surrounding the trunk acts as a sort of..." He paused as he seemed to search for the right word that my tiny brain could understand. "Interface, you see? Once infused with magic, the circle will act as an extension of myself to visualize and examine the spells that have been wrought upon the trunk."

"Oh. Neat." I noted smartly.

"Fachnan, will the circle be able to detect what may be inside of the trunk?" Braun asked.

Fachnan shook his head. "There's no way to tell just yet. I will need some time to examine the enchantments."

"Take a guess for us, please." Braun encouraged.

Fachnan sighed, clearly already exasperated. "The exact nature, I have no clue. But if this trunk is as tightly sealed as you say, then whatever is sealed within is extremely powerful."

"A weapon, then?" Bishop asked.

"That is one possibility, but not necessarily a likely one." Fachnan said. "Like I said, I will need to examine the trunk first before I can begin crafting any meaningful hypotheses."

I puffed out a breath. "Alright, well then let's get to it then."

"I will get to it, yes." Fachnan corrected with pointed emphasis. "You all will leave me to do my job. When I have something to share, you will hear from me."

I scoffed. It seemed Fachnan was still as cheery as ever. I opened my mouth to protest, but Bishop placed a firm grip on my good shoulder. "Come on, Tobias. Why don't we get some grub while Fachnan does his thing?"

My stomach rumbled at the thought of food, and I couldn't help but agree. When was the last time in all this mess that I'd had a decent meal? A couple days ago, perhaps? I nodded in agreement, and Bishop, Braun, and I left Fachnan to his work.

Light Haven's cafeteria wasn't unlike one you'd find in any typical high school. Long community tables were lined up side by side, with a narrow path between the two rows. On the other side of the far wall was the kitchen, connected only by a few service windows, each with a long line of people from various parts of the world, along with a handful of dwarves and elves.

Off to the side, separate from the long lines was another window that was currently closed. Twin wooden doors blocked my view inside. Braun walked straight for it, ignoring the lines of people.

"Uh, this one looks closed." I said.

"Not exactly." Braun replied as he walked up to the closed window. He rapped the back of his hand against the wood.

A moment passed before I heard the shuffling footsteps of someone approaching from behind the window. The doors swung open and we were greeted with the chest of a very large, very plump figure. His belly filled the entire view through the window.

"Uh, hello?" I said inquisitively.

The figure backed up a few steps before crouching down to peek through the window. The man peeking through had a baby face, but that was the only thing about him that was child-like. The man had to be huge, probably pushing ten feet tall from what I could tell.

"Oh, 'ello Mister Braun. You have guests with you today?" The big, portly man said. He spoke with an accent that I couldn't quite place. His short O sounds sounded more like an "aw" sound.

"Hello there, Andhrímnir." Braun said politely. "Yes, I wanted to spare my guests the pain of the public lines today. Three of the usual, if you don't mind?"

The man called Andhrímnir nodded happily, almost eagerly. "Yes, of course. One moment then. I will bring your food out shortly. Please, sit."

And with that, the big man stood up and closed the window. I could hear the sound of his lumbering footsteps fading away as he retreated into what I assumed was his kitchen. Braun led us to a table nearby and we all sat down and waited.

"Who was that?" I asked. "You called him Andrehmeer?"

"Andhrímnir." Braun corrected, speaking with a perfect accent. One that I now realized was reminiscent of Norway. "He's on contract with the Mystic Order as the personal chef to the High Elders."

"How'd he get so damn big?"

"Andhrímnir is a sort of a minor Norse god." Braun explained, as casually as explaining a fork was a tool with which to eat food.

I babbled for a second, trying to come up with words that made sense. "You just...you just have a god cooking your meals for you?"

Bishop stepped in. "Once upon a time, it is said he cooked for the Norse pantheon, but with those gods missing or in hibernation, he needed a new purpose. So, the Mystic Order offered him a position here just a few hundred years ago."

My uncle and the High Elder spoke as if this were just a normal everyday thing, which to them, I suppose it was. We waited for a few more minutes until those lumbering footsteps approached. Andhrímnir approached from behind me, and his arrival shocked me. For one, I have no idea where he came from. From what I could tell, there was no door leading out of the kitchen. Not to mention I hadn't even noticed him approaching until he was already upon us. Then there was the fact that he was even bigger than I'd realized.

Andhrímnir was closer to twelve feet tall and half as wide. Despite this, his limbs were far from stubby in comparison. He may have been a rather fat fellow, but I had a feeling behind all that weight was nothing but pure strength. On one arm, he balanced three plates, each with a bowl of something hot and steamy. In his other hand he held three large mugs by their handles.

"Three of the usual, boss." Andhrímnir rumbled.

"Thank you." Braun said with a respectful bow of his head.

Bishop echoed the sentiment, and Andhrímnir set the plates and mugs down in front of us. We distributed them evenly and I saw now that the bowls contained a piping hot stew with bits of vegetables and meat floating in the broth. The mugs held a white liquid that I assumed was milk. But it had a faint sweet smell I couldn't quite describe.

"So you're really a god, then?" I asked. "Andree...Andreh...screw it, I'm going to call you Andy."

Bishop and Braun both shot disapproving looks at me. But Andy only laughed. It was a big, bellowing, hearty laugh that shook my teeth.

"I know my name can sometimes be hard for the young'uns to pronounce. Lucky for you I'm not one of those old, sensitive-type gods. Andy will do." Andy said, clearly amused.

Phew, for a second there I thought I might've offended the god, judging from the continued disapproving looks that both Bishop and Braun gave me. I inspected the stew with an investigative stir with my spoon.

"What is this, exactly?" I asked him.

"Boar stew and goat's milk." Andy said simply.

The rumbling in my stomach conflicted with the hesitation I felt. It sounded gross, especially the goat's milk, but I didn't want to risk another opportunity to offend the god. Andy must've noticed this, because he spoke again, still sounding rather amused.

"Give it a try." Andy urged. "The stew is made from a divine boar that has been my rival since the beginning of creation. And the milk comes from one of my most loyal companions. You will not taste anything quite like it, even amongst the elven food cooked in the other kitchens here."

So, I did as Andy suggested. I scooped up a spoonful of broth, meat, and veggies and brought the spoon to my mouth. After another second's hesitation, I took a bite.

The taste was...well, no words I could put to it would do it justice. It was sensational. The flavors of the meat, veggies, and broth mixed so well and the meat practically melted on my tongue. It was beyond delicious. Gordon Ramsay himself would've wept at the taste. After I swallowed the concoction, I reached for the milk and took a sip. It was the icing on the cake. It tasted like sweet cream and reminded me fondly of Christmas cookies. Despite it being served cold, it filled me with a rush of warmth and comfort.

"Holy crap." I sputtered as I gulped down the milk. "This is...I can't even..."

Andy let out another hearty belly laugh, clearly pleased with my reaction. "Always a pleasure to see someone's reaction to my food and drink the first time around. Now you know why the gods ate this for every meal."

"Yeah, no kidding." I said as I took another bite.

Braun smiled. "Don't get used to it but enjoy it. It's not everyday that someone outside of the High Elders gets a chance to taste Andhrímnir's cooking."

We all turned our full attention to the food in front of us. I practically inhaled the broth. As much as I wanted to take time to savor it, I couldn't help but get it all down as fast as possible. After I'd gulped down the last of the broth, I dumped the remainder of the milk down my gullet. I leaned back in my chair, hand on my stomach, and let out a satisfied burpy breath.

"My compliments," I paused again to let out another low burp. "To the chef."

Andy laughed, a cheerful noise that rose deep from within. "I am glad you liked it, little wizard."

"Thank you very much, Andy." I bowed my head slightly to express both my gratitude and my respect. It felt like the appropriate thing to do when talking to a god. Even if he was supposedly a minor one.

"Of course, Tobias Leight." Andy returned the gesture before rising from where he'd been seated. "If you all need anything else, you know where to find me."

With that, the rotund god made his way back to the service windows from whence he'd came. I didn't see him go through a door or anything. I simply lost track of him in the crowd, which was weird, considering how massive he was. I chalked it up to spooky magic powers and thought nothing else of it.

"So, what now?" I asked, looking between my uncle and Braun.

"Well, should we check in with Fachnan?" Bishop looked to Braun.

Braun raised his wrist as if to check his watch. He wasn't wearing one, but that didn't stop him from looking at his wrist with an inquisitive look. "I wouldn't bother. It will only irritate him. If he hasn't gotten to us by now, I suspect it may be a long wait. You may as well head home. When he has something to share, either he or I will get in touch."

Phooey. I really wanted to find out what was inside that chest, or at least an idea as to why exactly it was locked up so tight. I let out an exaggerated sigh. It had been a long day as is, and we still hadn't really learned anything about this whole ordeal. I'd have to sit down and really think through everything we knew now. I suspected Bishop was thinking along the same lines.

"Alright, no problem." Bishop said, as he rose from his seat. Braun did the same and I followed suit. "As soon as you learn something, please let us know. We need something to act on before we can move on the vampires."

"Of course, Bishop. But remember, patience is key. Anything else only leads to disaster. Remain calm, cool, and collected, and let things work themselves out. Given time, I'm sure Fachnan will be able to provide us with actionable information." Braun lectured.

How refreshing, someone besides me being told to cool their jets and be patient. With that being said, Bishop and I dismissed ourselves and said goodbye to Braun and we headed back towards the Portal Nexus.

"When do you think we'll learn something about the trunk?" I asked Bishop. The sound of my voice echoed down the maze-like hallways of the Light Haven. If you paid too much attention to the echoing, it got disorienting very quickly.

"Fachnan's the best of the best when it comes to this sort of thing, but the wards on that trunk are extremely complicated and have several layers of protection. It'll probably be a while before we hear anything. Tomorrow morning at the earliest, but that's under the best of circumstances." Bishop explained.

It sounded like extremely technical magic. Both the wards themselves and the examination process that Fachnan was performing to unwind them. I wondered how long it would take me to get even close to that level of skill. So far, I was pretty decent at the quick, kablooey kind of magic, but the more technical magic like my disappearing act or tracking spell were still things I couldn't do without intense focus or assistance.

"What do we do until then?" I asked him.

Bishop smiled. "I'm sure there's some trouble we can stir up."

Chapter 17

We emerged from the Gum Wall into a crowd of seemingly oblivious tourists. They seemed more annoyed that we were blocking their view, when they should've been dumbfounded at the fact we'd just walked out of a gum-covered wall. We shuffled out of the crowd and into the rain. It wasn't raining nearly as hard as it had been when we entered Light Haven.

I checked the time on my phone. It was just after 5pm. We had to find Maria Grimaldo before the clock struck midnight on Friday night. That gave us less than 36 hours to work with. With any luck, Fachnan would have something for us to go off of in the morning. Were we supposed to wait until then?

"You know what, Bishop?" I said. "I feel like we've been running around looking for these trunks that we've forgotten our main objective."

Bishop seemed to think about that for a second. "You're right. These trunks were never our main priority."

"I mean sure, we assumed that if we found the trunks, we'd find her. But we haven't had too much luck with the trunks in the first place." I scratched my chin in thought. "What if we shifted our focus back to finding her? Maybe she'll lead us to the other two trunks."

"Flipping our original idea on its head, eh?" Bishop chuckled. "Not a bad idea, kiddo."

"Only problem is, we don't have any leads on Maria herself." I grumbled.

"Not necessarily. There's one place I wanted to pay a visit to again." Bishop said speculatively.

"Hm, where's that?"

"The warehouse that we tracked down using those bullets." Bishop explained. "We didn't really get to investigate much before having to retreat. Because someone couldn't keep their cool."

His pointed gaze said it all. "Right," I said sheepishly. "Well, second time's the charm right?"

"Uh huh." He said through a chuckle. "I say we make our way there and take another look around. I think there's a good chance we'll find Maria there, or at least a clue to her whereabouts."

"And I promise to be on my best behavior this time around." I held up my hand with my first three fingers raised. "Scout's honor."

"Best behavior doesn't necessarily mean good behavior, now does it?" Bishop cocked an eyebrow. "And you never did Boy Scouts."

"Drat, ya caught me." I held up my hands and shrugged. "Oh well, guess you'll just have to take my word for it."

We called an Uber and made our way to the industrial complex where the vampires' warehouse was located. The complex was actually pretty busy at the moment, as a lot of people were getting off work and heading home. So Bishop and I found a secluded corner to bide our time in while people cleared out.

"Okay, so what's the game plan?" I asked him.

"Second verse, same as the first." He said.

I looked at him skeptically.

Bishop let out a sigh. "We go in under a veil and take a look around. All the different flavors of vampire have remarkable senses so we'll still have to be pretty sneaky, even under the veil. Not to mention if they have any warlocks on staff."

He was talking about Kat, of course. She was working with the vampires in order to get whatever was in those trunks. So if this was the alliance's base of operations, there was a good chance she was here. It made me wonder though, what exactly had Kat promised the various vamps that would convince them to betray their clans? Whatever it was, it had to be pretty enticing. From my experience with the three clan leaders, none of them seemed like they took kindly to traitors.

"Okay, let's do this thing." I said.

We made our way casually through the maze of buildings. Bishop cast a see-me-not spell. How he described it, it wasn't quite a veil, but it did make us extremely dull and not worth noticing.

It didn't take long for us to arrive at the vampire hideout. It was about as unremarkable and nondescript as a building could be. Large, rectangular with an off-white coat of paint. Large windows lined the upper levels, no doubt the office level of the building. There was a small entryway, also lined with windows, that led into a lobby. There was a lot of caution tape and tarps around it now though. No doubt to hide the damage from our narrow escape last time. There were no guards outside, and I didn't spot any cameras either. Which I found somewhat strange. No guards, sure. But no cameras, that was odd as hell.

But not as odd as what I found near the building's perimeter. Forcing their way out of the concrete were several outcroppings of flowers and toadstools. Each grouping was an almost perfect circle of randomly placed daisies and mushrooms. There was maybe half a dozen of the strange circles.

"Bishop, what do you make of those?" I pointed towards the circles. As I stretched out my hand, I felt a subtle power emanating from the plants and fungus. They were definitely magical in nature.

Bishop narrowed his eyes. "Fairy circles."

"Uh, what are fairy circles?" I asked.

"They form in the presence of the fae, usually wherever they may be residing in the mortal world." Bishop explained. His eyes didn't waver from the circles.

I didn't know much about the fae, except that they weren't something to be messed with. They ranged from mischievous to murderous, and were tricky as hell to deal with. I'd only come across a faerie on one occasion, and it had been one tough son of a gun. It had almost killed me when I was just starting out.

"What would the fae be doing here?" I asked him.

“Nothing good, I know that much.” Bishop said. There was a hint of tension in his voice that hadn’t been there a moment before. “If the fae are involved somehow, this got a whole lot more dangerous. We need to be on high alert. That means no fooling around.”

I gulped. “Right, got it. No funny business.”

As we approached, Bishop spoke. “A fae presence here would explain the lack of mortal security measures. Like cameras or an alarm. Faeries tend to muck up modern technology just by being in the same room.”

“Why’s that?”

“No one knows for sure. Faeries eat, sleep, and breathe magic. And that much magic in one spot seems to interfere with technology for some reason. Only extremely powerful mortal wizards can achieve the same passive effect. I count maybe a dozen in the world. For wizards like you and me, we have to actively try to disrupt technology.” Bishop explained in a quiet and quick tone.

I nodded. “Uh, anything else I should know about faeries before we head in?”

“They’re weak to salt and iron. The purer the iron, the better, but most alloys will do.” Bishop said patiently, like a teacher explaining a subject to restless students.

"Uh, I don't have any salt or iron."

Bishop held out his hand and twisted his wrist. One moment, there was nothing, The next, his staff appeared in his hand. He gripped the top of it and gave it a light twist. A six inch blade that I assumed was pure iron extended out of the bottom with a satisfying metallic sound.

"Leave any faeries to me." He said plainly.

I raised my eyebrows appreciatively. "Got it."

"One more thing, veils are useless when dealing with the fae. Their relationship with magic allows them to see the presence of veils plain as day." Bishop explained. "So we're going in as is. It'd be a waste of time and effort to do otherwise. That means stay low and stay quiet. And do exactly as I say."

I took out my eskrima, holding them ready by my side as I crouched behind him. "Okay, let's do this then."

Bishop peeked through the tarps obscuring the doorway. He signaled the all clear and slinked through the tarp and into the lobby. I followed suit. I was careful to keep my steps as light as possible. It only took one echoing footstep to alert a horde of vampires to our presence. We weren't armed with any vampiric weaknesses, only our magic. Any altercation would be out of our favor. We crouch-walked through the lobby and approached the door leading into the warehouse itself.

I rose to look through the small window on the door. I had to stop myself from flinching in surprise. There were two Jiangshi with their backs to us on the other side of the door. The mossy green hair was a dead giveaway. We needed a way to take them out quickly and quietly.

“We don’t know how many others might be nearby.” Bishop hissed in a nearly inaudible whisper. “We have to draw as little attention as possible when taking them out.”

I looked up at the window and then back at the lobby. “We could lead them in here and take them out from behind. They’re slow enough that by the time we’re on them they won’t have a chance to retaliate.”

Bishop nodded. Then his eyes traveled over to the desk positioned off to the side of the lobby. Sitting on the counter was a silver desk bell. His mouth curved up into a smile.

He pointed towards the bell. “Remind me, what are one of the Jiangshi’s weaknesses?”

“Bells. It’s said that the chime of a handbell can stun them, right?” I said, not entirely sure I’d remembered it correctly. "Would a desk bell count though?"

"Only one way to find out." Bishop said.

I shrugged. It was a better plan than nothing at all. Bishop snuck over to the desk, retrieved the bell, and then returned to his position off to the side from the double doors, opposite of me. I held out my eskrima, holding the metal-tipped end about an inch from the tile floor. Bishop gave me the go ahead and I lightly tapped out a quick shave and a haircut beat. The sound wasn't terribly loud, but the echo was enough to garner a response.

I heard the two Jiangshi converse in Chinese. It probably went something like:

"What was that?"

"I don't know. It came from the lobby."

"Let's go take a look."

"Man we sure are dumb and ugly."

"I know, right?"

The doors creaked open into the lobby, momentarily obscuring us from view. The Jiangshi looked around before taking several steps forward. It was one of the first times I got a good look at them when they weren't trying to kill me. Their bodies seemed to stutter, like watching an internet video with a bad connection. Their limbs moved stiffly and slowly. It took them nearly a minute, an extremely nerve-wracking minute at that, for them to make it to the center of the lobby.

The doors swung close, and I was barely able to see Bishop when he hit the bell. The chime echoed in the empty lobby and it took effect instantly. The Jiangshi shot upright and let out a creaky moan. Bishop rushed forward and I followed suit. He smacked the first Jiangshi on the back of its head with his staff as hard as he could. It made a hollow thunk sound and the Jiangshi began to crumple just as I came up on the second vampire. I swung both of my eskrima down from left to right across the vampire's head and struck true right behind its gnarled ear. It went down just as easily as its partner before it.

I got a closer look at the fallen vampires. They had been wearing cheap suits that didn't fit quite right. They were barefoot, and they had long claws where their toenails should've been. Their faces had locked up into a shocked expression. Their bloodshot eyes contorted into a look of both surprise and anger. Up close, I could see that their skin seemed to be flaking off. Not to mention, they smelled like roadkill.

"Ugh," I did my best to cover my nose with the back of my hand. "Man, they stink."

"An unfortunate side effect of being a walking corpse." Bishop said in a low tone.

"How much do you think these guys spend on cologne?"

Bishop neglected to answer my question. He crouched near the door, opening it slowly. The door didn't creak ominously or anything like that. On my uncle's signal, I slinked through the door and held it open for him.

Once we were both through, we hid under the large metal shelving, pressed up against a wooden crate. It seemed we had lucked out this time around. There were noticeably less vamps patrolling the warehouse. Bishop gave the hand signal to advance forward and then scuttled across the aisle to another crate ahead of our position. I followed suit. It was eerily quiet in the warehouse. The only sound I could make out was that of my own breathing. A fact I quickly became self-conscious of. I did my best to keep my breathing as quiet and as slow as possible. Don't mind me, just the sound of a draft. Definitely not the sound of a teenage wizard mucking about.

A loud banging sound came from somewhere in the warehouse. I froze instantly, trying not to focus on the fact that I hadn't taken a breath in. Had something fallen over? Or had someone just entered the building, letting the door slam because they had no reason to be sneaking around. I looked to Bishop, he had gone completely still. I couldn't quite get a read on him, since his back was facing me. His wizard's staff was held ever so slightly at an upward angle, as if he were preparing to attack.

Footsteps began to echo through the warehouse, but it was hard to tell from which direction. I counted three, maybe four, sets. The first set was a confident stride characterized by a smaller, but faster sound. If I had to guess, a woman wearing heels. The second set was a near match in pace, but accompanied by a sound that made me think they were wearing tennis shoes. The third was a little slower, but not by much, and each step made a much larger and deeper sound. Boots. The last set was the strangest of them all. It didn't even sound like proper footsteps. It was by far the slowest, and this person must've been struggling to keep up with the rest. It sounded more like a large *Thump!* sound, with a couple of seconds in between, before another *Thump!*

Bishop held up four fingers behind him, signaling that he too counted four individuals. I patted myself on the back for that. The footsteps were getting louder, the sound becoming easier to track. They were getting closer. My head was on a swivel as I tried to triangulate the noise. The last thing we needed was to get caught with our pants down. Bishop placed his free hand on the ground, whether he was using wizardly means to find the source or just feeling out the vibrations, I wasn't sure. Maybe a bit of both.

Finally, the footsteps rounded a corner, and I saw through the gaps in the metal shelving that they were in the aisle next to us. I recognized the boots immediately. It was Kat. She was dressed in the usual attire I'd come to associate with her. Combat boots, black skinny jeans with fashionable rips up and down the legs. Coming around the corner last was clearly a Jiangshi, living true to its "hopping vampire" name. Its legs were pressed firmly together, and it took the occasional hop forward to move. As it approached, I got a glimpse at its face, Feng Dài. The leader of the Jiangshi here in Seattle. He was wearing the same outfit I'd seen him wearing when we first met, a simple black gi with gold stitching. He wore no shoes, but he was wearing a pair of black sunglasses, the lenses were completely black as well. I wondered if his eyes were sensitive to light.

At the head of the pack, I saw Oliviana, the head of Seattle's Motus Vampires. She wore a skirt suit, all white of course, with matching white heels that looked like a nightmare to walk in. Her nearly white blonde hair went all the way down to her waist. I was right about my earlier estimations about her height. Even without the super heels, she looked to be nearly seven feet tall. Her business attire hid her supernaturally attractive features quite well, but even still, I felt a primal urge course through every muscle in my body. In nature, animals gain all kinds of adaptations to get a leg up on the competition. Cheetahs ran fast, the grizzly bear got so big that nothing else could mess with it, so on and so forth. Oliviana and her kind exuded an aura that made a man want to throw himself at their feet, screw the consequences. That probably made Oliviana the most dangerous person in the room, as far as I could tell.

The person walking alongside Oliviana was the only one I didn't quite recognize. She looked familiar, but where had I seen her? She was much shorter than Oliviana, closer to Kat's height. Her hair was dark and went just past her shoulders. She wore a form-fitting black dress that stopped at her knees, and she was wearing matching black Converses. She had light brown skin and dark eyes, making me think she might've hailed from Central or South America.

Bishop tapped me lightly, and pointed to the girl when he caught my attention. He was trying to tell me something about the girl. But what? I squinted at her. The realization came to me in a rush.

We had found our Maria Grimaldo.

Chapter 18

There she was. We actually found Maria Grimaldo. Now all we had to do was rescue her from two vampire lords and a dangerous warlock. It couldn't be that hard, could it? No, if memory served, the Jiangshi were far more dangerous than their meager, decrepit appearance let on. And Feng Dài was likely to be far more dangerous than his subordinates. Oliviana no doubt had a deep reservoir of power from her constant feeding at her strip club. I wasn't sure exactly how strong Kat was, but I'd yet to beat her in a straight fight. That left us with very little to work with. If fighting was out of the question, we'd have to find an alternative way of getting out of here alive with Maria in tow.

Bishop held up his hand to me, open palmed in a pacifying gesture. He wanted to wait and see how things played out before we made our move. The four of them continued down the aisle, seemingly oblivious to our presence. I did my best to peek down the aisle to see if I could guess where they were going.

Bingo.

At the end of the aisle was a room jutting out from the far wall. An office, perhaps? Or maybe a storage room where the other two trunks were being kept. If we were lucky, we'd kill two birds with one stone. I tried not to think how Bishop and I would get both the girl and the two trunks out. It had taken both of us to carry just one of the old trunks. Details for later. For now, we had to figure a way out of here that included staying alive.

Oh, can't forget the possible presence of at least one faerie. Vampires, faeries, and warlocks, oh my!

The four of them walked down the aisle and towards the room. Oliviana stepped forward and fussed with the door for a moment. A closer inspection revealed she was entering a code onto a keypad just above the knob. I heard a faint beep come from the door before it opened. They all filed in, Feng Dài hopping in last and closing the door behind him. Bishop shifted around me to sneak back out into the aisle. He waved his hand in a signal for me to follow him. We took it slow and easy. We didn't want to risk moving too quickly and noisily, even the smallest slip up would give us away to the sensitive hearing of the two vampires.

We approached the nearest wall of the room. The room itself was clearly made on the cheap, the walls were made of plywood with a window on each side except the far wall, which was made of concrete, like the rest of the building. I entertained the possibility of blasting through the wall with fire, should the need arise. But closer inspection revealed the wall had been enchanted with defensive spells. I was still a bit new at this, but I could detect the presence of magic laid into the wood. Despite its appearance, the cheaply made room was a fortress. It would take some serious firepower to punch through. Exactly how much firepower, I wasn't sure. And I decided it would be an option of last resort. I imagined that Bishop had come to a similar conclusion.

But if I were an evil vampire alliance, this would be exactly where I would store the mysterious trunks. Luckily for us, the room hadn't been soundproofed, and we could hear the conversation inside.

"-tomorrow night." Oliviana said.

"What of the meddling wizards?" Feng Dài asked.

"Funny you should ask, corpse. Considering they stole the piece of the spear that had been entrusted to your clan." Oliviana chided.

"Spear?" I mouthed to Bishop.

Bishop shook his head and pointed to the room.

Feng Dài retorted in an angry chain of Chinese.

"Don't get all high and mighty with me. You let your guard down, and now the wizards know you're involved somehow." Oliviana said. "It won't be long before they come back looking for you."

"Leave the wizards to me." Kat said. "When the time comes, I can handle them and retrieve the piece of the spear."

Oliviana scoffed. "Please, what's a mageling like you going to do against a wizard like Bishop Leight?"

"I can handle myself just fine, Oliviana. Or do I need to remind you what happened to your little goon squad after you tried to cut me out of this alliance?" Kat sneered. "How long did it take your cleanup crew to scrape the blood off the walls of that dump you call a club?"

Something crashed to the ground, followed by hurried footsteps. That must've pissed Oliviana off. "Watch your tone with me, girl. I am no thrall or underling. If it was you and me alone, you wouldn't get the chance to fling one spell before I had you under my own."

I could hear the smirk in Kat's voice. "Sorry love, but we both know you're not my type."

"No, you're too twitterpated over that scrawny wizard boy of Bishop's." Oliviana said haughtily. "For all we know, you're working for them. Why else would you have gone to see him without any backup?"

Scrawny? That was just rude.

"Because, you airheaded bimbo, if I could scare him off, it would be one less wizard to meddle in our plans." Kat said. "He might not look like much, but Tobias Leight is dangerous in his own right. And stupid enough to challenge us, despite the clear power imbalance."

"Now, now, let's not fight amongst ourselves. Not now, when our plan has almost reached its grand finale." said a feminine voice I didn't recognize. The speaker had a Spanish accent. Wait a second, was that...?

"Maria's right." Feng Dài said. "We cannot afford to be at each other's throats now. The plan is at a critical point. Everyone has a part to play in the ritual tomorrow night."

Something clicked in my brain. Maria wasn't a hostage at all, she never had been. She was in cahoots with Oliviana, Feng Dài, and Kat. They were all working together. Images of the attack on the Blood

Clan's safe house flashed through my mind. There hadn't been any signs of a struggle, besides the initial break-in. Just enough to make it look convincing. Maria must've gotten herself placed in the safehouse to lead them to the trunk, which she had acquired right under Grimaldo's nose. But what was going on tomorrow night? And what was this spear they were talking about?

Bishop's face had scrunched up, as if deep in thought. No doubt, he was putting all the same pieces together. Bishop came back into focus and made eye contact with me. He pointed towards the exit. It was time to leave. We'd learned plenty, now it was time to report back to Don Grimaldo and the Mystic Order with our findings.

We began to waddle out the way we came. Slowly but surely, we didn't want to risk moving too quickly and accidentally make a noise. We were only about a hundred feet from the exit.

Eighty feet.

Sixty feet.

Forty feet.

Then my damn phone rang.

Panic set in as I hurriedly jammed my hand into my pocket to grab the phone and shut it up. I declined the call so quickly I didn't see who was calling. There was a brief moment where nothing seemed to happen. Bishop and I stared at each other in complete silence. Both of us were momentarily frozen by the most ill-timed phone call in history. That's when the door to the meeting room exploded outward, flying down the aisle and wedging itself in the wall near the exit. If we had been down the other aisle, it would've taken our heads off.

"Time to go!" Bishop yelled.

Stealth was clearly out the window, so we took off running. A fireball roared passed me and blew the exit doors off their hinges in an explosion of light and sound. The doorway was ablaze, but Bishop wasn't slowing down. So neither did I, we jumped through, the flames biting at our extremities, but doing no serious harm. We cleared the reception area in two seconds and made our way outside. We didn't stop running. It was probably the fastest I'd run in my life. We would have gotten away, except three of our pursuers were vampires who could move like hell on wheels when they needed to, and the last was a warlock with a serious grudge.

A wall of flames erupted on the street, spanning the space between the vamps' warehouse and the one next door, completely cutting off our only avenue of escape. The wall of flame stretched up at least ten feet or so. It was going to be difficult to get past. We'd have to turn around and make our way around one of the other buildings. Sure it sounded like the best option, but upon turning around, that option very quickly went null and void.

Kat, Maria, Oliviana, and Feng Dài stood blocking our path. And of course, they were accompanied by a dozen or so Jiangshi, and another dozen Motus Vampires. Kat's hands were held up, preparing to throw lightning, judging by the crackling bolts bouncing between her fingertips. Feng Dài's hand was outstretched, and I could just make out dying embers and wisps of smoke. He'd called up the wall of flame. Oliviana drew a sword from a scabbard she wore on her hip. It was a long and thin blade that seemed to gleam despite the low light of the early night. Maria stood empty handed, but something about her stance made me wary. Despite her apparent youth, I had a feeling she was the most dangerous one out of the bunch.

"Wizards, so kind of you to drop in." Maria said. "I was just thinking about how we were going to retrieve our missing trunk, when you decided to grace us with your presence."

Bishop thrust his spear into the ground, a low thrum of power pulsed out. His eyes ablaze with a purple light. "Let us leave. Now. Before this gets ugly for you."

Oliviana let out a rich, throaty laugh. "Oh, Bishop, honey. Your intimidation tactics still leave a lot to be desired. You're not exactly in a position to make threats."

Unfortunately, Oliviana had a bit of a point, and I suspected even Bishop knew that. We weren't in a position to be making threats. Not yet, anyways. I pulled my phone back out, it was a miracle I hadn't dropped it. As quickly as I could, I sent a text. Hopefully my backup plan came through. For now, our only hope was to stall.

"What's this spear you were talking about?" I spoke up. "The one you have stored in these trunks."

Kat smiled. "Wouldn't you like to know, wizard boy?"

Maria shrugged. "The spear is an artifact of immense power. We need it for our plans."

"Your plan's tomorrow night. A ritual, right? What could this ritual possibly be that you'd all agree to work together?" Bishop asked. He looked at Maria specifically. "To betray your father, no less."

"What point is there in telling you, wizard?" Feng Dài spat. "There is nothing you can do to stop us. You're trapped and about to die."

Maria let out a girlish giggle. A sound far too innocent for a vampire who'd trapped them and was about to kill them. "I'll let you in on a few details. As a reward for all your hard work getting this far."

"Maria-!" Oliviana interrupted.

"Quiet!" Maria's voice boomed. Her eyes lit up like spotlights.

Oliviana growled but pulled back, clearly not wanting to challenge Maria further.

I narrowed my eyes. There was something not quite right about Maria. She seemed off, in more ways than one.

Maria composed herself, her eyes returning to normal. "Tomorrow night, we'll be changing the status quo. In times long ago, vampires of all breeds ruled this planet. They were your kings, your gods. Villages would offer their riches and their children to appease them. No one dared venture into the night, for that was their domain. But as time went on, you worms actually managed to learn a thing or two. You learned their weaknesses, how to hurt them. Vampires were soon hunted to near extinction, they had to go into hiding. Nowadays, a bold vampire is a dead vampire. They've all resorted to more underhanded tactics to survive. Selling drugs, running brothels, and hiding in the night hoping an unsuspecting victim comes wandering by. It took generations to rebuild their numbers. Now with the clans strengthened once more, it's time the tides shifted once more. Vampires will return to their rightful place as rulers of humankind. You all will return to your proper place, being livestock."

"That's a real great speech and all, I can tell you practiced it in the mirror." I said, trying to sound confident. "But how exactly do these plans of yours help you guys do all that?"

Maria smirked. "With the help of this artifact, a ritual will be performed. Something the vampire clans have theorized and pondered over for generations, but could never figure out how to pull off. A ritual that will make vampires into the gods they always were, by finally stripping them of their trivial weaknesses. No longer will the Jiangshi be compelled to count pocket change or be killed with a wooden stake. The Motus Vampires will no longer burn and cower before symbols of God. The Sanguine will become immune to the effects of sunlight and fire. They will all be invincible. And humanity will have no choice to submit or die."

Holy shit. If that happened, it would change the very nature of the world itself. Humanity would become slaves with about as much agency as farm cattle. It would be the collapse of civilization as we knew it.

"Your plan is insane, Maria." Bishop said, raising his voice. "The Mystic Order would never allow a world ruled by vampires to exist. It'd be total war!"

"A war the Mystic Order would have no chance of winning." Feng Dài countered. "Your numbers are few."

"Yes, but that will make the Mystic Order desperate. They'll call in favors from the other supernatural nations. Then the vampires will all call in their own allies." Bishop explained. "Before you know it, the Mystic Order will approve the use of forbidden magic. They will call on the power of gods and monsters of their own. A conflict of that scale will destroy the world! It's madness!"

"Madness is a word used by the weak and clueless to describe the strong and the visionaries. I guess you'll never know how it turns out though. You won't live long enough to see it." Maria cocked her head forward. "Kill the boy. Keep Bishop Leight alive, though. I think he's the perfect candidate for the final part of our plans."

Bishop's eyes widened, his head whipping around to me. I felt a surge of power bubble up from him. He stepped in between me and the vampires. Thrusting his free hand towards me, he shouted a word and a cyclone of wind exploded towards me.

"Wait-!" I yelped.

But I was too late. The wind swept me up and hurled me through the wall of fire, dispersing the flames just enough to let me through with minimal burns. I flew through the air about fifty feet before I hit the ground and rolled another ten feet or so. I groaned as I clumsily got to my feet. I stepped forward to run back to Bishop to help him, but my cage had thoroughly been rattled. I didn't even finish the step before the world started spinning and I fell on my face. I tried to rise, but my sense of balance and direction was completely out of whack. All I could do was look towards the wall of flame. In between the flames I could make out Bishop as he fought against the vampire horde. He seemed to focus on a million things at once as he fought. Deflecting leaping vampires and balls of fire while retaliating with his own violent displays of fire and lightning.

My heart stopped when I saw one vampire get through his defenses, slashing at the back of his leg, forcing him to a knee. He took out another two vampires before his defenses failed and they were on him. I couldn't see him under the dog pile of vampires.

"No!" I choked out, struggling to rise to my feet.

Six vampires flanked by Kat jumped over the wall of flame. No doubt they had spotted me. Shit. Again, I struggled to get to my feet, but my body kept failing me. One of my limbs would simply give out or lose balance and I'd be right back on my face.

I heard a loud crash from somewhere behind me. My vision was still spinning and starting to fade. But I could see a large canine shape approach from behind me. Someone was riding on its back.

I heard a bellowing roar right as my vision faded to black.

Chapter 19

I awoke with a start, sitting upright from where I slept. Only to be met with a stabbing pain in my shoulder that immediately made me recoil. I groaned, fighting through the pain as I tried to stand up.

“Oh no you don’t!” Claire’s voice came from somewhere nearby.

I was still pretty woozy, so I didn’t see her coming. But she forced me to lay back down on the couch as gently as she could. After a moment to gather myself, I realized we were back at my apartment. I was laid up on the couch and it dawned on me that I was shirtless. My shoulder had been bandaged. I counted another six or so bruises and scrapes, no doubt courtesy of being flung through the air by my uncle right before he...

Oh. Right.

"How'd you-?" I began to ask.

"Find you?" Claire finished the sentence. "Well you sent me a text that said 'Zend Scoot', which I assumed meant 'Send Scout.'"

"Oh, yeah. Sorry, I was kinda panicking in the moment."

"Anyways, I told Scout we needed to find you. He immediately hulked out and well, I hopped on and came along for the ride." Claire explained. "Good thing I did too, because it was all I could do to stop him from trying to fight that entire goon squad."

Scout was a hellhound, giving him all kinds of supernatural abilities. It's how he got there so fast. He's incredibly strong as well, but I suspected even he would've been outmatched against that mob of vamps. As much as it worried me that Claire had been so close to the danger, I was thankful that she'd come along, or I might've lost my dog.

"What the heck happened back there, anyways?" Claire asked.

So I brought her up to speed on everything Bishop and I had been dealing with. The vampiric alliance, the trunks that contained pieces of some sort of spear, and Maria's plan to start a new world order.

Claire shuddered. "You know, I didn't think this supernatural stuff could get any scarier, but this is something else."

"Trust me, I know how you feel." I agreed.

"So what are you going to do now?" Claire asked.

I paused to think for a moment. What was I going to do? Bishop had been captured and I didn't even know why. Why did they go out of their way to keep him alive? Furthermore, I had no idea where to even start looking for him. I seriously doubted they'd ever return to that warehouse again, not after we'd broken in twice.

"I'm not sure quite yet. Give me some time to think on it. I'll keep you in the loop."

Claire frowned, but nodded. "Okay, let me know when you plan to do something stupid."

Claire rose from where she sat and bent over to kiss me on the forehead. I felt myself heat up instantly but did my best to keep me cool. She smiled knowingly and headed for the door.

"Hey uh, where is Scout, anyway?" I asked her.

"I think he went upstairs." Claire said. "I'll see you later."

"Okay, see ya." I said.

Claire walked out the door and I sat up once more, wincing as my shoulder flared up.

I had a lot to think about. There was a lot riding on me not to screw everything up. My first instinct was to just start blasting the vampire bases left and right until I got answers. But that wouldn't do. For once, I had to keep my emotions in check and think about this critically. I couldn't do this alone, even with Scout's help.

Then I remembered something. Something obvious, stupidly so. I found my phone sitting on the coffee table and started dialing a number. I held the phone to my ear as it began to ring.

One ring.

Two rings.

"Come on, pick up." I muttered.

After the third ring, a tired voice answered, "Uh, hello."

"Jacob, it's Tobias." I said. Then I realized what time it must've been. "Oh crap, sorry did I wake you?"

Jacob yawned. "No, sorry. Just been a little busy and wore myself out."

Jacob Lewis had been my best friend for as long as I could remember. We'd grown up together and got into all sorts of shenanigans and trouble when we were kids. It wasn't until last year that I learned what he really was. Jacob was a golem, a magical construct that had been tasked with protecting me. I was the subject of a prophecy that involved the devil himself possessing my body and taking over the universe. Together, we had managed to stop that from happening. Jacob had been out of town for a couple months on some mundane mission for the Mystic Order. His words, not mine.

"Sorry, it's been a long couple of days and my head's a bit scrambled." I said. "I forgot to check the time before calling."

Jacob let out a yawn, but when he spoke, I recognized that he'd gathered his focus. "Really, it's no big deal. What's up?"

I explained the events of the last few days for the second time in the last fifteen minutes, right up until the point when I called him. "And now, here we are."

Jacob blew a breath out. "Vampires, man. I leave for two months and you find a way to get this deep into trouble."

"Yeah, which is why I could use you back here." I said.

"While I appreciate your confidence in me," He began. "why don't you just ask the Mystic Order for help?"

"I plan to." I clarified. "But I don't really know anyone from the Order that well. If I'm going into this, I want to make sure I have someone with my best interests at heart by my side."

"Just say you don't trust the Order."

I shook my head. "I'm not saying I trust them or don't, but I definitely trust you."

"Fair enough." Jacob said. "Okay, my work out here has pretty much reached its end, anyways. I just have to handle something before I go. I can be back in Seattle by the morning."

I breathed a sigh of relief. "Thanks. It means a lot. I'll see you in the morning."

"Get some rest." Jacob said, stifling a yawn. Then he hung up.

Get some rest. Yeah, right. My uncle was captured. The vampires had possession of two-thirds of a relic that would make them all nearly invincible. And I had no idea where this ritual of theirs was going to go down, or what it entailed.

I decided that sitting here and feeling sorry for myself would get me nowhere, and decided to head upstairs to take a shower. I felt awful and a shower would probably do me some good. I rose from the couch and headed for the stairs. Climbing the flight of stairs was a trial of its own. Everything hurt. I'd been beaten and tossed around a lot in the last couple of days, and as a result, my entire body ached with a wary pain that no young adult should have to go through.

I stopped at Bishop's room. On the bed, Scout lay on my uncle's bed, in his mundane doggy form. He was curled up near the pillow that Bishop slept on every night. I frowned. The mutt was loyal to a fault. I wasn't sure exactly how smart Scout was, but I could tell he missed my uncle and was worried about him deeply.

"Don't worry boy, we're going to get him back." I assured the hellhound.

Scout thumped his tail on the bed three times. I knew it was an answer of some sort, but I couldn't be sure as to what exactly the dog was thinking.

I smiled, trying to reassure him. But I don't think I even convinced myself.

I continued down the short hallway and went into my bathroom. I turned on the shower and began to undress the rest of the way. My legs were tender. Every effort to get out of my pants was met with twinges of pain, but I ignored them. I'd have time to moan and groan about the pain when this was over.

Showering while avoiding getting the bandages on my shoulder wet was a tricky thing, but for the most part I managed. The shower felt like a ritual, in a way. Scrubbing all the dirt, grime, and dried blood off of me was therapeutic. In the process, I felt my mind clearing. The worry and shame of my recent failure seemed to recede to the back of my mind. Still present, but not as overbearing as it had once been. It was replaced by a steady resolve to see this through. To prove myself.

I stayed in the shower for over half an hour, just enjoying the hot water as it washed away my pains and worries. As much as I wanted to stay here forever and get lost in the comforting heat of the water, I knew eventually I had to get out and get back to the task ahead of me. I shut off the water, instantly being hit by the comparatively frigid air of the apartment.

My teeth chattered as I fumbled for my towel. I scrubbed my body with the towel and wrapped it around my waist. I stepped out of the shower and approached the sink. The mirror had fogged over from the steam. Seriously, you would think they would've invented steam-proof mirrors by now. Wait, had they? Something to Google later, I supposed. I took a small hand towel resting near the sink and put it up to the mirror. I carved a path through the steam, allowing myself a view in the mirror.

The view I got nearly tumbling to the floor as I jumped back in shock. If it hadn't been for the door behind me, I would've surely fallen to the ground.

Reflected in the mirror's image was not me, or even my bathroom. It was a dark room of some kind. I wasn't able to make out any details through the steam that remained. Standing where my reflection should be...was Kat.

"Hello, love." Kat purred.

I thrust my hand out at the mirror in a way that I hoped look threatening. "Where's my uncle?" I growled.

Kat looked amused. "Oh relax, wizard boy. You're not scaring anyone while you've got a towel wrapped around your waist. I only wish to talk."

"Talk? Okay, let's talk about you releasing my uncle!" I snapped back.

"Not gonna happen if you don't work with me." Kat tossed her hands up in a shrug. "I have something you want. And you have something I want."

"The trunk." I said.

"Well, more so, what's in the trunk. But yes." Kat nodded. "The last piece of the spear. If you want your uncle back, you'll bring it to me tomorrow night."

"The Mystic Order has the trunk." I said. "Do you really think they're just going to give it up now? To me, of all people."

Kat shrugged again. "I dunno, but you better figure it out. Otherwise, your uncle is vampire food. Trust me, Oliviana has been wanting revenge on him for betraying her all those years ago. It's all we can do to keep her from ravishing him."

I held back a tinge of rage. "Assuming I can get this spear piece, where am I supposed to bring it?"

"The Needle." Kat said simply. "That's where the world will change forever, my love."

"Stop calling me that." I snapped. "Why there?"

"The ritual in question is best performed as close to the sky as possible. It will allow us to tap into the coming storm in order to magnify the magical energies at work." Kat explained.

"I don't get it, Kat. Why help the vampires?" I said. "You're mortal, just like me and every other human on the planet. How do you stand to benefit from creating super vampires hell bent on taking over the world?"

"I don't." She said, as if it was obvious. "But after the ritual is done, Maria has promised me the spear. After you ruined my attempt to bring Azazel into this world with the Holy Grail, it was magically spent. It wouldn't hold up through another attempt to bring my lord back from Hell. I needed another artifact. I was looking for information on the spear when Maria and I crossed paths. We formed a partnership. If I help her, I get the spear after she's done."

"And you get another chance to bring the devil back." I concluded. "Surely, you have to know she's going to betray you in the end. This won't end well for you."

For a split second, her image changed. It was so quick, I thought I was seeing things. For a brief moment, she was replaced by my reflection. Or so I thought. I caught a glance of the wicked smile adorned on my face. And I realized it wasn't me at all. It was Azazel.

"I think you'll find that I'm far more capable than the last time we met. After you ruined my plans. It changed me." Kat said. Her voice had a strange quality to it. For every word she spoke, I heard mine as well, superimposed under hers.

"What happened to you that day, Kat?" I asked her. Though I had a sneaking suspicion I already knew.

When the dust had settled after my encounter with Azazel last year, Kat had disappeared. As well any evidence that Azazel had been there at all. I'd overcome his mind control and forced him out. I had assumed he had gone back to Hell or wherever he'd been trapped, but maybe that wasn't the case at all.

"I can tell by the look on your face that you're starting to figure it out. I always knew you were smarter than you looked." Kat said, a false sense of praise to her words. "You forced Azazel out of your mind. In the chaos of the moment, in the magic rich air, Azazel's essence had to go somewhere, and the door to Hell was closed behind him." She pointed to her temple. "So he's been trapped in here, for a year. Do you have any idea what it's like having a damn fallen angel trapped in your head for a YEAR?" Her voice had risen to a shout.

At a point in time, I'd really liked Kat. She seemed to sympathize with me and my frustrations towards the Mystic Order when I first started out. Even now, the Mystic Order's cryptic and haughty way of handling things drove me crazy. But she had been there to tell me I wasn't unreasonable for feeling that way. So as much as I didn't want to sympathize with her situation, I understood. I really did. Azazel had possessed me for a much shorter time, not even ten minutes, but it had been the worst experience of my life. Not because I was tortured and chained up in my own mind or anything like that, but because it had felt nothing close to the sort. When Azazel had taken over my mind, I hadn't even realized it had happened at first. I'd still felt lucid, even though he had been the one in the driver's seat. His thoughts had been indistinguishable from my own. If my friends hadn't been there and in harm's way, I'm not sure I would've been able to snap out of it.

So yeah, I got it.

"Kat, let me help you." I pleaded. "The Mystic Order can help you. We can get that demon out of your head and back behind bars where he belongs. But you have to let me help you. I know what it's like, better than anyone. Please, Kat."

Kat paused. I saw in her eyes that a part of her was genuinely considering it. An almost imperceptible flash of light lit her eyes up for a moment. To anyone else, it would've been a trick of the light. But I knew better. Azazel was pulling the strings.

"No, you still don't get it." Kat spit, her words coated in pain and frustration. "Those old bastards don't care about the little guys, like you and me. You don't know them like I do. They won't help me, they'll lock me away and leave me to suffer."

"Damn it, Kat. That's not true!" I retorted. "Please Kat, don't do this."

She ignored me. "The Space Needle. Tomorrow at midnight. Bring the spear or else the vamps declare open season on Seattle. And if I see a single wizard, I'll kill your uncle myself."

Then she was gone. The mirror only showed my reflection now. The look of horror and sadness on my face I saw that day would remain etched into my brain forever.

Well, shit.

Chapter 20

Frustration and rage overwhelmed me. I punched the mirror as hard as I could. With my emotions running wild, I lost control of my magic. Kinetic energy exploded from my fist and completely shattered the mirror, sending shards flying in every direction. Whether I'd redirected the shards with the kinetic magic or it was just dumb luck, I managed to come out of the moment with only a few new scratches. What Kat was proposing was crazy. Either I handed over the last thing the vampires needed to become demigods, or the entirety of Seattle was going to become one giant buffet for supernatural predators.

I followed the trail of logic. If vampires were allowed to run loose, what would stop other supernatural predators from coming out of the woodwork and following suit? In my lessons on magic and maintaining balance in Seattle's supernatural ecosystem, Bishop had told me there were far more supernatural beings inhabiting human cities than the Mystic Order could ever hope to account for. Goblins, ogres, ghosts, demons, faeries, vampires, and even more monstrosities that weren't nearly as cute and cuddly. If the vampires got the green light to run rampant through the city, it wouldn't be long before every other monstrosity would come out of the woodwork and do the same.

It would be chaos.

So I had to figure out how I was going to keep the final spear piece from the vampires while also bringing it right to them. I had to figure out how I was going to stop two vampire lords, a vampire lord's daughter, and a warlock from killing my uncle and pulling off a ritual that would send the balance of the supernatural world into total havoc. All without having any wizards along as backup. Which is why I'd called Jacob in, of course. But one apprentice wizard and his golem friend weren't going to be enough against a vampiric alliance on this scale. Sure, I had Scout too, but I was debating putting him back on Claire guard duty. If things got bad, she would be in danger. I had no idea how I was going to pull this off.

I shuffled out of the bathroom, carefully stepping over the mess of broken glass on the bathroom floor. I'd have to remember to clean that up before going back in there. The last thing I needed at this point was to spike my foot on a bunch of glass shards. But the shower had soothed my body a bit and I felt fatigue setting back in. My head hurt and I just wanted to lie down. I traded my towel in for a clean pair of underwear and flopped gracelessly onto my bed. Sleep came almost instantly.

I had nightmares of sparkling vampires and mushroom fairies chasing me through the hallways of my school. And when I next awoke, the sun was shining brightly through my curtains. Upon waking, I felt as though something was wrong. You know how you can just tell that your home is occupied, and you usually have a pretty good guess as to exactly who should be there? Well, as far as I was aware, it should only have been Scout and I. It was quiet, but the house felt full.

I reached for one of my eskrima, which I usually kept on my nightstand. But they weren't there. I slapped myself on the forehead. I'd left them downstairs when Claire and Scout had brought me home. I hated to go into a confrontation unarmed, but it seemed as though I'd be doing exactly that. I rose up out of bed as quietly as I could and exited my room into the hallway. As I passed the bathroom and approached the stairs, I noticed that all the broken glass had been cleaned up. The mirror was still shattered, so I definitely had not dreamt up my encounter with Kat last night.

Who would've cleaned it all up? I knelt at the top of the stairs. I couldn't see anyone in the living room, but I definitely heard movement. I heard pots and pans clanging together as someone opened and closed a cabinet. Were we being robbed? Who robs someone's kitchen?

I could see my eskrima on the edge of the table near the couch I'd woken up on yesterday, along with my charms bracelet. If I could get to them without being spotted, I'd have a fair chance against whoever had invaded my apartment. Wait a second, where was Scout? I leaned back to peek my head into my uncle's room. The dog was no longer there. And he hadn't been in my room either. So he had to be downstairs. But there didn't seem to be any signs of a hellhound rampage against home invaders. Throwing caution to the wind, I hopped down the stairs two at a time, turning on a dime to face the kitchen once I'd reached the bottom.

At the dining table, sat Claire. She was reading a book. I'm not sure what she was reading, as the cover was facing away from me. Scout was laying at her feet, curled up. When he saw me, he lifted his head and thumped his tail happily against the floor. My gaze wandered to the kitchen, where I saw Jacob. He was in the process of making pancakes.

"Hey man, hope you're hungry!" Jacob said gleefully.

Jacob Lewis had been my best friend ever since I came to Seattle. He was a big guy, especially for his supposed age of seventeen. Jacob told me that golems didn't age the same as humans, so I wasn't quite sure how old he actually was. He was built like a large oak tree. A wide chest and thick arms, but not an ounce of excess fat. His body was sculpted, quite literally, to be dense and strong. Jacob loaded up the last of the pancakes onto the comically large stack and brought the plate over to the table. He sat down and loaded two flapjacks onto his plate.

"You going to get dressed before joining us?" Jacob asked. "Or are you comfortable in your undies?"

I glanced down. I'd momentarily forgotten that I hadn't gotten dressed before investigating the disturbance downstairs. I felt my face grow hot as I glanced from my boxers to Jacob, then to Claire, who was keeping her eyes firmly on the book she was reading. Her cheeks had grown a shade or two redder.

"I'll uh, be right back." I stammered before rushing back up the stairs.

Once I got dressed, I came back down dressed in jeans and a black t-shirt featuring the boxart from the original Castlevania. I figured the shirt was appropriate, given the foes we'd be facing soon.

I sat down next to Jacob and across from Claire, eagerly loading up my own plate with three pancakes. I drenched them in syrup, and began devouring them without a moment's hesitation. I hadn't noticed how hungry I was, but given all the craziness I'd been dealing with the last couple of days, I supposed it made sense.

"Hungry, mister?" Claire asked, amused. Not looking up from her book once.

"You could say that." I tried to say, but it came out muffled through the doughy deliciousness. I narrowed my eyes at her book, finally getting a good look at it.

It read *A Guide to Vampires: Nosferatu, Lamia, Strigoi, and more!* I recognized it from one of my trips to Light Haven's library.

I swallowed a large mouthful of pancakes. "Hey, where'd you get that?"

"I brought it over." Jacob explained.

"But why?" I asked.

"Because, you're gonna need all the help you can get." Claire said. "I'm not going to be the damsel in distress or cheerleader from the sidelines this time around."

"Nuh uh, no way. It's too dangerous!" I protested. "There's no way I'm letting you throw yourself in the middle of a conflict with bloodthirsty vampires!"

Claire set the book down, crossing her arms. She glared at me something ferocious. "I don't remember asking for, or hell, even needing your permission."

I looked to Jacob, hoping he'd back me up. He shrugged. "Sorry man, she's made her mind up. How I see it, we can either help her be ready, or reap the consequences when she jumps in woefully unprepared."

"You've got to be kidding me." I let out an exasperated sigh as I rested my head in my hands.

"You don't have to worry about me." Claire said. "I've been studying vampires since Jacob got here a few hours ago. He told me the kinds we would have to worry about, and I've been preparing." She rose from her seat and started walking towards the garage.

"Preparing?" I rose to follow her.

Upon entering the garage, I realized exactly what she meant. Lined up in a row were a dozen crudely carved wooden stakes. I picked one up to examine it. It wasn't anything fancy, but nothing from my limited knowledge told me it needed to be.

"They aren't made from peach trees, but Jacob said it didn't matter too much." Claire said.

Piled up next to the stakes were a pile of leather pouches. I picked one up and it jingled as the contents shifted. Each pouch was filled with coins. If you were to loosen up the drawstring, it would act like a distraction grenade. The Jiangshi wouldn't be able to resist.

"You really have been busy." I said, genuinely impressed.

"And as for the Motus Vamps, that's where I came through." Jacob's voice came from the doorway. He approached the opposite side of the table. On the other side of the table were two paintball guns, each with a couple extra tanks off to the side. As opposed to paintballs, the clear tanks were filled with orbs containing what looked like water.

"Let me guess, holy water?" I asked, examining one of the tanks.

"Correctamundo." Jacob smiled with pride. "These should do well to keep the Moties off of Claire, giving me and Scout time to take them out."

"This is impressive." I said. "We might actually stand a chance at beating these guys."

"I didn't worry too much about preparing for Sanguine Vamps, because from what you've told me, the only one we have to worry about is Maria herself." Jacob said.

"Yeah," I nodded. I remember that I had a couple of things to take care of before the meeting with Kat and her vampiric friends. "Look, I have to go to Light Haven before this all goes down."

"Oh, maybe I should come with you." Jacob suggested. "I doubt the higher-ups are going to be too thrilled about giving you the spear piece. You'll want some backup."

I raised an eyebrow. "You think we're gonna have to fight for it?"

"No, but you're known to be a bit hotheaded. And I think you could use a cooler head to help convince them to go along with your plan." Jacob clarified.

"That's...a fair point." I conceded.

"You're damn right it is." Jacob smiled broadly.

I turned to Claire. "In the meantime, you and Scout stay here and sit tight. Regular mortals aren't allowed in Light Haven, anyways."

Claire puffed up her cheeks. "Fine, but don't even think about cutting me out of the action."

"Wouldn't dream of it. At this point, I doubt I could stop you if I tried." I smiled.

Honestly, I was getting really sick and tired of the trek to and from the Gum Wall. It was a tedious process going there and back constantly. I really needed to get a car or something. I'd armed myself with all my magical gear. My sheepskin jacket, my charms bracelet, and my eskrima amounted to a miniature magical arsenal that mortals wouldn't bat an eye at. But any gung-ho vampire assassins would think twice upon seeing the magical ensemble.

Jacob didn't need to carry anything on his person to look like a threat. To mortals, he was a huge guy with an expression that said he was looking for a fight, and supernatural predators would be able to sense his true nature. Golems were incredibly strong defenders of the magically attuned. The Mystic Order used them to seek out and protect fledgling wizards. They were also known to do the same for those who'd already dabbled with and been corrupted by dark magic; warlocks. But instead of protecting them, they were told to apprehend or eliminate them, whichever came first.

We arrived at the Gum Wall just as the storm front rolled in once more. It had been a muggy few days with some light rain. But something in the air told me this next storm was going to be a doozy. This was the storm that Maria planned to use for their ritual. I could hear the thunder beginning to rumble just as I opened the way into Light Haven. Jacob and I stepped through the glowing passageway. The sudden shift in atmosphere and climate always caught me slightly off guard. It induced something similar to vertigo, momentarily disorienting me as my body got used to the sudden change in light and temperature.

Wizards bustled about the Portal Nexus without paying us any mind. The crowd was an unusual one. You saw those whose ensemble reminded you of a typical wizard from fairy tales and Lord of the Rings, old men wearing long, billowing cloaks. Then there were people like my uncle and I, just unassuming, normal-looking people. They carried various magical implements and stuck their noses in large, worn books. I also saw a few elves amongst the crowd, though they had a mastery over a tricky type of magic that made them extremely hard to notice. Orbs of light flew through the air, flitting through the crowds in an erratic manner. I recognized them as pixies. The room was full of doors opening and closing, letting in brief flashes of light as the passerby came and went from all over the world. It took me a second to realize that this is probably how Jacob got to Seattle so fast, and still had time to help Claire with preparing our anti-vampire weaponry.

"Come on, it's this way." I ushered him out the main exit and into the halls of Light Haven. "Uh, I think." I added under my breath.

Jacob followed after me. Light Haven was a confusing place to get around. It was an ever evolving maze that seemed to be actively attempting to thwart you along the way. Over the last year, I'd grown accustomed to its mannerisms and so long as I focused on where I wanted to go, the halls usually cooperated.

"So you just willingly handed over an unknown artifact to the Mystic Order?" Jacob asked, his tone one of weary surprise.

"To be honest, it was Bishop's idea." I said. "And we couldn't risk the vamps tracking it back to our apartment and causing all kinds of havoc. Not just for us, but our neighbors too."

Jacob nodded approvingly. "I'm just surprised is all."

He was referring to my general distrust in the Mystic Order. Don't get me wrong, I didn't think they were some nefarious, evil organization or anything like that. However, history dictates that you can only allow a governing body so much trust. I'd paid attention in history class, and I saw what happened when a population placed too much trust in their government. But Bishop had made the right call in entrusting the trunk with Fachnan. Fachnan was the only person we knew who had a chance at opening up the trunk. So no matter how you sliced it, it was the only call we could've made. I just hoped that it paid off.

Fachnan had been busy. He'd taken over the training room for his work with the trunk. There were fresh scorch marks on the walls and several rows of bleachers had been crushed. The trunk sat in the middle of a complex circle that was composed of several layers with strange arcane symbols arranged between the several smaller circles that made up the larger one. My eyebrows raised when I realized that the trunk was sitting open. Its padlock had been unlocked, and was sitting near the trunk on the ground. I noticed the ring of the padlock was red hot, as if someone had taken a blowtorch to it.

Fachnan was sitting at a desk he'd set up nearby, with a strange pair of spectacles on. They had several magnifying glass attachments and he was studying something on the table intently. As we approached, I tried to get a look at what he was examining, but the desk was cluttered with various books and strange objects that I assumed were tools he'd used to examine and eventually open the trunk.

"Uh, hey Fachnan. Whatcha got there?" I asked as we approached.

Fachnan lifted his head to look at us. His face was covered in soot and ash. His orange hair was very disheveled, a stark contrast to its usual neat cut that he meticulously kept it in. “Oh hello, Leight.” His magnified gaze shifted to Jacob. “Oh, and Jacob. You’ve returned from your assignment.”

“Yeah, I wrapped it up just in time to find a mess back home.” Jacob said. “Tobias has brought me up to speed, but I see you’ve managed to open the trunk.”

“What’d you find?” I repeated.

“Ah, right.” Fachnan muttered. He took off the strange spectacles and held up what he had been examining.

It was a stick. A perfectly straight length of wood, maybe about two feet long or so. The ends were fractured, as if someone had snapped off the ends. The elusive spear piece we’d been hearing so much about.

“That’s what all the fuss is about, a stick?” I asked in genuine disbelief.

Fachnan sighed, clearly not amused by my lack of reverence for the mysterious stick. “This isn’t just a stick, Leight.”

“Okay, then what is it?” I asked skeptically.

Fachnan frowned. “Well, to be honest, I’m not exactly sure what it is.” He admitted.

I resisted the urge to facepalm. "Can you be a bit less vague? That stick has gotten us in a lot of trouble the last few days."

"Well, as you can tell, it's only a piece of a greater whole. And it's exuding a massive amount of power, even fractured. There are some runes engraved into the body, but I can't quite make them out. They could be Greek, or Celtic perhaps."

"Mind if I take a look?" Jacob asked, holding his hand out for the stick.

Fachnan eyed Jacob, but gave him the stick anyways. Jacob took the stick in both hands, holding it close to his face to examine it. From where I was standing, I couldn't see any runes or sigils on it. It just looked like a plain, old stick. But after a moment, Jacob's eyes let off a faint blue light. The stick seemed to respond, and small symbols began to come to the surface, glowing with the same blue light.

Jacob shook his head, his eyes returning to normal. The symbols on the stick seemed to disappear as well. "They're not Greek or Celtic. If I'm seeing this right, these symbols, at least some of them, are Enochian."

"What's Enochian?" I asked.

"Enochian, of course." Fachnan said, as if he had known it all along. "The language of the Angels."

"Angels? Like, THE Angels?" I asked, pointing up towards the ceiling.

"Yes, like from Judeo-Christian mythology." Jacob confirmed. "But there were other symbols I couldn't quite read or bring to the surface."

A lightbulb seemed to go off in Fachnan's head. "Hmm, give me a moment. I'll be right back."

Fachnan removed his magnifying spectacles and left the room. A few moments later, he had returned, and with someone I had not been expecting to see again so soon. Andhrímnir shuffled through the door with a bit of difficulty, due to his larger-than-life size. The chef of the Norse gods ambled his way to meet us, following Fachnan back over to the table.

"Andhrímnir, good to see you." Jacob nodded politely. He pronounced the god's name perfectly, without so much as a stutter. Jerk.

"A pleasure to see you as well, young golem." Andhrímnir said, with a hearty laugh of greeting.

"Uh, what's your guys' personal chef doing here?" I asked. "Uh, not that I'm not happy to see you, Andy."

Andy smiled at me, amused by my bluntness and honesty.

"I've asked Andhrímnir here to take a look at the artifact. If my theory is correct, his examination may provide us with answers as to what the true nature of this object is." Fachnan explained. "Andhrímnir, if you please." He gestured to the stick that Jacob was still holding.

Andy held out his large hand politely, and Jacob handed it over. My golem friend looked absolutely tiny by comparison, which I hadn't thought possible.

The stick responded immediately to Andy's touch. Runes and sigils lit up with a golden light, although different from when Jacob touched it.

"Interesting, very interesting." He said. "Golem, would you mind?"

Andy offered him one end of the stick. Jacob looked from Fachnan to me to the stick, and then reached his hand out. Upon touching it, the sigils from before lit up as well, until the stick was casting motes of gold and blue light. Andy nodded in comprehension, and Jacob took his hand away.

"So what do we have here, Andhrímnir?" Fachnan asked.

"Something I believed to be lost to this realm long ago." Andy nodded, a hint of excitement threatening to overwhelm him. "It goes by many names, and has been passed to many hands over the generations. But long ago, I knew it as Gungnir."

“Gesundheit.” I said, but Jacob and Fachnan seemed to be too stunned to appreciate my quip.

“Are you sure?” Fachnan asked.

“Certainly. I’d recognize it anywhere.” Andy said.

“Okay, I’ll bite. What’s a Gungnir?” I asked.

“In my time, Gungnir was the spear wielded by Odin, the Allfather.” Andy explained. “He wielded it in battle with a precision that no other god could replicate. He once used it to impale himself against Yggdrasil to gain knowledge of magic.”

“Woah.” I said. No wonder the vamps were so desperate to get this spear. A magical artifact of that magnitude was nothing to scoff at, and would act as the perfect channel to funnel the magic required for their ritual.

“That doesn’t explain the Enochian though.” Jacob said.

Andy nodded gravely, giving it some thought. “Well, like I said, the spear has been passed down over the ages as the Norse gods faded into obscurity.” Andy seemed to study the piece of the spear closely for a second. “This spear has come into contact with the blood of more than one god, and not just those of the Norse.”

I raised an eyebrow. “What are you saying?”

"I'm sure you are familiar with the story of the Crucifixion, yes?" Andy asked.

We all nodded, inviting him to continue.

"Well I can't be sure, but judging from its magical aura, and the presence of Enochian writing alongside the Norse runes, I believe that Gungnir also served as the Lance of Longinus." Andy explained.

No one said anything for a moment. "Okay, I give up. Who's Longinus?" I asked.

Jacob had a bitter look on his face. "If legend is to be believed, Longinus was the one who pierced the side of Christ after he was crucified. Which would make Gungnir..."

"The Spear of Destiny, or the Holy Lance." Fachnan said.

Jacob nodded in grim agreement.

"I believe so." Andy said. "Gungnir, the Spear of Destiny, a worthy title to be sure."

"So just how dangerous is this thing?" I asked.

"The Spear of Destiny, in the right hands, can remake the world in the wielder's image." Fachnan explained. "If it is truly Gungnir as well, its wielder would be unstoppable. If someone like Azazel were to get their hands on it, it would truly be the end of the world as we know it."

That's when it all clicked for me. The one thing I couldn't understand about all this. Why Kat was involving herself with the vampires' plans. Once the ritual was complete, there was nothing stopping her from wielding the spear herself. She could use it to finish what she and Azazel had started last year. Azazel would be able to take my body over once more, and with the spear in hand, he'd be unstoppable. There wasn't a power in the world that could oppose him. It wouldn't matter if the vampires had shed their weaknesses, so long as it all ended with the spear in Kat's hands.

I looked at Fachnan. "You're going to want to sit down for this."

I began explaining everything I'd learned, carefully omitting my revelation of Azazel's involvement, as indirect as it may be. I focused on the details I'd learned about the vampire's plans to become demigods in their own right. Then I mentioned Kat's ultimatum regarding the last piece of the spear and Bishop's capture.

"Absolutely not." Fachnan said at once.

"Fachnan, you have to listen to me." I pleaded. "Whether or not they get the remaining piece of the spear, the vampires are going to go on the offensive. The vampires will cut loose on Seattle, killing millions."

"One city to save the world? It's a grave cost, but one we may have to pay." Fachnan said simply. As if millions of lives just didn't matter.

"And you really think they'll stop at Seattle. Sure, it starts with Seattle. But what will stop them from expanding? Attacking other cities. First the state, then the country, then the world." I growled.

Fachnan seemed to consider this for a moment. "And you have a plan? One that meets her demands?"

"Just enough to get me close to the ritual." I said. "I wreck the ritual, save Bishop, and get out of there with the rest of the spear."

"And you think they're just going to let you make off with the Spear of bloody Destiny?" Fachnan spat in retort.

"No, but like I said, I have a plan." I said.

"And this plan would be?" Fachnan trailed off, waiting for an explanation.

"Trust me, you're not going to like it. But if everything I've learned is correct, it will work." I promised.

Jacob raised an eyebrow and looked at me, his arms crossed across his chest. I hadn't let him in on my whole plan just yet, because odds are, he wouldn't like it either.

Andy grumbled to himself and then inclined his head. "Trust the boy, Fachnan."

Fachnan whipped his head towards Andy. "What?" he asked with a crazed look in his eye.

"I trust the boy." Andy said. "The end of the world has been foretold, and I don't see it happening today."

"On what authority?" Fachnan growled.

Andy only smiled. It was a smug look, but the god seemed confident in his information.

Fachnan turned back to me, eyeing me with a smoldering glare. We'd come to an uneasy friendship since the end of last year. He knew what I was capable of, and as much as he claimed to dislike me, to a certain degree he trusted me.

"And if you're wrong, Andhrímnir?" Fachnan said, without taking his gaze off of me.

"Then we all die, and it doesn't matter much anyways." Andy said. "Whether we bring the spear or not, the vampires plan to lay siege to the world. At least, if we go out, we can say we tried to do something about it."

Fachnan stared at me for a long moment. "Give the spear fragment to Leight, then."

Andy turned and offered me the piece of the spear. A tiny thing in his hands, I took it carefully. “Thank you, Andy.”

“I trust you, young wizard.” Andy nodded. “I’ve seen many a mage, druid, and wizard in my time. None have had the heart or the conviction that I see in you.”

That level of praise made me uncomfortable, and I shifted my feet nervously. “Uh, right.” I turned to Jacob. “We should get going. I have another stop to make.”

“Why do I have the feeling I’m gonna hate this?” Jacob asked ironically.

“Trust me, I do too.”

Jacob and I walked out of the training room, leaving Andy and Fachnan behind. It wasn’t long before we found our way back to Seattle. It was midday when we returned, judging by the time on my phone. Trips to Light Haven always did funky things to the flow of time. It felt like we’d been in there less than an hour, but we’d easily killed at least two hours during our visit.

“So, where are we going now?” Jacob asked me.

“To see a mob boss.” I said.

Chapter 21

Jacob studied the unassuming building, a look of recognition on his face. I was no expert, but it didn't seem to be a positive reaction. He scowled at the building without saying a word. His only other response was to cross his thick arms across his chest.

"You've got to be kidding."

"Well, judging by that reaction, I'm guessing you know where we are." I said.

"Yeah, and I don't like it." Jacob grumbled.

"Come on, Jacob." I said. "They have just as much stake in this as we do."

"We can't trust them."

"To save me from a burning building? No. To do my taxes? Also no." I countered. "But to act in their own self interests? Yes."

"If you say so." Jacob muttered.

And so, we entered the local headquarters for the Blood Clan of vampires. Tina was manning the doors again today, like she had been on our last visit. She opened the door wordlessly, all the while maintaining a painfully stretched smile. Sitting at the receptionist's desk was a young blonde woman, she couldn't have been much older than me. She too brandished a painfully wide smile. Her name tag labeled her as "Julie".

"Hi, Julie." I said pleasantly. "We're here to see Mr. Grimaldo."

"Mr. Grimaldo doesn't have any appointments today." Julie said in an eerily pleasant voice. "Perhaps you can come back next month? I can pencil you in for an appointment...oops, never mind. It seems he's completely booked next month as well."

"I think he'll want to see us now." I said. "I'm Tobias Leight, here with information regarding his daughter."

Her unnaturally happy expression almost cracked for just a moment. She typed something into her computer for a moment and paused as she read something on the screen. Then the elevator dinged as it opened.

"Mr. Grimaldo will see you now." Julie said, without taking her eyes away from her screen.

Jacob raised an eyebrow and looked over at me.

I shook it off. "Come on."

I headed for the elevator, twirling the spear fragment like a baton, as if I were taking a relaxing walk in the park. Jacob and I stood shoulder to shoulder in the elevator, patiently waiting for the elevator to arrive at its destination.

"I still think this is a bad idea." Jacob said.

Before I could respond, the elevator dinged again. The doors opened up, revealing we'd arrived in the office of Don Grimaldo. Grimaldo sat at his desk exactly how I'd found him the first we'd met. His head resting on the steeple of his hands. The painting behind him serving as an ominous backdrop. He looked at me the way a tiger might look at a big, juicy steak. There was hunger in his nearly black eyes. I gulped. I couldn't let him unnerve me.

"Hello, Mr. Grimaldo." I said, trying not to stumble over my words.

"Ah, the little Leight. I can't help but notice your uncle isn't here." Grimaldo's eyes narrowed. "And neither is my daughter."

I looked at Jacob for some reassurance. He shrugged. "Hey, this was your idea. Don't look at me."

Gee, thanks buddy. I turned my attention back to Grimaldo. "That's why I'm here, Mr. Grimaldo, sir. The situation's changed. I'm here to request your help."

"That wasn't the deal, was it?" Grimaldo raised an eyebrow.

"No, but I think you'd be inclined to help, after you hear what I have to say." I said. "Based on everything I've seen in the last few days, it seems that your daughter is actually the brains behind this entire ordeal."

Grimaldo bared his teeth in a growl. "That's a bold accusation, son."

I held up my hands in a pacifying gesture. "I realize that, sir, but just let me explain."

Grimaldo settled for a moment. "Explain yourself, and quickly, before I lose my patience."

I nodded. "My uncle and I witnessed your daughter consorting with the heads of the other two clans. They're working together to make the other two clans more powerful, to shed all their weaknesses. In the long term, I believe they plan to become the dominant powers of the world."

"But why would my daughter do this? And how?" Grimaldo asked.

"It seems Maria was coordinating with the other clan leaders to gather fragments of a powerful artifact they plan to use as the focal point for a ritual. A ritual that takes place tonight. As to why, well that's where things get interesting." I explained, and this next part was my biggest gamble. "Based on evidence I found at one of their facilities, I believe your daughter may be under fae influence."

"You believe she's being controlled by the fae? To what end?" Grimaldo asked. He seemed remarkably calm.

"There were fairy circles at this same facility. She was also demonstrating odd behavior and traits that aren't typical of a Sanguine Vampire. Glowing eyes, and a sense of authority that she shouldn't have, considering her age and supposed status compared to Oliviana and Feng Dài. It seemed like she was the one in charge, and that the others were wary to cross her. I can't be 100% sure on the details, but I believe the fae are meddling in some way." I said. Man this was nerve-wracking. He was taking this all in so calmly. "I won't know for sure until I confront her tonight. But it's just a simple fact that none of the other vampires are acting in the way they should. An alliance like this is unheard of. I don't think it could be done without an outside influence."

Grimaldo nodded once. He didn't seem pleased with the information I'd presented him. "And what do you think, is the purpose the fae have in mind for all of this? Why manipulate the vampire clans to work together? In an attempt to make them more powerful, no less. Furthermore, why exclude the Blood Clan at large from their plans? You've yet to mention my own people in all this, outside of my daughter."

My uncle had taught me a little bit about the fae. The first thing he made sure to drive home was that you couldn't trust the fae to operate on mortal logic. They were tricky and mischievous at their best. At their worst, they were malevolent and cruel. But even without the fae as a factor, I'd already figured out what the motivation was.

"I believe this is all in an attempt to throw the supernatural world, followed by the mortal world, completely out of balance. They're attempting a power shift, they want to turn humans into cattle, and become too powerful for anyone to be able to stand in their way. If they succeed, the Emotion Clan and the Soul Clan will be too powerful for any other supernatural nation to oppose. And I think they plan to eliminate the Blood Clan as competition."

Grimaldo stayed quiet for a moment as he seemed to process everything I'd told him. He looked from me to Jacob and back to me. "What about your uncle?"

"I'm sorry?" I stuttered.

"Where is your uncle? And who is this?" Grimaldo waved a hand at Jacob.

"Jacob Lewis, golem." Jacob said without looking at Grimaldo.

"My uncle's been taken, by Maria and her allies. They mean to use him as a sacrifice for their ritual." I said honestly. There was no point in lying.

"So, if all you've said is true, if I simply do nothing, I can eliminate one of the most powerful wizards in the country?" Grimaldo mulled the idea over, a smug look on his face.

"If you do nothing, my uncle dies, and your rivals become powerful enough to wipe your entire species off the face of the Earth." I snapped back. I took a deep breath, centering myself again. "I'm asking for your help, Grimaldo. The Mystic Order's hands are tied, and I need allies if I'm going to fight this enemy. Our enemy. Work with me, and we may be able to rescue your daughter. I think she can still be saved from whatever influence the fae have on her."

Grimaldo stayed quiet for a long moment. I was sweating. If Grimaldo didn't agree to help, I had no idea how we were going to pull this off. I gripped the spear fragment in my hand so hard my hand started to cramp. I'd completely forgotten I'd been holding it this entire time.

Grimaldo nodded. "Very well, young wizard. I will assist you in this matter. For my daughter's sake."

I could breathe again. I let out a huge sigh of relief. "Thank you, sir."

Grimaldo held up a business card. "Call this number when you are ready to make your move. My scourge and I will join you then."

Jacob took the card from him and put it in his pocket.

"Understand this, wizard. I still expect the safe return of my daughter. If any harm comes to her, or I find out you have been lying about any of this, it will be your head. The consequences be damned."

"Noted." I said.

"Time to go." Jacob said with a firm tone.

"Yeah, you can say that again." I muttered as I headed for the elevator.

Jacob followed after me. He didn't say anything until the elevator doors had closed again. "How sure are you of the fae's involvement?"

"There were fairy circles at the warehouse where the alliance has been meeting." I said. "It can't be a coincidence."

"And what about their alleged influence over Maria?" Jacob asked.

"Admittedly, I sort of pulled that out of my ass." I admitted. "But how else do you explain her behavior? Like I said, she seems to be the one in charge here. And I highly doubt Oliviana or Feng Dài would listen to her unless there was more going on with her."

"Fair, but you're still taking a couple leaps of logic there." Jacob said. "If you're wrong about Maria, Grimaldo is going to go ballistic."

"Well then let's hope I'm at least somewhat on the money." I muttered. "Bishop's life is depending on it."

Thunder rumbled overhead as we exited the building. I looked up at the sky just in time to see a crackle of lightning jump between clouds. It was only midday, but the storm clouds covering the sky brought with it a darkness I'd associate with late afternoon.

I'd managed to retrieve the spear fragment from the Mystic Order with little opposition. I wonder if Fachnan felt as though he owed me, and as a result, put up less of a fight. No doubt Andy's expertise helped with that. Though, if Braun had been present, I suspect it would've been a much bigger issue to surrender the spear fragment into my custody. I held up the spear fragment in my hand, observing it closely. It was a mundane, unassuming thing. Much like the Holy Grail before it, if I wasn't told exactly what it was, I'd assume it was nothing of importance. It could've been a broken mop handle for all I knew. It was only when I reached out with my magical senses that I detected a faint thrum of power. It pulsed against my magical senses, almost imitating a heartbeat. I pushed my senses to investigate more deeply.

That's where things started to get interesting. The well of power that only a fragment of the Holy Lance contained was baffling. It wasn't overwhelming like the Holy Grail had been, to my surprise. The Holy Grail had knocked me on my ass when I'd observed it under the magical spectrum, literally. But the Lance of Longinus, at least the fragment of it, was a much quieter, deeper power. It felt as though my senses were diving deep into the ocean, with no end in sight. It was an immeasurable well of magical power. I got impressions of the wielders it had passed through.

Powerful warriors, mighty tyrant kings, gods, and demigods alike.

I felt someone shake my shoulder. I felt a rush as I came back to my senses. Jacob was staring at me with a look of concern. "You took a peek at the spear's power, I'm guessing?"

"Uh, yeah." I stammered. "This thing's power is insane, and this is only a fragment of the spear."

"Word of advice. Proceed with caution when observing ancient magical artifacts. You can get lost in their well of power. If I hadn't been here with you, you could've been standing here for hours before you snapped out of it." Jacob said.

"No kidding." I said. I held the spear fragment tucked against the length of my arm, so that one end nearly poked at my armpit. "We should probably get back to the apartment."

"Yeah, if I had known you were planning to come to an evil vampire lair, I might've suggested dropping it off first." Jacob said.

"Whoops, my bad." I half-shrugged.

Jacob rolled his eyes. "Let's get moving. I think it's starting to rain again."

We arrived back at the apartment just as rain began to fall. It started off as a light sprinkle. But judging from the dark clouds looming overhead, I was expecting it to get much, much worse. Claire was sitting where we'd left her. She'd traded in her book on vampires for a carving knife and several thick tree branches. Off to the side, were six neatly carved stakes. She held a half-carved stake in her hand. As we opened the front door, Scout lifted his head up to greet us, his tail wagging happily.

Claire set down the half-finished stake on the table. "Hey boys, welcome back." Claire smiled at us. Man, she had the kind of smile that could just melt all your troubles away.

"Hey." I smiled back. "You've been busy it seems."

She'd changed clothes since we'd left. Before she had been wearing comfortable loungewear. Now she looked like she was getting ready for a hike. She wore a plain black t-shirt with fitted brown cargo pants. The pockets looked large enough to hold at least three stakes each. It made her otherwise petite form look bulkier and a bit awkward in places. Draped over her the back of her chair was a brown canvas jacket. It looked thick enough that it would deflect an indirect swipe from vampire claws, but thin enough so as to not restrict movement.

"I see you're embracing your inner Vampire Hunter Barbie." I smirked.

“Ha, ha.” She said with an exaggerated tone. “I had a feeling that sweat pants and giant sweaters weren’t the best outfit for going vampire hunting.”

I was still uneasy about bringing her with us. But there wasn’t a lot I could do to stop her. In a way, she’d be in more danger if we didn’t bring her along. If we failed, trying to keep her away from the danger would only leave her in a more vulnerable position.

“Well if you’re going to be going along with us, maybe we should do a crash course on self-defense.” I said. “Stakes and holy paintball guns are nice and all, but I want you to be prepared in case something gets too close and personal.”

“Finally!” Claire cheered. “I’ve been trying to get you to teach me some of your Kung Fu for years.”

I sighed. “It’s not Kung Fu.” Then I reconsidered the thought. The martial arts discipline I’d been trained in was called Kajukenbo. It was an American mixed martial art that did in fact take the best qualities of Kung Fu. “Okay, well it does involve Kung Fu. But that’s not the point. After you finish with the stakes, I’ll run you through the basics.”

“Yes!” Claire giggled with excitement. She returned to working on the wooden stakes.

Jacob smiled at her excitement.

In a way, I was excited too. Sure, we were facing incredibly dangerous odds, but we were doing it together. It felt good to have a team of sorts who would have my back. Jacob's absence had come with a sense of loneliness. I had missed having the big guy around, not just for his combat prowess, but also because he was a steadfast and loyal friend. It reassured me to know he had my back. I'd sidelined Scout over the last few days as well. Sure I'd had a reason, but he was a force to be reckoned with. Between Scout and Jacob, my team was not something to be sneezed at.

Then there was Claire, who had been helpless during last year's conflict with Azazel and his minions. But that was beginning to change. She was educating herself on the supernatural world, learning how to defend herself. Sure, she was just a vanilla human, but now she was gathering the tools and resources to defend herself against whatever went bump in the night. I couldn't help but admire her strength and renewed confidence. I'd also changed a lot in the past year. When everything had gone down last year, I was completely out of my element. I'd had to learn a lot all at once, and even then, I'd gotten very, very lucky. But this time was different. I was stronger, smarter, and far more prepared. No longer was I Episode IV Luke, I'd changed and grown into Episode V Luke. Still a lot to learn, but no longer the farm boy on a backwater planet.

It took a couple of hours to finish preparing our anti-vampire arsenal. By the time we were done, we had three dozen wooden stakes carved. Jacob had prepared a couple of extra holy paintball tanks, and even fitted fresh iron caps for my eskrima. If I was right about Maria being replaced by or under the control of the fae, they would certainly help.

After that had been done, Jacob and I ran Claire through some basic self-defense techniques. We showed her the basic blocks, punches, kicks, and takedowns, with a strong focus on how to get your enemy off balance. Jacob was our vampire stand-in, as he was the only one who would have comparable strength to the opponents Claire would have to face. We trained for another couple of hours until I was confident Claire had committed the movements and techniques to memory.

By the time we were done, Claire and I were both sweating and out of breath. Being a golem, Jacob didn't have to worry about getting stinky and sweaty, but it was still clear he had grown tired.

I checked the clock. It was only 6PM. There was still so much time. I was starting to grow anxious. I knew a fight was coming, there was no way to avoid it. I'd done everything I reasonably could to prepare. But nerves overwhelmed me all the same. I wasn't sure how the hell I was supposed to pull this off.

Jacob seemed to sense my anxiety, or maybe it was the look of existential dread on my face. "Hey, why don't you take a shower and try to get some rest?"

"No, I'm fi-"

"You're not fine." Jacob shook his head. "You're about to head into a battle you feel woefully unprepared for. The stakes are high and it's getting to you. That's normal. Trust me, take a shower and just close your eyes for a bit. It'll help."

"Plus, you stink." Claire added.

I glowered at her. "Fine." I sighed and made my way up the stairs.

So I did as I was told, taking a brief but therapeutic shower. Luckily there was no mirror for Kat or any of my other enemies to make a surprise appearance in. I walked back to my room, dressed only in a pair of sweats and flopped into my bed. I laid there for an hour without a wink of sleep. There were too many thoughts going through my head, too many worries and anxieties. I let out a heavy sigh and sat up.

"A wizard works best when his mind is clear." My uncle Bishop had once told me.

I scoffed at the memory. How was I supposed to have a clear mind when there was so much at stake? I felt a childish sense of resentment bubble up in me. Why had my uncle thrown himself to the wolves like that? We could have fought our way out together. We could have come up with a plan. When I saw him, I was gonna punch him in his stupid face.

I shook my head. No, this wasn't his fault. And reasonably, there would've been no way we could've fought our way out together. There had been too many of them. I needed to clear my head, and clearly sleep wasn't an option. So I rose from my bed and moved to the center of the room, where I sat down cross-legged. I rested my hands in my lap and closed my eyes.

If I was going to pull this off, my mind needed to be clear. Fear is normal. Fear can be useful. It can be the driving force that's the difference between life and death. But I had to use the fear, not be controlled by it. I'd never put much stock in what Bishop had tried to teach me about meditation. Until now, it just seemed like some zen, hippie nonsense. But now I realized what a useful tool it really was. So I sat there, taking slow, rhythmic breaths. I did my best to think about nothing at all. Soon, the fear began to recede into the back of my mind, no longer running wild and unchecked. It never disappeared, still lingering at the edges of my consciousness. But it was no longer overwhelming my thoughts. I would use that fear, anger, and rage as a tool for my enemy's destruction, not my own. I took one last deep breath, a sense of finality to it.

There was a knock at my door as I opened my eyes. A moment later, Claire opened the door. "Hey, Jacob says it's time to get moving."

Claire had showered and finished getting ready. Her hair was in a ponytail pulled through a baseball cap. The large pockets of her cargo pants were heavy with their contents, most likely stakes and paintball tanks. I glanced over at the clock sitting on my nightstand. I was shocked to see several hours had passed. By the time I'd gotten settled in my room, it had been 6:30PM. But somehow, during my meditative state, four hours had passed.

"Oh, sorry." I stuttered. "Give me two minutes to get dressed, and I'll meet you guys down there."

Claire smiled. "Okay." She retreated back into the hall, closing the door behind her.

So I got dressed. I pulled on black jeans and the Castlevania shirt I had been wearing earlier. In my closet sat some steel-toed hiking boots. I'd be doing a lot of running, but the idea of kicking some sorry vamp in the face with steel-toed boots satisfied the caveman in my brain, so I pulled them on and tied them tight. I slipped into my bomber jacket and headed downstairs.

Jacob was wearing a tight black t-shirt, jeans, and heavy combat boots. I wondered if they were steel-toed as well. His t-shirt accentuated the muscles of his chest and arms. Man, I needed to work out more. He seemed content without a jacket. Another benefit of his golem abilities, resistance to cold and heat.

We'd prepared two backpacks filled with our arsenal. Claire was shrugging one on and I did the same. The fragment of Gungnir stuck out of mine, it was a little too long to comfortably fit into the bag. I pulled the shoulder strap of the paintball gun over my head so that it hung comfortably by my left hip. I strapped my eskrima onto my right leg, making sure they were in easy reach so that I could grab them in a flash. I clipped my charms bracelet onto my right wrist. It made a satisfying jingle as I moved my arm back to my side.

I looked at Claire and Jacob. They looked strong and impressive, but most importantly, they looked ready. Scout rose from where he'd been lounging, shook his body once, and looked up at me with a doggy grin.

I took a deep breath. "Okay guys, let's do this."

Chapter 22

Thunder boomed and lightning cracked overhead. The storm had settled in and rain was coming down hard. Raining cats and dogs? Nah, it was raining tigers and wolves. The wind howled and ripped at my clothes, and it took a bit of effort to not get blown away in the chaos of it all. My jacket kept most of the weather's bite off, but my hair was soaked and plastered to my head. I really wish it came with a hood.

Claire looked absolutely miserable. She was shivering and had a tight grip on the baseball bat she'd brought along with the rest of her anti-vamp arsenal. Jacob looked completely unphased, he wasn't even wearing a jacket. Being a golem definitely had its perks. Jerk. Scout shook his body in an attempt to dry off. But it was no use. He looked up at me with a grumpy glare.

I'd gotten in contact with Grimaldo as soon as we left the apartment and laid out a bare bones plan that would most certainly go to hell within the first five minutes. But that was sort of the point. Maria and her alliance had a plan that they needed to see through tonight. So my plan was simple. Cause as much havoc as I could while working my way to the Needle. My best guess was that they had Bishop at the top of the tower, where they could get as close to the storm as possible.

I suspected Maria and Kat would be the only ones at the top of the tower, though it was possible Oliviana and Feng Dài would be up there as well. My gut told me though that they would act as the last line of defense, at the base of the tower.

We stood across the street from the Space Needle, huddled under a bus stop to take advantage of its minimal protection from the rain. When lightning flashed and lit up the world, I could see figures milling about around the Howard S. Wright Memorial Fountain and the surrounding courtyard. No doubt about it, those were vampires of both the Emotion and Soul clans. It looked to be about an even split between the two clans. I recognized the stiff hopping motions of the Jiangshi and the tall, lithe forms of Motus

Vampires. The latter carried guns and long, thin swords.

I felt a rush of nerves as I prepared to make my move. I looked to my friends. “It’s not too late to back out.” I said.

“Wouldn’t miss this for the world, buddy.” Jacob said, placing a strong hand on my shoulder.

“Yeah, me neither.” Claire said through chattering teeth.

“Okay, here’s the basic game plan.” I began. “We’re going to try and settle this diplomatically.”

“Diplomacy, huh?” Claire said with a hint of teasing surprise. “I’m surprised you aren’t going to just charge in guns blazing.”

“When diplomacy eventually fails we’re gonna have a fight on our hands.” I continued, ignoring her comment. “Claire, keep the vamps in front of you. I can’t have you charging head first into a swarm of vampires. Even with all of our preparation, you’re still swinging way too far out of your weight class here. Scout, I want you to stick to Claire like gum on a shoe. Run interference for her so that she doesn’t get overrun. If things get too dicey, get her out of there.”

Scout replied with what I assumed was an affirmative woof. He wagged his tail and kept his eyes on me, listening intently.

"Jacob," I said, turning my attention to him.

"I know, punch every vampire within reach." Jacob said.

"Actually I was thinking you could use your affinity to earth magic to keep these guys off balance." I countered. "Earthquakes, quicksand, whatever you can muster. Otherwise yeah, punch them all in the face."

Jacob grinned. "Sounds like a party. What are you going to do?"

"I'm going to fight my way through the crowd and head to the top of the tower. I'm guessing that's where my uncle is and where the ritual is gonna go down." I said.

"That sounds easier said than done, Toby." Claire commented. "Do you really think you can fight your way through a vampire horde?"

"I appreciate the vote of confidence." I grumbled. "That's what you guys are for, to be big, loud distractions. Between Jacob and Scout, the vampires should be plenty distracted. Which gives you all the more opportunity to pick them off, Claire."

"What about Grimaldo?" Jacob asked.

"He'll show." I said. "He and his goons will be your guys' backup. Then I rescue Bishop, stop the ritual, fight fight fight, and then we go home."

"No room for error in that plan." Jacob raised an eyebrow.

"Y'know, I really don't appreciate your guys' lack of confidence." I grumbled.

Claire punched Jacob's arm playfully. "Don't worry, Toby. We got your back."

Jacob feigned pain. "Yeah, we trust you."

"Okay, so let's get this done." I said.

We began our approach towards the plaza. Once we'd crossed the street, all the goons that had been milling about turned and locked onto us. They didn't move or attack, they just stared at us.

"That's not creepy." Claire said. Her voice sounded small and wary.

"No kidding. They sure do know how to set the scene." I said. It was like a scene out of a horror movie. Dark figures standing in the storm ominously. I did my best not to let on how nervous I was. My friends needed a confident leader. I couldn't afford to let my nerves get to me.

"Oi, stop wizardling." One of the vampires barked in a Chinese accent.

We stopped walking. The nearest vamp was less than twenty feet away. A Motus Vampire, I assumed. She was tall, wearing a white leather bodysuit. She was holding an assault rifle of some kind in her hands.

"You were told to come alone, wizard," she said.

"No, I was told not to bring any other wizards along." I corrected, making sure to insert a sense of confidence into my voice. I pointed at each of my allies. "Golem, human, dog."

The Motus Vampire glared at me through the rain. An even taller woman came up from behind the vampire. I recognized her immediately. Oliviana, the head of the Emotion Clan. She was dressed identically to her henchwoman, but instead of a gun, a long sword hung in a scabbard on her waist.

"Tobias Leight, did you bring the artifact?" Oliviana asked.

I reached over my shoulder, pulling the spear fragment out from where it was sticking out of my bag. "You mean this twig?"

"Hand it here." Oliviana held out her hand.

"I want my uncle back." I said flatly.

"The artifact first." She demanded.

My free hand rested on my eskrima. I unbuckled the clasp, making sure I could pull one free at a moment's notice. "How do I know you'll free my uncle once I hand it over?"

"I am many things, Tobias." Oliviana said. "But a liar, I am not."

I laughed out loud. "That's rich. You've been lying to us from the very start. Claiming to have nothing to do with this conspiracy."

Oliviana curtsied mockingly. "Tobias, it need not be this way. Just come with me, and I'll guarantee safety for you and yours."

As she spoke the words, I felt an odd sensation come over me. Oliviana seemed to radiate heat and light. I felt my eyes go heavy and I couldn't help but focus on the curve of her hips underneath the body suit. She traced one finger up her stomach to the zipper that stopped just underneath her generous chest. Her eyes locked with mine and she pursed her lips in such a way that...

"Knock it off, bitch!" Jacob's voice boomed.

The magic that Oliviana had been using on me seemed to shatter. She pouted at Jacob. "Oh, you can't blame a girl for trying."

Oliviana was so beautiful and seemed so human, that I had let my guard down. I'd practically walked right into her sexual mind whammy. If Jacob hadn't been here to back me up, to intimidate the vampire into dropping her seduction magic, I might've been suckered into going along with whatever she had planned.

"Not on your best day." I growled. She didn't need to know how well her plan had been working. "My uncle. Now." My voice grew louder with each word.

"It seems we've reached an impasse." Oliviana shrugged. Almost too quick to see, she unsheathed her sword and pointed the tip at me. "So I'll make it simple. Hand over the artifact. Now!"

I heard Claire suck in a nervous breath.

"You want it? Come take it." I said, pointing the spear fragment at her. On pure instinct, I channeled my magic through the fragment. "*Kaze!*"

I'm not sure what had possessed me to use the spear fragment as a focus, but it paid off. The cyclone that erupted from the spear fragment was more powerful than any other I'd called up before.

Oliviana was sent flying across the plaza towards the fountain. She crashed into the fountain's base, shattering the side of it. Water poured out and around her. She was dazed for a moment. But the other vampires got the message.

The fight was on.

Chapter 23

The plaza immediately erupted into chaos. The Jianghsi leaped at us deceptively fast. Half of the Motus Vampires followed suit, unsheathing their blades. While the other half leveled their automatic weapons and opened fire. Matching their speed, Scout shifted into his monstrous hellhound form and shielded us from the initial volley of bullets. They did little more than annoy the beast and he let out an angry roar in response. To the vampires' credit, they were smart enough to hesitate at the sight and sound of an angry hellhound.

Scout's hellhound form was an odd mix of man and beast. His forelegs were closer to brawny human arms, giving him a bulldog-like stance. His jaws were full of giant, mismatched teeth. Flames trailed his spine and his thick muscles deflected the bullets like they were Nerf darts.

The vampires didn't hesitate for long before resuming their assault. They charged again and Scout leapt into action, batting aside various vampires who had attempted to swarm him. Jacob followed Scout's lead; his arms began to glow with a golden green light as he charged into the fray. A Motus Vamp slashed at him with her sword. The sword clanged as if it had collided with stone. The vampire looked at him in stunned surprise, just long enough for Jacob to deck her in the face and drive her head into the ground.

I looked to Claire. "Remember the plan. Stay on the outside and be safe! Scout will protect you!"

Claire nodded, readying her holy paintball gun in one hand and a wooden stake in the other. I rushed past Scout as he retreated to be closer to Claire, freeing one of my eskrima along the way. I hadn't anticipated using the spear fragment as a magical weapon tonight, but I sure as hell wasn't going to question it.

I ran to where I last saw Oliviana. She was pulling herself from the rubble of the fountain as I approached.

"You stupid, arrogant child!" Oliviana said through clenched teeth. "I was actually going to let you live, too! You would've made such a nice play thing, like your uncle!"

I pointed the spear fragment at her again. "*Kaze!*"

A blast of wind so ferocious that I had to take a step back to brace myself erupted from the spear piece. Olviana was ready for it this time. She didn't have enough time to dodge the attack, instead she braced her arms in a defensive position and took the brunt of the attack. The wind hit her like a runaway train and forced her back against the centerpiece of the fountain.

As the wind died down, I charged, not giving her any time to recover. I swung my eskrima at her head. She caught it on her forearm with a wince of pain before sucker punching me in the face. Bishop had told me that vampires of all flavors were strong, but I'd underestimated the Motus from the start. I stumbled back, my vision clouded by stars and flashing lights. I shook my head free of the daze just in time to see Oliviana charging me with her sword held high. I managed to get my weapons between my head and certain death as she swung down with the sword. I charged my eskrima with pure magic energy just before our weapons clashed and it took all my strength not to give way. Arcane light sparked from where my eskrima met her sword, causing spots to dance around in my eyes. Oliviana gritted her teeth and leaned into her sword harder. My arms shook and I was forced down to a knee.

"Do you really think you can stop what's about to happen here?" Oliviana growled.

"At the very least, I can annoy the hell out of you guys." I grunted under the strain of blocking her attack.

Oliviana spun her blade as she shifted her stance and made a shallow cut through my jeans and into my calf. I cried out in pain and rage, retaliating with a swing of my eskrima to her knee cap as hard as I could. It made a sickening crunch sound and she bellowed out in pain.

I seized the opportunity to aim the spear fragment directly at her stomach and howled "*Kaze!*"

The runes of the spear flared up once more and a miniature tornado burst forth and sent her hurtling across the plaza like a rag doll. I fell to my hands and knees, careful to not lose my grip on the spear fragment. I panted heavily, trying to catch my breath. The spells I channeled through the spear were powerful but draining. I wouldn't last long if I kept relying on it. The cut on my leg was messy and bloody. It alone wouldn't kill me, but it added to my growing fatigue. And the fight had only just started.

I slipped my backpack off one shoulder, taking the brief reprieve to open it up and pull out one of the pick-me-up potions I'd brewed a couple of days ago. I untwisted the cap and dumped the contents sloppily into my mouth. It coated my chin and soaked part of my shirt. But I instantly felt the difference. It felt like I'd just chugged twenty uber espressos. My body was tingling with newfound energy. Now I understood why Geralt of Rivia swore by those Swallow potions.

"Woohoo! Alright!" I cheered drunkenly as I stood back up, putting my backpack back on in the process. Vampires were closing in all around me as a cocky grin spread across my face. "*Kaze orbitae!*"

I drove my eskrima into the ground as I forced the magic through. Wind exploded out in all directions in the shape of a shallow bowl, twelve feet in diameter. Vampires were lifted into the air and thrown back several feet away.

"Yeah, take that you Twilight rejects!" I taunted.

Just in time for Feng Dài to hit me from behind with a ball of fire. I was flung forward onto the ground, losing my grip on the spear fragment and my eskrima. They rolled out of reach near the rubble of the fountain. The hair on the back of my head was a bit singed, but my spell-laden jacket had taken the brunt of the attack.

"Thank you so kindly, young wizard," Feng Dài's mocking voice came from somewhere behind me. "For returning what you had stolen from me."

The Jiangshi lord took several stiff steps past me to where the spear fragment was lying on the ground. I thrust my arm out, reaching for the piece of the spear. But it was way too far. As I pulled myself into a less prone position, I managed to grunt out: "*Kaze minimus!*" A small gust of wind picked the spear fragment up off the ground just as Feng Dài was reaching for it.

And flung it away to my left.

Okay, not what I had been going for. But it bought me a couple of seconds. I stood back up, grabbing my second eskrima as I did. Feng Dài was making his way slowly to where the spear fragment had fallen. I rushed to intercept him, reaching over my head into my bag as I did so. I pulled out one of the wooden stakes and gripped it in my hand. If both of the vampire lords were left unattended, I didn't have a chance at succeeding here. I had to take at least one of them out.

Feng Dài turned to meet me as I rushed at him. He raised his clawed fingers, ready for a fight. I swung my eskrima towards his head. He easily blocked it, but I had no intention of the strike making contact. It had been a distraction for my next strike. I thrust the wooden stake towards his heart. But you don't get to be the local lord of the Jiangshi by painting pottery. With a swift sweep of his other arm, he deflected the strike hard enough to knock the stake out of my hand. It went tumbling uselessly away.

He struck at me with his claws and I flailed my eskrima arm frantically to deflect his strike. It struck him on the wrist and I heard brittle bones crack. I took a wide step around him, spun into a kneeling stance and struck his kneecap with my eskrima. Again, brittle bones crunched and snapped. Feng Dài howled in pain. As he spun to meet me, I rolled backwards, conveniently landing by my other eskrima. I took it in hand just in time to see Feng Dài fling another fireball at me. I crossed my eskrima in front of me, channeling energy through them. The fireball clashed with the defensive energy I'd gathered and burst around me. I deposited one of the eskrima into its holster and pulled another of my trinkets from the bag. I tossed the pouch full of coins towards Feng Dài and it fell open, a handful of pocket change clinking against the wet concrete.

"Bastard!" Feng Dài cursed.

I heard a *pop pop pop* sound and Feng Dài's head jerked and sizzled. I turned to my right to see Claire aiming down the sight of her paintball gun, grinning like a mad woman.

Even as a lord of the Jiangshi, he couldn't resist the urge to properly count the coins. He fell to his knees in a stiff, almost robotic motion and began sorting the coins. It was the breather I needed. I rushed past him, intending to retrieve the spear fragment. But I wasn't the only one. Oliviana had recovered from the whirlwind that had sent her flying. She was moving like a blur towards the spear fragment, and even though I was closer, there was no way in hell I'd beat her to it.

That's when a screeching howl pierced the night. Dark shapes rushed into the fray to meet the rogue vampires. They slashed with viciously sharp claws and blades and our enemies began to fall. Even though he moved as a shadowy blur, I recognized Grimaldo as he rushed to meet Oliviana. They met in a clash of blades that shook the ground around him. Oliviana's katana-like blade contrasted sharply, no pun intended, against Grimaldo's double-edged sword.

"You witch!" Grimaldo's voice boomed over the storm. "You dare to usurp the balance! To doom my clan while yours and the dirty zombies of China ascend and thrive!"

"Dirty bloodsucker!" Oliviana spat. "You're one to talk, siding with this wizard! This mortal!"

"You know, I know you're not technically wrong." I spoke up. "But the way you said it made it sound derogatory."

Grimaldo glared daggers at me. His Sanguine vampire traits were bleeding through, again no pun intended. His face had partially morphed into something bat-like. His ears had grown and become pointed, his nose was upturned and his lips receded to reveal pointed canines.

"Foolish boy!" He growled. "This is no time for jests! Retrieve the artifact!"

I giggled, the sound bordering on mania. The energy from my potion must've still been coursing through me. "Right, I'll get right on that!"

Feng Dài was nearly done counting the coins. A sudden tremor shook the earth, nearly knocking me off balance. The Jiangshi cursed as the coins rattled on the ground and scattered amongst themselves once more. I recognized the tremor as Jacob's earth magic.

While I ran to retrieve the spear piece, Grimaldo and Oliviana renewed their clash. They struck at each other with their blades at blinding speeds. Each strike shook the earth and scattered rain droplets like a broken sprinkler. I scrambled to pick up the artifact, the pure giddy energy running through making me fumble with it before I finally grabbed it. With

Oliviana occupied, I stuck the spear fragment into my bag and pulled out another stake.

I took a moment to locate my friends in the chaos. Jacob was engaged with three Jiangshi. One of them got within range of his enlarged clay fists, Jacob swung at the vampire, but it narrowly dodged away. The other two took the opportunity to hurl elemental magic at him. I could hear Jacob yell in frustration as he tried to pin them down. The Jiangshi repeated this process twice more before Jacob decided he'd had enough. He raised one of his fists into the air, glowing power gathering around it, before striking the ground as hard as he could. Stone spikes erupted from under the Jiangshi. One was impaled on the spike, twitching like a dead bug, but the other two managed to evaded the attack at the last possible second.

Claire was busy with her own mob of Motus Vampires. It was strange watching them move. Their movements were too quick, too smooth to be human. They tried to rush in, but Claire kept them at bay with the weapons we had provided her. My heart stopped when I noticed one had slipped passed her defenses while she was occupied with its allies.

That's where Scout came in. The hellhound let out a roar that shook the ground as he leapt through the air, crushing the vampire before it had the chance to attack Claire.

Feng Dài was still counting coins on the ground, in spite of the fact that he'd love nothing more than to rip my head off. I sprinted towards him, running faster than I ever had before. As I got closer, he tore his eyes away from the coins. I had a split second to realize that the coins were all sorted on the ground. He'd finished counting them! But it was too late, if I stopped my charge now I'd be left wide open for a counterattack. I leapt towards him, rearing my arm up in preparation to strike with the stake.

Feng Dài turned to meet me and thrust his arm forth. A fireball exploded outwards towards me and I realized I was gonna get a first-hand experience on how a cut of steak felt on the grill.

Oh fucking well, I guess.

The fireball flew, I struck out with the stake, and the next thing I knew, I was tumbling through the air.

Chapter 24

I lay on my back in the middle of the plaza. The sights and sounds of battle were distant and muffled by the ringing in my ears. My chest hurt like hell. It was a deep, stinging pain that I had only a small familiarity with. I'd burned myself before, not with fire, but when I'd once spilled boiling water on my hand while trying to make ramen. It wasn't even close to how excruciating this pain was now though.

I tried to gather myself, lifting my head just enough to get a view off my chest. The front of my shirt had completely burned away, revealing raw, red skin with black charred bits around the edges nearest the shirt. The rain granted me a sense of soothing relief, but it also stung and drew my attention to the pain more. Why hadn't I zipped up the damn jacket?

Nevertheless, it had protected me from most of the blast.

I mustered my strength and managed to roll onto my side, propping myself up with one arm. I looked to where I thought I'd left Feng Dài. Thankfully, my second degree burns hadn't been for nothing. Feng Dài lay on the ground nearby, unmoving. A wooden stake stuck out of his chest.

"Suck on that, you soul-sucking freak!" I gasped. I got onto my hands and knees and struggled to rise. I stood shakily, taking inventory of myself. Everything was still attached, and despite being thrown through the air, the contents of my bag hadn't spilled everywhere. The spear fragment still stuck out of where I'd left it. I winced as another lance of pain radiated through my chest. That was definitely going to be a problem.

But it was not a problem for right now. Right now, I had to stay focused on the task at hand, no matter how much I was already hurting. There'd be time to lie down and bitch and moan about how much my body hurt. I figured I should count my blessings. Between the adrenaline coursing through me and the potion I'd drank earlier, I was feeling better than I should have.

A glance to my right revealed that the eskrima I'd been holding had rolled a short distance away.

I walked over to it, still trying to shake off the daze. Everything was slowly coming back into focus. To my right, I saw Claire and Scout engaged in combat with a handful of Jiangshi, who were currently oblivious to the fact their master had been slain. Claire was spearing the hearts of the incoming Jiangshi one by one. When too many got close, Scout would jump in and promptly dispatch them. It paid to have a hellhound on your side, even if he was considered a runt for his kind. Scout seemed to be having a field day with the vampires. He ran through a crowd of them, knocking several over and crushing even more with his giant paws. Claire followed after him, stabbing several Jiangshi who'd survived Scout's charge.

To my left, Jacob was busy fending off three Motus Vampires. Jacob was bathed in an earthen-tone light. His right hand had morphed into a spiked mace made of hardened clay. A shallow half-dome had expanded from his left arm, acting as a shield to protect himself with. He smashed in the head of a male Motus Vampire, the flying blood and brain bits made my stomach turn, and it took all I had to not spew chunks everywhere.

Jacob made a circular motion with his arms and shouted a word I couldn't make out through all the noise. The two remaining vampires suddenly sank up to their necks in the ground. Jacob had used his quicksand spell to immobilize them. Without a second thought, he swung his mace hand at the vampires' heads, finishing them off.

I heard a pained cry and before I could turn to look, Grimaldo was flying over my head. He hit the ground in a roll before going still, his sword clattering nearby. Damn it, he was my trump card against Oliviana. Speaking of...

I turned to face where I'd last seen Oliviana. To his credit, Grimaldo had worked her over pretty good. Her white bodysuit was torn in several places, pale blood leaking from several long wounds. She was breathing heavily, and if I wasn't incredibly terrified at the moment, I'd find the berserker warrior chick look to be extremely hot. But I had to remember she was a predator. An incredibly dangerous, yet incredibly attractive, predator. I suppose that's what made her so effective.

"You stupid brat...you couldn't just leave well enough alone." Oliviana's voice was strange. It had grown a shade or two deeper. Had her teeth always been pointed like that?

"What can I say?" I shrugged cockily. "I'm just a nosy guy."

"And now it's going to get you killed." Oliviana growled. Her body began to shift.

That's when I remembered a detail about Vampire 101 that I'd glossed over when all of this started. When the Motus Vampires were backed into a corner, they had a much more powerful, demonic form.

Oliviana began to grow. Her stance widened as her legs grew an extra foot in length. Bones crunched and rearranged as her feet burst from her boots and turned into cloven hooves. White fur covered her legs as her body suit shredded and gave way to her transformation. She put on an extra fifty pounds of pure muscle, her skin turning a bright pink color. The body suit had been completely destroyed, leaving her completely naked. The fantasy of the sexy seductress was completely ruined for me as I watched her transformed. Long, obsidian claws extended from her fingertips. She arched her back as large goat horns curled out of her head. Oliviana faced me, a secondary pair of blood red eyes cracked open above her normal set.

"Oh crap." I muttered.

Oliviana rushed forward at impossible speeds. Before I even had a chance to move, she was looming over me. I moved to defend myself but I was too slow, and she backhanded me across the chest and sent me hurtling across the plaza.

"I'll allow you this much, Tobias Leight." Oliviana purred as she walked towards me. "It's been quite a long time since anyone's forced me to assume this form. Consider it an honor."

"Oh yeah," I spit out a bit of blood. "I feel so honored."

I groaned in pain as I forced myself to rise. I pocketed one of my eskrima and pulled out the spear fragment. I was going to need every advantage I could get. I'd never faced something quite like Oliviana, even the demonic henchgoons that Azazel threw at me last year. The difference came down to intelligence, not to mention the vendetta Oliviana clearly held for me.

I leveled the spear fragment on Oliviana. My shoulder hurt like hell, the burns on my chest were screaming with pain. But if I was going to get out of here alive, I had to push past those injuries. Oliviana was less than ten feet away. I gritted my teeth and snarled, "*Hinote!*"

Fire wasn't my strong suit. I'd been getting better at it, but I usually needed the assistance of my charms bracelet. But I'd gambled on the spear fragment making up for it. And hoo boy, had I gambled good. A column of white hot flames erupted from the spear fragment and engulfed Oliviana. The flames roared in my ears, and the heat they radiated made my instincts scream "Run away!" But I held fast, not letting up for several more seconds. The flames erupting from the spear fragment didn't seem to be too bothered by the torrential downpour. Finally, the flames ceased and I paused to admire my handiwork.

My stomach dropped as the flames surrounding Oliviana sputtered out. Besides some charred skin and roasted hair, she was nearly fine. To further my dismay, even those injuries were healing before my eyes. She was smiling, mouth full of serrated teeth.

"Oh you've got to be kidding me." I muttered.

"What a shame, Tobias." Oliviana said, her voice was deep and she spoke with a bit of a lisp through the needle-like teeth. I wish it detracted from how intimidating she was. It didn't. "You had so much potential, such a shame to see it go to waste."

I held my weapons up, ready to defend. She rushed me again, and before I could move to defend, she slashed at my stomach with her claws. I screamed at the top of my lungs as she ripped my burned flesh open. Coursing with rage, I swung at her head with my eskrima. She caught it absentmindedly, and yanked it out of my hand. With one quick squeeze, the wood of the eskrima splintered and exploded.

"No!" I screamed. I pointed the spear fragment at her stomach and cried out. "*Hinote fordun!*"

A cannonball of fire and kinetic energy exploded from the spear and sent Oliviana skidding across the concrete. I hit her again, and she was sent screeching across the concrete farther back. I reached over my shoulder to where the holy paintball gun was strapped to my backpack. I took aim and squeezed the trigger. The paintball gun hissed as it fired off pellet after pellet. Oliviana screamed as the holy water pellets burst on her skin. It left burn marks like my flames had, but deeper. Each pellet left behind a pitch black cauterized wound. I didn't let up until the paintball gun clicked empty, then I lifted the spear fragment again and let loose another cannonball. Oliviana was off balance and disoriented, so the third flaming cannonball threw her on her ass.

I panted heavily, tossing the paintball gun to the ground. Nearby was some old construction equipment left over from when the plaza had been under renovation. Sitting in a large wooden crate were a pile of metal stakes. I hobbled over, stretching my hand and grabbed four of them. Oliviana was still stunned and sprawled out on the ground. I stepped over her and let out a defiant, angry cry as I drove one of the stakes into her left wrist.

The scream she let out could never be mistaken for human. It was the sound of a mindless beast, driven insane by pain. She flailed, trying to fling me away, but I deflected her desperate strikes, stomping on her free wrist and pinning it to the ground. Then I drove another metal stake into her forearm, careful not to pierce her other wrist.

"Oliviana, you damn idiot!" I screamed at her. "Stop now before I have to kill you too!"

As the words came out of my mouth, I shuddered. I'd killed Feng Dài. Sure, he was a monster. But he'd still been a person, in the most technical sense. It didn't sit right with me. Monstrous demons was one thing, but something that walked and talked like a person...

Oliviana roared in pain and anguish. She struggled desperately against her bonds, but it was no use. I'd gambled on the stakes working at all, but I'd soaked her in holy water beforehand, so it apparently counted.

"It doesn't have to end this way!" I yelled over the rain. "Yield now and you can live! Call off your men! The Jiangshi too, they'll listen to you! No one else has to die tonight!"

Oliviana locked eyes with me, they burned with hatred. But she wasn't an idiot. I had her dead to rights, and if she died, it wouldn't matter if Maria's plan succeeded. She stared at me for another long moment, breathing hard with her teeth bared.

Finally she said, "I yield."

"Louder!" I screamed.

"I yield!" She roared.

"Swear it, a truce until this ordeal is over." I said, so only she could hear.

"And twenty four hours after. I swear it." Oliviana seethed. It cost her something to give in, especially to someone she considered lesser than her.

I nodded, then I stepped off of her. "Call off the other vamps."

Oliviana nodded. Then she let out a bellowing roar that drowned out the sound of the rain completely. Almost instantly, the other Motus Vampires and the Jiangshi stopped fighting. My Sanguine allies followed suit. Two of Grimaldo's associates were helping him stand. I turned to face him.

"That means you two. A truce until this is over, and twenty four hours after." I told him, my face locked in a scowl.

Grimaldo grimaced, but he nodded in agreement. "I swear to it, wizard. But what of my daughter? And the rogue wizard?"

I took a deep breath. "Don't worry, they're next."

As the battle ceased, I scanned my surroundings in an attempt to find my friends. It wasn't hard, Scout stood out like a sore thumb. He was standing defensively over Jacob and Claire. My eyes widened when I realized that Claire was on the ground. I took off at a near sprint towards them, much to my body's protest.

"Oh would you shut up, already?" I cursed at my body. "There'll be time to bitch about the pain when this is all over."

Jacob was tending to Claire, who was laying flat on her back. It took me a moment, but I finally made it over to them.

Claire's arm was bent sharply at a sickening angle. Her face was pale with pain and it took all of my self-control not to go back over to the crowd of vampires and let loose on them.

I knelt down beside her, breathing hard. "Claire! It's okay, we'll get you to a hospital."

Claire coughed and managed to smile at me. "My dumb fault, I let one of those leather-clad freaks too close."

"She'll be okay, Tobias." Jacob reassured me. "I used a spell to dull the pain, and otherwise, she isn't in any serious danger for the moment." He jerked his head to the crowd of vampires. "How'd you manage that?"

"I made Oliviana realize that she'd be too stupid to die over this." I explained. "Called for a ceasefire."

"You humiliated her in front of her people. She won't forget that." Jacob's eyes landed on Feng Dài's still corpse. "And the Jiangshi definitely won't forget that. They'll be out for blood, sooner or later."

"I wasn't given much choice." I said.

Jacob nodded. "I know."

Claire coughed again. "What happens now?"

I rose to my feet a little shakily. "There's still Maria and Kat to deal with. I'm assuming they're at the top of the tower. They're probably not even aware of what's gone on down here."

"You shouldn't go alone." Jacob pointed out.

"I know, but I need you here." I said. "To make sure these vamps don't go crazy again, and to get Claire some help."

Claire shook her head. "I'm not going anywhere until you come back!" She said, a look of stubborn determination in her eyes.

I sighed. "I'll be okay, I promise." I turned to the tower and began walking. "Plus, I still owe you a dance."

I walked away before they could say anything in response. I heard Scout whine as I went, an odd sound coming from a hellhound. I had half a thought to bring him along, but decided against it. For one, the observation deck of the Needle would be too cramped for him to be useful. Not to mention, I wanted Claire and Jacob to have as much backup as possible. As I walked, I stared at the top of the tower in concentration.

"Don't worry, Bishop." I said. "I'm coming for you."

Chapter 25

To my surprise, the elevator was still functioning. I don't know why I expected it to be shut off or busted, but it zoomed up the tower like chaos wasn't raining down around us. While I waited, I pulled my second pick-me-up potion from my bag and chugged it. I was going to need it. The burns and wounds on my chest nagged at me, distracting pain radiating from my body. I took off my ruined shirt and wrapped it around my stomach to slow the bleeding from the cuts that Oliviana had left. Thankfully the defensive spells of my jacket had held together, otherwise I would have felt a bit naked and vulnerable going into this. I held the spear fragment in one hand, my remaining eskrima in the other.

I felt a pang of sadness in remembrance for the one Oliviana had shattered. Sure, it was just a thing, but they had been a gift from Bishop and marked the start of my journey into wizardhood. I still had the one, but they'd been a matching pair. I'd grown comfortable using them and learning to fight with them. Maybe Bishop could help me with a replacement, after this was all over.

The elevator dinged and then opened slowly. I stepped out and took in my surroundings. The viewing platform was dark and seemed to be completely empty. I frowned and moved forward cautiously. I held my eskrima and the spear fragment at the ready, prepared to blast anything that popped up. The potion had settled and took effect, making my fatigue fade away.

"Hello?" I called out into the darkness. "Kat? Maria?"

No one answered. Typical.

"I kicked your lackies' asses. Now it's just you two." I taunted the darkness. I took slow, quiet steps and kept my head on a swivel. Where were they? I had a bad feeling about all this.

"Come out, come out wherever yo-" I felt the hairs on my neck stand up. Through blind instinct alone, I dove forward into a roll. A bolt of electricity crackled and boomed right through where I'd been standing a moment before.

I rolled into a kneeling position and turned to face behind me. Kat was standing there, pointing a smooth staff of white wood in my direction. Residual electricity crackled around her before slowly dissipating.

"Well hello there, Tobias." Kat mewled. "So glad you could join us. And you even brought the artifact with you."

"Where's my uncle?" I growled.

Kat leaned on her staff casually. "Oh, he's around. The ritual is almost set to begin." She pointed at the spear fragment. "We were just waiting on that."

"Come and get it then," I challenged.

Kat frowned. "It doesn't have to be this way, Tobias. There's still a chance to fix all of this. Work with me, accept your destiny. With you and Azazel merged together, we can—"

"Forget it." I cut her off. "I'm not gonna let the vampires succeed, and I'm definitely not going to get in bed with you and Azazel either."

Kat smirked. "Interesting choice of words."

"Oh screw off." I groaned. "Listen, I'm giving you one chance. Stand aside, and I'll let you live to regret it another day."

Kat's face hardened. "You know I can't do that, Tobias. I need that artifact. I need him out of my head!" As her voice rose, it seemed to change. As if another voice was speaking over it. The voice of Azazel, the fallen angel that was currently living in her head rent free. It was creepy as hell to hear, mainly because his voice was nearly identical to my own.

"Kat, please let me take you to the Mystic Order. They can help you." I pleaded. I didn't want to fight her. Not because I was afraid of hurting her, okay maybe a little bit. But also I'd never actually beaten her in a fight. She was at least as powerful as I was, most likely stronger. And she had a fallen angel inside her that would certainly amplify her power.

Kat let out a cackle. "Tobias, you naïve fool. Still trusting those old bureaucrats." She mocked. "Last chance. The artifact."

I sighed. "I'm sorry it has to be this way."

"*Raiko!*" Kat's voice echoed. Lightning zig-zagged from her staff and rushed toward me.

My hands seemed to move on their own, crossing the eskrima and spear fragment into a defensive position. The lightning struck my foci and the force sent me skidding across the floor a few feet, but I managed to hold my own. I threw my arms out to the side, dispersing the attack.

I aimed my eskrima at her and shouted, "*Kaze!*"

A wind funnel roared forth towards her. She spun her staff in her hands, chanting a magic word. A wall of wind spread from her spinning staff, perfectly countering my spell. But I hadn't planned on the attack actually making contact. Just a simple distraction. I ran towards her while the wind obscured her vision.

"*Duro!*" I yelled. I felt my skin harden immediately as I closed the distance. I deposited my eskrima and swung my fist at her face in one fluid motion. My hardened fist struck her in the mouth and sent her stumbling back. She cried out in pain but I didn't let up, rearing up for another punch. She swung her staff and hit my wrist. It didn't hurt much, thanks to the hardening spell, but it was enough to deflect my attack. Kat pivoted and swung her staff into my gut. Again, it didn't hurt much, but it made me stumble. But I rolled with it, stepping down and then swinging my left leg in a wide roundhouse kick. I caught Kat in the stomach and I heard the air escape her lungs as she went tumbling to the ground. She rolled on her side and twisted to a kneeling position, aiming her staff.

"*Raiko!*" Kat cried.

I was too close to dodge or defend myself effectively. The lightning struck and sent me flying into the air. I cried out in surprise and pain as the hardening spell failed. I lost my grip on the spear fragment and crashed into a diorama of the Space Needle. It crumbled underneath me and I hit the ground hard, the impact knocking the wind out of me.

Kat chuckled, picking up the spear fragment from where it had fallen. "Gotta say, Tobias. You've got a mean right hook, but I've been hit harder."

I tried to gather my senses, but the room was spinning and my entire body tingled from the electric blast. I moved sluggishly, trying to get my feet under me. I groaned as my body protested. Everything hurt, and the pick-me-up potion was only able to do so much for me.

"Kat..." I groaned. "Where's my uncle? Where's Maria?"

"Oh, you thought they were up here, didn't you?" Kat taunted. She was walking towards the viewing deck.

"What? What do you mean?" I said, every word coming out shaky.

"I figured you'd be stupid enough to try and make your way up here." Kat said. "So we adjusted our plan a little." She cocked her head towards the viewing deck as she walked. Kat walked out onto the viewing deck and approached the glass barrier.

Then she threw the freaking spear fragment over the edge.

"What!" I gathered my senses and ran out onto the viewing platform.

Kat made no move to stop me, leaning against the railing nonchalantly as she watched me. I pressed my face against the glass and looked down below. The spear fragment fell towards a figure. And even from here, I could tell it was Maria. She stood near the center of a large magic circle. It was a bright red color, vivid and easy to spot even in the storm. Something told me it wasn't paint. Something lay in the center of the circle.

Bishop...

Kat had tricked me. Lured me to the top of the tower to duke it out one on one. A match-up she was confident she could win. Meanwhile, Maria had been hiding out somewhere below, just waiting for me to head up. I took my eskrima in hand, the wood creaking in my grip.

"Damn you..." I muttered.

Kat perked up, holding a hand to her ear. "Hm, what was that?"

"I said DAMN YOU!" I roared, aiming my eskrima at her. I channeled energy from my charms bracelet, activating the fire spell etched within. "*Hinote!*"

A fireball soared from my eskrima and detonated as it hit her. But I didn't pause to see the results. I took a few steps back from the edge of the viewing platform. The elevator was programmed to return to the bottom floor after each trip. I couldn't afford to wait for it.

"*Duro!*" I yelled as I ran towards the edge.

I jumped forward, my hardened body shattering the glass easily.

"Tobias!" I heard Jacob's voice from somewhere far down below.

Then I fell. Hurtling towards the earth, it dawned on me how stupid of an idea this had been.

Chapter 26

Yeah, this had been a really bad idea. Believe it or not, it doesn't actually take long to fall from a height of six hundred or so feet. Six seconds, give or take. Trust me, I counted. I had only a couple of seconds to react and figure out how I was going to stop myself from splatting onto the concrete. My hardening spell wasn't strong enough to save me from an impact like this. I was tumbling wildly through the air, struggling to right myself and screaming the whole way. I managed to right myself into a dive, and I aimed my eskrima at the ground as my hardening spell faded. Here goes nothing.

"*KAZE MAXIMUS!*" I screamed desperately, slamming as much power as I could into the spell.

I held onto the eskrima for dear life as hurricane winds erupted forth. As the winds made contact with the ground below, I felt my fall slow. But would it be enough? Either it would, or it wouldn't matter anymore. It was the longest six seconds of my life. Then I hit the ground.

Good news, I lived. Bad news, something was definitely broken. Maybe multiple somethings. Nevertheless, I was alive. And I was here. I tried to get my arms under me to rise, but my left arm refused to respond. A searing lance of pain struck my chest and it took all my willpower not to scream out. I managed to rise, and I found it to be a miracle my legs weren't broken. My left arm hung uselessly.

"Tobias, are you okay?" Jacob ran over to me, his voice urgent and concerned.

"Uh, yeah." I said, slurring my words a bit. I gestured to my left arm with my eskrima. "I think I uh, dislocated my arm."

Jacob pointed to my eskrima. "You may want to bite down on it." He said and then grabbed my wrist.

With one swift motion, he pulled on my arm and I heard a loud pop and another wave of pain ripped through me. I screamed through gritted teeth, then tested my arm a bit. It hurt, but it would work.

Then I turned to where I'd seen the magic circle. Maria stood in the circle, Bishop unconscious at her feet. He'd been beaten savagely. His eyes were swollen shut and his face was covered almost entirely in bruises. The painted runes and markings were glowing with an eerie red light. The three spear fragments floated in front of her. The bottom end of the shaft, the middle piece we had been using, and the tip of the spear. The spear tip itself was pretty big, about two feet long and a foot wide. It had three points with very little space in between. If the points had been much wider, I'd have said it was more of a trident. The pieces floated together, glowing light shined brightly from the cracks, then faded away. The Spear of Destiny was complete, unmarred by any sign it had ever been broken.

"Maria!" I called out. "Stop this now!"

Maria glared at me, her eyes glowed with a white light. "You can't stop me now, wizard. The ritual is nearly complete." Her voice was devoid of emotion. She took something out of the pocket of her skinny jeans. "There's only one more thing before we can begin."

It was hard to see through the storm and the arcane light. But the way she held it, I realized it was a syringe. Inside it was a red liquid, almost like blood. No wait, it wasn't just like blood. It WAS blood.

"Blood from a vampire of the Blood Clan." Maria said, sounding completely detached from the situation. As if this were just a normal Friday night.

A vital piece of information rushed to the forefront of my brain. "If you're injected with the blood of a Sanguine Vampire..."

"You become one." Jacob finished the thought.

"In order to complete the ritual, the sacrifice must have a wizard's magical aura and the blood of a vampire." Maria explained.

Oh shit.

I rushed towards Maria, preparing to blast her to kingdom come. Her body tensed and I felt a ripple of energy through the air. Something grabbed my arms, stopping me from moving. On my left, a Motus Vampire held onto me. To my right, a Jiangshi did the same. Both their eyes were glowing with the same white light as Maria's.

I looked to Jacob, several vampires had restrained him and pinned him to the ground. He had no leverage to fight back with. It didn't stop him from trying, but it was useless.

"Maria!" Grimaldo's voice rang out.

I'd nearly forgotten about the Don with everything else that was going on. He'd attempted to approach his daughter as well, but he too was restrained by rival vampires. He gritted his teeth, his features were bestial, but I could still recognize the desperate look in his bloodshot eyes.

"Maria!" Grimaldo yelled. "Why are you doing this? Why have you betrayed your own kind?"

Maria chuckled. The first sign of emotion she'd shown since she had revealed herself. "You silly, little blood feeder." She said. "You still don't get it, do you?"

Grimaldo stared, still straining against the other vampires. How the hell was she controlling them?

"Your daughter, precious thing she is, has been dead for a long, long time." Maria explained, as if her very presence wasn't a contradiction to the statement.

"What nonsense do you speak?" Grimaldo's voice filled with rage. "Who are you, witch? And where is my daughter!?"

"Didn't you hear me, you dolt?" Maria rolled her eyes. "Your daughter is dead. I killed her myself. And I'm not a witch."

Without another word, Maria began to change. Her features melted and shifted. Colors swirled and the girl I'd known as poor, missing Maria disappeared before my eyes. New features began to take shape. She had shiny, bronze skin and long nails painted red. Her hair was golden brown and trailed down to her bare feet. It seemed to flow serenely in the wind, even though the rain and wind was raging around her. A tiara of petrified wood with a golden leaf as the centerpiece adorned her head. She wore an amber-colored dress that seemed to shimmer despite the lack of sunlight. Her eyes were like kaleidoscopes, shining bright with a thousand colors. She was the most beautiful thing I'd ever seen, and also the scariest. And that was saying something.

What the hell was she?

"You're one of the Sídhe." Jacob grunted from under his captors.

I shot a look at him and then turned my attention back to her. I didn't know much about the Sídhe, except that they were the ruling class of faeries. They were the most human of the fae, yet the most alien. It was impossible for a mortal to understand the inner machinations of any faerie, but especially the Sídhe. From my lessons, I'd learned they had been toying with humanity for thousands of years. This Sídhe had been playing the vampires for suckers, but why?

Her presence explained why I'd seen fairy circles back at the warehouse. And why she had held so much authority amongst her cohorts, quite literally. The Sídhe were pure magic incarnate. I could buy that she had managed to enthrall the lesser vampires with magic. It was a fail safe, in case her lieutenants Oliviana and Feng Dài failed or turned traitor.

"Yes, I am one of the Sídhe." Faux-Maria said. "You may call me Queen Medb."

"You wretch! Surely you know this means war!" Grimaldo roared. "Me and my kind will hunt you to the ends of the Earth!"

Medb laughed heartily, holding a hand to her mouth. "Oh I'm sure you would, Grimaldo." She gave the Spear of Destiny a twirl. "Which is why, I must see this ritual through. With these vampires under my control, and their weaknesses shed, you and your kind won't stand a chance." Medb turned her attention to me. "And neither will the Mystic Order. Or any of the other supernatural nations. What happens here tonight will shake the balance of the world. And this is only the first step in our plans."

Our? Did she mean the other Sídhe?

"Ah, but here I go, getting distracted again." Medb turned her attention to my unconscious uncle. "It's time to begin."

I struggled against my captors, but their grips were unyielding. Medb knelt down beside my uncle, holding the syringe in her hand. She pulled up one of his sleeves and lowered the needle towards his forearm.

"No!" I screamed. Power surged through me. I felt electricity coursing through my veins. Thunder clapped loudly in my ears, and suddenly, I was free. The vampires who'd been holding me had crumpled to the ground. I didn't bother trying to figure out how I'd done that. I started sprinting, oblivious to the accumulated injuries I'd earned for myself tonight.

I was twenty feet away from Medb. I'd only just learned of her existence, and all I knew was that I wanted to kill her. The needle was less than an inch from my uncle's arm. I sped up, it felt like lightning was pumping energy into my muscles. I looked down for a split second, and realized lightning WAS pumping through me. Electricity zipped and zapped around me, hopping from limb to limb. My magic, combined with my desperation, had allowed me to call up the same power that Kat used against me.

Only ten feet away now.

I saw Medb pierce Bishop's skin with the needle. "No!" I bellowed and jumped through the air towards her, my leap propelled further by the lightning that emitted from my body. I saw her press on the syringe, and its contents began to flow into my uncle.

I hit Medb like a cannonball, an explosion of electricity engulfed us both. We went tumbling past my uncle and stopped just at the outer edge of the circle. Medb tried to rise but I decked her with a lightning powered punch. She swept the Spear across the ground, cracking against my ankles and causing me to fall on my face.

"No! I won't let a child like you stop me!" Medb leveled the spear at me and a bolt of blue energy flashed outwards. It hit me like a truck and I went tumbling across the ground. My uncle's unconscious body interrupted my roll.

The electric power that had fueled me seemed to fade. My vision was blurry, but I could make out Medb's silhouette sauntering to stand over us. I could feel energy gathering around us in the circle. The ritual. It was happening now.

"You've impressed me, for someone so young." Medb's voice echoed weirdly, as if I were hearing her from far away. She raised the Spear into the air, chanting in a language I'd never heard before. As my vision focused, I saw the clouds directly overhead swirling. They were perfectly orbiting Medb and the Spear. "Now, Spear of Longinus, Gungnir, the Holy Lance, grant my wish this night!"

The spearhead began to glow and she twirled it so now the tip was directly over Bishop's body. Then she drove the Spear down towards his heart. Everything seemed to slow down. Medb moved like molasses, her face twisted in a maniacal look of glee. All I had to do was...

With the last of my strength, I thrust my hand out and struck the spear shaft with my palm. It was just enough to deflect the Spear and drive it into the ground. There was a booming sound and the ground shook. The light gathered around the Spear faded to nothing, and the eerie glow of the circle followed suit.

The rain seemed to let up then. Not entirely, but it settled down from a torrent to a drizzle. I was draped across my uncle, and for a second, I thought I felt him stir. A bloodcurdling scream of rage pierced the night. I turned my head to see Medb, and oh boy, was she pissed.

"You insect!" Medb kicked me as hard as she could, the strike landing directly against my broken ribs.

I cried out, I couldn't help it. Everything just hurt too much and I was completely drained. I couldn't even call up enough wind to imitate a blow dryer. Medb grabbed me, pulling me up to a standing position. With one swift motion, she pressed her palm against my chest and blasted me with pure kinetic energy. I would have cried out if it weren't for the fact she'd completely knocked the wind out of me. I hit the ground a few feet away and crumpled, doing my best to curl into a ball. Congratulations Tobias, you'd foiled the secret faerie plot. Now you're going to die. Medb floated towards me.

"You think you've accomplished something here, boy?" She spat. "I still have the Spear of Destiny! I can do whatever I want with it! I'll make the vampires my invincible servants! I'll curse the world with an eternal full moon, letting the werewolves run free! I'll cleanse every monster on this planet of their weaknesses and set them loose on humanity! Starting with that little girlfriend of yours."

"You..." I coughed, blood splattering the ground near my head. "Bitch..." I moaned. I had to do something. But I couldn't move. I was tapped. I closed my eyes. I'd done all I could. That had to be enough, right?

"You forgot one thing." A new voice said. Wait, I knew that voice. I picked up my head just enough to follow the sound. Medb turned towards the voice's owner as well. Bishop was standing weakly in the circle's center, using the Spear to balance himself. "You don't have the Spear right now. I do."

With a grunt, Bishop yanked the Spear of Destiny from the ground, twirled it once and pointed the tip at Medb's head.

"No!" Medb screamed and surged through the air towards my uncle.

Bishop smiled, and I realized he was missing a tooth. His eyes gleamed through the swollen skin on his face. "Medb of the Unseelie Fae!" Bishop's voice boomed with power. Magic coated every syllable he spoke. "I, holder of the Holy Lance Gungnir, henceforth banish you from this Earth for three years and a day! Your meddling has no place here! Begone with thee, witch!"

"I'll kill you!" Medb screeched.

The Spear of Destiny glowed with golden and blue light as the runes carved into it lit up. A beam of light fired from the Spear's tip and struck Medb directly in the heart. She stopped in midair, completely unmoving.

Then she spoke. "Hear me now, Tobias and Bishop Leight. I will not forget this insult. I will spend every day planning my revenge and fantasizing about all the ways I will cause you misery and pain. There will be nowhere you can hide from me or my subjects. This is only the beginning!"

Medb arched her back and let out a wail like a banshee. Her body stretched and dissolved into mist in every direction. Until there was nothing left but a wisp of smoke. Then that too faded away.

The rain stopped. The clouds parted. The day had been won.

I tried to keep my eyes open but it proved to be impossible.

Chapter 27

My eyes shot open and I jolted awake, rising to a sitting position. Oof, big mistake. The world spun and I felt nausea threaten to overwhelm me. A firm hand on my shoulder gently pushed me back to a laying position. I glanced at the hand on my shoulder and followed the arm up to see Bishop. Man, did he look like crap.

My uncle, who was usually full of life, now looked drained of it. It seemed that all the bruises and swelling had healed, but his skin had become a shade or two paler than I last remembered, and his eyes were rimmed with dark circles. The wise glint in his eye that'd I had grown so used to was gone as well. Now they just seemed distant and tired.

I took a quick look around. I knew this place. We were in the Alfheim infirmary that was connected to Light Haven, the Mystic Order's headquarters. It was a forest full of glowing green moss and thick-rooted trees. My hospital bed was the only mundane thing about the place.

"Bishop, you're okay." I said with a weak smile as a sense of relief filled me.

He nodded. "Thanks to you."

I frowned as I tried to recall what had happened.

Bishop, seeming to sense what I was thinking, spoke. "You managed to save the day, nephew. The vampires' plan to evolve failed and they've all retreated to their hiding places, for now."

Images flashed through my mind. Feng Dài's corpse with a wooden stake sticking out of it. The bound Oliviana at my feet. Grimaldo fighting desperately to save his daughter. Maria turning out to be...

"Bishop, about Maria..." I began.

Bishop grimaced. "Yes, I'm aware. Jacob filled me in."

"I don't get why Medb would have gone to all this trouble though." I said. "Especially to help the vampires of all things."

"No idea." Bishop shook his head. "Faeries are hard to understand on the best of days, but the Sídhe are even more confusing to us. They're known as deceivers, tricksters, and manipulators. Their way of thinking is completely alien to us."

I twisted my face in thought. "She was trying to raise an army. She spoke of the Sanguine Vampires and the other supernatural nations as if they were enemies she needed to fight. And she said this was only the first step in her plans." I paused. "Well, she said 'our' plans. Makes me think that she's not acting alone."

Bishop considered this. "Perhaps she's talking about the other Unseelie Fae?"

I shrugged, my shoulders ached, and I instantly regretted it. "I mean sure, but she was willing to work with two different breeds of vampire. Who's to say she doesn't have allies outside of the fae?"

Bishop smiled, seemingly proud of the chain of logic I'd strung together. "I was thinking the same. I just wanted to see if you'd come to the same idea."

He grimaced suddenly, and then tucked his face into his arm, coughing violently for a moment.

I frowned. "Are you okay?"

Bishop cleared his throat. “Uh, no. While you did save me and stopped the ritual, I’m afraid I didn’t come out unscathed.”

I raised an eyebrow. “What do you mean?”

He frowned deeply. “As part of the ritual, Medb injected me with the blood of a Sanguine Vampire. A full dose would have turned me into one of them. You interrupted her, and thus I only got a partial dose. But it was enough to induce a...partial transformation.”

My eyes widened. “You’re part-vampire?”

He rolled his neck uncomfortably. “Simply put, yes. Fachnan has been performing tests to learn the full scale of what’s happened to me.”

“And?” I urged.

“Fatigue being the most notable.” Bishop said, letting out a tired sigh. “I’ve developed sensitivity to sunlight, enhanced reflexes, partial night vision. And most unfortunate, a thirst for blood.”

I shifted uncomfortably.

“It’s nothing I can’t handle.” Bishop clarified. “And it doesn’t seem to be a consuming urge, or even a necessity for survival. It’s been a week since it happened and I haven’t needed...” He hesitated. “To feed. Fachnan and Sylf are trying to concoct a cure. But there’s no record of a vampire being cured.

They're considering supplements to curb the negative side effects."

I couldn't imagine what he was going through. My uncle had worked so hard to become a powerful wizard and a defender of humanity. Sure, he'd once done Oliviana's dirty work, but this was different. Now he had become, at least partially, one of the very monsters he'd sworn to fight. And there was no known cure. I wondered how it would affect his work as a wizard.

A realization dawned on me. My eyes widened. "I've been asleep for a week!"

"Yes, you were kept in a magically induced coma while you recuperated. Your injuries were extensive and you'd damn near killed yourself from over exerting your magic." Bishop explained.

Prom. I'd missed freaking prom. I was supposed to take Claire to the prom. Oh God, Claire. She'd been roughed up pretty bad during the fight. Last I'd seen her, she was lying on the ground with her arm broken.

"Claire." I sputtered. "How is she?"

"All things considered, she's okay." Bishop said. "Jacob got her to a hospital, where she's been resting since. Scout's been sticking close to her. I think he likes her. As far as her parents are concerned, you both got roughed up by some extra aggressive thugs trying to rob you."

"We missed prom." I sighed.

"I know, I'm sorry." Bishop said genuinely. "Once you're cleared to leave, I have an idea to make up for it."

"Oh yeah?"

He held up a hand. "Later."

I puffed out a breath. Being a wizard was cool and all, but it had seriously taken a toll on the typical high school experience. Multiple attacks on campus, missing prom, what's next? My mind wandered for a moment before it decided to focus on arguably more important things.

"The spear." I said. "What happened to the spear?"

"It's in good hands." Bishop assured me. "I brought it to Braun and he made sure to split it back into pieces and store them away. We can't risk it falling into the wrong hands again."

There was some cynical part of me that wasn't so sure that the Mystic Order was the right hands for it to be in either, but I didn't tell my uncle that. I'd fought enough battles for the year. I didn't need to make my grievances with authority into a bigger issue, for now.

"Just one more thing." I said.

"What's that?" Bishop asked.

"I'm freaking starving." I groaned. "What's a guy gotta do to get some grub around here?"

Bishop smiled and patted me on the shoulder. "I'll see what I can do."

My uncle managed to pull some strings and get me some steaming hot stew from our resident Norse god, Andy. All things considered, it wasn't a bad victory meal. I'd saved my uncle and stopped the bad guys. Not too shabby, Tobias, not too shabby at all.

The Jiangshi seemed to go completely into hiding since their leader met his tragic end. Bishop told me that they hadn't been seen since the incident, and their usual stomping grounds were abandoned. Oliviana had survived my makeshift crucifixion, and while she hadn't made an appearance, Heaven's Door resumed operations pretty quickly. Grimaldo and his scourge had gone back to business as usual. He'd even sent me a card, the sentimental guy.

"*Wizards,*

While the outcome of this ordeal was not ideal, your assistance in this matter cannot go unnoticed. You have done a service to the Blood Clan here in

Seattle. If you ever need our assistance, I believe in balancing the scales, and will do whatever I can to provide aid. One time only.

Don Matías Grimaldo"

The letter had been written in red ink. Definitely ink. I didn't think about it too hard and I didn't want to. I wasn't sure how I felt about being owed a favor by a blood-sucking vampire, but I decided it couldn't be the worst thing in the world to have in my back pocket. Grimaldo was a proud man, and he didn't feel comfortable leaving a debt unpaid. I could respect that.

A few days later, Jacob came by the apartment.

We clasped hands and pulled each other into a bro hug. Even though he was careful with his immense strength, I still winced in pain as we embraced. I hadn't fully healed from my injuries, especially the burns. The healing salves I'd been given could only do so much.

"How are you feeling?" Jacob asked.

"I'm alright, especially for someone who got into a fight with a few dozen vampires and a faerie queen." I said. "But I didn't call you to talk about me."

Jacob's eyebrow raised.

"You really came through for me, buddy. And on such short notice too." I said. "I wouldn't have been able to pull this off without all of your help. Thank you."

He smiled. "Yeah, you probably would've gotten yourself killed. Even with my help you just couldn't help but go in guns blazing."

I rolled my eyes, but I smiled. "Shut up, man. I'm trying to thank you here."

Jacob let out a barking laugh.

"Oh, there's one more thing I need your help with." I said.

I stood in the dark gymnasium of King's View High School. The tux I was wearing wasn't a perfect fit, and itched in all the wrong places. But it was worth it. I waited, nerves making me giddy. Where were they?

The metal door creaked open on the far side of the gymnasium, letting in a shaft of light that threatened to reveal my presence. I took a half-step to the left to ensure I stayed shrouded in darkness a few moments longer. Claire walked in, Jacob following closely behind her. In the light, she looked absolutely stunning. She was wearing a beautiful baby blue dress that reached her knees. Her hair was done up in a bun.

Her broken arm was in a cast and sling, but it did nothing to detract how beautiful she looked.

"I still don't understand what we're doing here, Jacob." Claire muttered, sounding slightly annoyed. "Or why I have to dress like this."

I heard Jacob chuckle. "I know someone who can answer that." He reached to a light switch on the wall near the door, and flicked it into the on position.

Purple lights illuminated the gymnasium. A globe with multiple flashing lights spun, mixing more cascading colors into the mix. The speaker system overhead played a slow song perfect for dancing, the melody beckoning me to sway and two-step. I stood in the middle of the gym, my hands crossed in front of me. I couldn't help but grin stupidly at how excited I was.

"How did you-?" Claire stared in disbelief, shifting her gaze from Jacob to me, then back to Jacob.

Jacob shrugged, as if he had no idea. Then he smiled. "Have fun."

He retreated back through the door, closing it behind him. Claire and I met each other halfway and she smiled at me gleefully.

"What is this?" She asked.

I extended my hand to her. "I believe I owe you a dance."

She took my hand and I placed my other one on her waist, pulling her close. We began to dance, slowly turning and stepping. Claire looked into my eyes, smiling the whole time, and I did my best to keep my cool.

As the song ended and went on to the next, she asked. "So how did you pull this off, Toby?"

I gave her a wry smile. "Magic."

She giggled and I took the opportunity to lift our hands and twirl her, before resuming our dance.

"I'm really sorry we missed prom." I said.

"That's okay, fighting vampires is a pretty close second." Claire assured me.

I raised an eyebrow. "Really?"

She considered that for a moment, a playful look on her face. "Eh, sorta. Definitely exciting. We should definitely do it again sometime."

"Sort of a weird first date." I noted.

"Definitely not a date." She clarified. "Jacob was there. And technically, your uncle." As if their presence was what made monster fighting a bad date.

"You were pretty badass. I saw you staking all those Jiangshi," I praised.

"Yeah I was, huh? I might just become a monster hunter." Claire said mischievously.

"Really?"

"You never know." She shrugged innocently.

We went silent after that, enjoying each other's company and the atmosphere. It wasn't prom, but I wouldn't have traded that night for the world.

Epilogue

I took Claire home and Jacob graciously agreed to clean up our mini-prom. I still wasn't sure how he'd managed to make it happen in the first place, but he'd pulled it off. I walked up to the front door of the apartment and fussed with my pocket until I got my keys loose. I found the key to the apartment and stuck it in the knob. But to my surprise, it was unlocked. I frowned, but pushed the door open and stepped inside. The apartment was shrouded in darkness, there was no sign that Bishop or Scout were home.

"Maybe he needed something at the store." I shrugged. It didn't seem likely, but where else would they be?

I reached for the light switch and flicked it. Nothing. My frown deepened. Was there a power outage or something? I sighed. Just what I needed to end a perfect night. I shut the door behind me, then tried the light switch again. Still, nothing.

"Well this is just great." I muttered.

I pulled out my phone and turned on the flashlight. At least that still worked. I made my way through the dark living room and towards the kitchen. As I bent over to open the fridge I heard a noise. I paused, my hand an inch from the fridge door, straining to hear whatever had made the noise.

Sure enough, there it was again.

Someone coughed.

I shot up straight, now on full alert. I scanned the room slowly. I held up my phone to light my surroundings, but it suddenly flickered and died. You've got to be kidding me.

"Who's there?" I spoke to the dark room.

That's when I noticed that Bishop's recliner was turned so that its back was to me. Usually, it would've been turned ninety degrees to the right so that my uncle had a view of the kitchen and the front door.

"Hello?" I repeated.

Then the chair turned. It wasn't even that kind of chair, which made it all the more peculiar. But as it turned, I realized that someone was sitting there. I grabbed a knife from the knife block and pointed it at the intruder.

"I don't know who you are, but I've had a long last couple of weeks. And I've been feeling a bit jumpy. Makes me liable to stab you first and ask questions later." I said, trying to sound tough and intimidated. Truthfully, I was scared out of my wits.

"There won't be any need for that." The intruder said. His voice was calm and gentle. Not the sound of a burglar or a hitman. The intruder's eyes lit up with a soft golden light.

"Did you uh, break my lights too?" I gestured with the knife vaguely at the ceiling.

"Oh right, I didn't want to freak you out right away."

"Kinda failing at that buddy." I retorted.

The intruder held up his hands and clapped twice. Light returned to my apartment, and I finally got a good look at the intruder. He had long, rust red hair that went down to his shoulders, with a beard to match. His skin was the color of bronze and wore a maroon t-shirt. A green cloak clasped with a silver ornate buckle rested on his shoulders. The glow in his eyes never faded.

"Who the hell are you?" I demanded.

The strange man stood up, and I realized that he was taller than me. Much taller. He had to crane his head awkwardly to avoid bumping it on the ceiling. "Tobias Leight, it's a pleasure to finally meet you. Truly an honor."

"Who are you?" I repeated, trying not to sound intimidated by his imposing stature.

"My name is Lugh." He said, introducing himself.

I frowned. "Is that name supposed to mean something to me?"

Lugh chuckled. "No. No, I suppose it wouldn't."

"Then?"

"I'm one of the Tuatha Dé Danann." Lugh explained. "I guess you could call me an Old God of Ireland. I'm here to talk to you about Medb, and the trouble she caused with my spear."

His spear? Was he talking about the Spear of Destiny?

"Medb, you guys buddies or something?" I asked.

Lugh shrugged. "Or something."

Okay, that didn't really answer my question at all.

"Medb has set something in motion. And I think you can help me stop her." Lugh said.

Oh. Oh boy, what the hell had I gotten myself into now?

So I sat down with Lugh and we talked.

Author's Note

Hey there! Thanks for checking out Fang Wars, the second book in the Chronicles of Leight series. I hope you had as much fun reading it as I did writing it. Tobias' early adventures have almost concluded.

As always, I'd like to extend a huge heartfelt thank you to all my friends and family, especially those who gave this story an early read to help iron out the minor spelling and continuity mistakes.

A special shout-out goes to my mom who keeps a busy schedule and rarely sits down to watch TV, let alone read a book about wizards and vampires. Thank you Mom, I love you!

If you have a moment, please consider leaving this book a review on Amazon and GoodReads. Small indie authors like myself are incredibly dependent on word of mouth, so a little review would go a long way!

Scan the QR code below to find links to all my social media pages so you can stay updated on future projects!

Also consider signing up for my newsletter to receive a FREE exclusive ebook. *Gorgon's Blood* is a prequel story following Bishop Leight a hundred years before the main series.

If you enjoyed *Fang Wars*, consider checking out other books by the author!

Chronicles of Leight Series

Fallen Son (Book 1)

Fang Wars (Book 2)

Gorgon's Blood (Book 0.1)

Dreambound Fae (Book 3) *Coming Soon!*

Tales of Leight Novellas Series

Wizard Rising (Book 1)

Reading Order

Gorgon's Blood (Chronicles of Leight Book 0.1)

Fallen Son (Chronicles of Leight Book 1)

Fang Wars (Chronicles of Leight Book 2)

Wizard Rising (Tales of Leight Novellas Book 1)

Dreambound Fae (Chronicles of Leight Book 3)
Coming Soon!

www.ingramcontent.com/pod-product-compliance
Lightning Source LLC
Chambersburg PA
CBHW010726100726
47899CB00009B/2937

* 9 7 9 8 9 9 8 6 6 3 6 1 1 *